Under the Windowsill

By

Elizabeth Wehman

Summit Street Publishing

UNDER THE WINDOWSILL
Published by Summit Street Publishing
131 West Grand River
Owosso, Michigan 48867

ISBN 978-0-9905580-0-2

ISBN 978-0-9905580-1-9 (electronic)

Publishing in the United States by Summit Street Publishing, Owosso, Michigan.

Library of Congress Cataloging-in-Publication Data
Wehman, Elizabeth
    Under the Windowsill/Elizabeth Wehman-1st ed.

2014945666

Printed in the United States of America
2014

10 9 8 7 6 5 4 3 2 1

I would like to dedicate "Under the Windowsill" to my parents, Fred and Jeanette Habermehl for their unfaltering support and desire to see me succeed in fulfilling my life's dreams. I wish they were here to share in the joy of this moment. Thank you for instilling Christ in my life, at an early age, and teaching me to give everything I do, my best.

Acknowledgements

The birth of a book is an incredible process. From the idea's inception through to its printing. Often, I found myself alone, with only spell-check and a good thesaurus. Yet, my cheerleaders were numerous.

My fervent encourager, by far, was my dear husband David, who often would tell me to "keep going," "don't give up," and always "I'm so proud of you." Without his love and understanding regarding how important this novel was to my life's aspirations, this book would not have been something for you now to hold. Thank you, my forever friend.

To my Emily Elizabeth, who put up with, many afternoon's in the sun, which included a copy of my latest version. Thanks to her, my character's words ring true to their age. Someday, she is going to be a great writer. To my Rebekah Leigh, who seemed to understand that a writer's conference was more important than her sixth grade speech and who faithfully kept copies of my latest version on her computer for safe-keeping. To my Ethan Paul, who kept telling me, "don't give up, Mom" and will now be my partner in helping others achieve their dreams. All three of these greatest blessings, cheered me through every single accomplishment of this book. I love them and thank them for their encouragement.

To every single friend and family member who told me to never give up. Asked me, even when I would tell them that nothing was happening in my book writing, to keep trying. Many who told me to say "no" to other things in life so I had time to write. Thank you for not giving up on me.

Thank you to former co-workers: Karen Mead-Elford, Ruby Mitchell, Ed Buskirk, Terri Brown who helped me with their skills and always told me I was a good writer. To Deb Love who never, ever, stopped asking me if I had found a tree to sit under to release my inner creativity.

Thanks to all my prayer warrior friends, who have kept my writing endeavors, "before the throne" for many, many years. To my writing friends who sat through classes with me at writer's conferences, and kept up with me through this twenty three year writing journey. May I be as encouraging to you, as you have been to me. Especially, Cecil Murphey, Jim Hill, Kathy Frazier, Arlene Knickerbocker, Sally Bradley and Donna Poole.

To all of my newspaper writing fans who were excited to learn of my last career step and didn't hold it against me. To each and every one of you who inspired me, without even knowing it, by commenting on a newspaper article which delighted you. And to all of you who believed in me even when I didn't believe in myself. Thank you.

And to the Lord of my heart who gave me a desire to write from as early as first grade. You truly do give the "desires of our hearts." My ultimate hope is that, some small part of what I write for others, will lead them to You. Thank you for this gift.

Elizabeth Wehman
Psalm 34:8

Chapter 1

Kenna McNeil found disappearing easy, but staying lost would be the true test. Even though losing herself in the midst of all these people shouldn't be difficult, keeping herself hidden would prove a harder task. She now knew those late night school play rehearsals would finally be put to good use.

Kenna glanced over the railing of the bobbing ferry at the clear water swirling underneath the dock. The surge of fellow ferry passengers departing the boat left her only one choice; begin her journey, or go back to her life of utter suffocation.

Opening her bright green purse, she felt for her sunglasses. Flipping them open, she pulled them on, and filed in behind the other tourists exiting the boat. Months of training in front of her bedroom mirror, and occasionally flirting, even with just the cows, would now be reality.

A metal ramp, deflecting the Michigan sun, led up to the dock. Safely on the dock, Kenna glanced up toward the boathouse in front of her.

She flipped her stylish purse onto her elbow, adjusted her white designer sunglasses, and headed down the dock. For some reason, the sound of her stilettos hitting the dock gave her a sense of confidence. She strutted beside the bobbing ferry and smiled. Her new demeanor would take concentration, but she found determination to give it her best try. She kept bumping into others as the ferry continued to unload tourists scurrying to pass her.

Everyone seemed eager to disembark, almost charging to explore the famous island. Many tourists grabbed hands of wide-eyed children, sprung open strollers, or wheeled their bicycles down the wide dock heading toward the boathouse.

The day's sunny rays reflected on Lake Huron causing it to glisten every time a wave formed on the water. The ferries lined up along the docks like horses getting ready for a race. White foam emerged from the back of the departing boats, churning water like washing machines. Gulls squawked overhead. Kenna strolled behind a group of tourists marked by matching bright yellow t-shirts with, "Let's just do it," printed on their backs. A guide shouted out directions, "We need to meet back here by five-thirty to catch the six o'clock boat." She screamed louder, cupping her hands around her mouth like a make-shift megaphone. "Don't be late. The boat won't wait for you to swallow your last fudge sample." Other passengers, carrying heavy coolers or slinging backpacks over their shoulders, chattered on about the weather.

Kenna's eagerness to get off the dock and into the boathouse stalled behind a slow moving woman. The woman held up a brochure and recited sites Kenna knew as main attractions on the island. A gray-haired, balding man beside her went at the same pace.

"Harold, we just have to get close to the Grand Hotel. I've wanted to see it for years."

The man shuffled along while trying to wipe his eyeglasses with his shirt. "We will, dear. We will. But first we have to figure out the best transportation to get there."

The woman snapped, "I'm not riding a horse. I told you that."

"I know, I know, Thelma. Horses are out. I think you can rent bicycles somewhere." The man waved a skinny, crinkled hand toward shore, then turned to glance back at Kenna.

"Sweetheart, you know I haven't been on a bicycle since before Michael was born."

"Come on, Thelma. I know. We'll figure something out. Now get out of this nice lady's way." The man grabbed his wife's elbow and pulled her closer. Nodding at Kenna he said. "I'm sorry. We're just excited to be here."

"A slow, moving lane might be appropriate," Kenna lingered on the 'slow, moving' then sashayed her way around the older couple. She grimaced at her harshness, yet smiled at the same time. Her Iowa heritage now hidden, the slick girl from New York City emerged.

As she neared the doorway, she stopped, pulled down her D&G's to the end of her petite nose, and looked over them to read the sign gracing the gateway. Its bright blue letters caused Kenna to sigh. "*Welcome to Mackinac Island.*"

The sign's welcome gave her courage and propelled her forward. Mackinac Island. If she never fit into another place, this one location could possess the charm she sought for her life. Could it repair the pit in her stomach and the ache in her heart whenever she thought of her father? She drew in a deep breath and looked around the crowded boathouse for her luggage.

The dim house bustled with every kind of passenger imaginable. Brawny, young dock-hands pulled luggage carts, just unloaded from the boats, into the dim area. Soon they shifted pieces of luggage from the carts to the awaiting horse-pulled carriages lining the sidewalk. To see clearer, Kenna pulled her sunglasses up and secured them on top of her head. She noticed only two things about these men. Not only cute, they were built like Marines just out of boot camp. Could she truly pull this off and even attract one of these in the process? She smiled, thinking of the challenge.

"Ride to the Lilac Tree Suites and Spa located over here!" One young man shouted, but another shout, from another dock-hand a few feet away, tried to shout louder. "Hotel Iroquois lodging cab. Boarding here!" Ferry passengers scattered to grab their bags and hustle to the closest carriage awaiting their tour of the island. Many of the younger families entered the street directly off to one side of the boathouse.

This would be the place. It had to be. Despite the chaotic scene, she felt new energy to surge forward. Here she could establish her new life. No turning back.

She saw her pink bags being jerked off a luggage cart and rushed to practice what she now knew as her destiny. "Hey!"

The young man grabbing her luggage off the rolling carts turned to her. His blue eyes showed bright underneath blonde bangs plastered to his forehead. "Hey," he said back. He grinned with white, straight teeth.

"Do you think you could help me find the closest Grand Hotel carriage?" Kenna gave him the sweetest smile she could muster and then licked her lips.

"Absolutely. These yours?" He pointed to the pink suitcases she stood by.

"Yes they are. You are so smart," Kenna giggled. She let her shoulders droop and answered in a quiet, smooth talking voice, "I'd really like that."

Before the young man could pick up both pieces of her luggage she turned and pointed to the street. "Is it over there?" Even though her blonde hair was recent and from a bottle, she suddenly felt like cheerleader Nicole Poindexter from school. And it felt empowering.

"No, ma'am. The Grand carriages are back here." He picked up one of Kenna's suitcases and lugged it over a shoulder, then flipped open the handle to pull the other. "Follow me."

Kenna spun on her heel and winked at the young man. "Do I have to? Why don't you follow me?"

She watched the boy's face now turn a bright red as he smiled. "With pleasure."

3

Kenna made sure each step provided the young man following her the nicest view of her size six backside. She noticed other young men stopping their work to watch her. A few whistled. As soon as she reached the curb she turned and thrust a ten dollar bill into his hand. "Thanks, I'll take those now."

The man looked down at his hand and smiled. "Ma'am, I'd be glad to help you." More confidence surged through Kenna like water through a lawn sprinkler on a hot day.

"No, really. I have them." Kenna grabbed the handles of one of her bags and waited for the boy to deposit the other at her feet. She wasn't sure how long she could keep this up without suddenly bursting into a fit of laughter.

The boy smiled again, giving Kenna an unofficial salute. "Okay. Have a good day." But then he stepped back. Kenna watched as he sized her up from the tip of her nose all the way down to her sling-back sandals. Breaking out in an almost instant sweat, Kenna turned, feeling her face flush. Yet she smiled.

Maybe this could work. The encounter was her first assurance that she could make people think she was something different than the person she had just left back on the mainland. Watching those Hollywood reality shows was going to be a great advantage to her. She found it came just a little too easily.

That's when she heard it. "Last call for the Grand Hotel carriage!"

She looked in the direction of the shout and saw a rather large group of tourists heading in the same direction. Her trip had started so early the day before, she grew more anxious to get to her final destination. Her toes screamed in her shoes and a growling stomach demanded a future call for room service. She needed to concentrate on her hot pink silk pajamas instead of longing to fit back into sweat pants and a t-shirt discarded in a trash container on the mainland.

Leaving the dim boathouse, Kenna found a crowded street bustling with all kinds of activity. She glanced to the right, and then left. Bicycles with confident and even shaky drivers maneuvered past Kenna in both directions. Draft horses hauled carriages down both sides of the street. Tourists, munching out of little white boxes, bustled along the sidewalks and scoured the glamorous shops. This was it. Her father's dream world. A place he always wanted to visit. But dairy cows never take a day off.

For years she wondered what magnetic draw this island had on her father. Now she knew. It was a place back in time. *"Somewhere in Time."*

4

She felt freedom for the first time, and that freedom reflected the fresh air of the blue Michigan sky drifting in off Lake Huron.

She stood on the edge of the curb. This needed to be it. The step that would change her life. Her plans which began months before, were now becoming reality. She closed her eyes as she took one step off the sidewalk ready to experience the rush of an exciting new life. Her life. Not some life contrived by her domineering mother. Her foot instantly sunk into something warm and mushy. Looking down she saw a brown substance, like pudding, begin to seep over her sandal and slowly surround her freshly-pink, manicured toes. An unfortunate familiar odor replaced the fresh air she had breathed in just seconds before. She felt something breathing over her head. She tipped her head up and back and looked into the biggest, most beautiful brown eyes she'd ever seen. A toss of his head and a snort made her realize it wasn't quite the brown eyes of her Prince Charming.

A voice startled her. "Uh, need a ride?" She looked past the brown, brushed, manicured mane and into the face of the driver. He smiled wide and his eyes sparkled. "Bad step, eh?"

Kenna's head fell. She felt her cheeks grow warm and imagined them as pink as her luggage. Trying to compose herself, she pulled her foot out of the goo. Thankfully, it wasn't the same manure texture left from a cow.

"Here." The handsome driver, complete with black top hat and red coat, tossed her a large roll of paper towels. "Catch."

She glanced up just in time to drop the handles of her luggage, but not in enough time to catch the roll that dropped beside her shoe. She bent down to grab it before it unrolled and went under the Percheron standing guard over her right shoulder. Memories of the Iowa State Fair flashed through her thoughts.

"Where ya headed?"

Kenna raised her foot off the ground and did her best to wipe the smelly, tar-like substance from between her toes, while balancing on her other foot. "Grand Hotel."

"Perfect. You found the right carriage." The man jumped off his perch and patted the large horse beside Kenna. "Guess you've met Butch."

Kenna nodded.

"He means well. Actually, that was from one of his other buddies up there. The manure scoopers didn't quite get to it yet." The man with the tanned face and adorable smile pointed down the street. "Let me get these for you."

Kenna continued to wipe away the manure from between her toes then picked up her new, white, now brownish, sling back, and commenced wiping off the sticky, now smelly shoe. The paper towel stuck to her hand and she realized it now held little hope of wiping up the mess. She turned back to the sidewalk to see the dockhand and some of his friends, standing in a row, smiling at her from inside the boathouse. She wasn't in any mood to flirt anymore. Ignoring them came easily.

The carriage driver lifted her luggage onto another cart behind the distinguished black carriage. He opened the carriage door, and pointed inside. "There's an open seat right here." Smiling, he took off his top hat, and tucked it under his right arm. "Ma'am? When you're ready."

Kenna tossed the half-used roll back to him and limped to the back of the carriage with one shoe off. He tucked the paper towels under his arm with his top hat, then turned and held out his hand to help Kenna up onto the back step of the carriage.

"Let me help you." Kenna thrust her brownish shoe back into place and reached for the man's hand just as he pulled it away. "Not that hand." He pointed to her other one. "That one, please."

Kenna must have had an expression of shock and audacity on her face, because the carriage driver just grinned. The other guests seemed too preoccupied with looking at the main street activities to notice her dilemma. She held out her clean hand and the driver helped her into the carriage. If she wasn't trying to act more mature, she would have dug her sharp heel into the top of his foot on the way up the steps.

She squeezed into the seat next to a large, elderly woman. The woman leaned over to her, waving her hand in front of her face. "It's a nice place, but the smells are a bit different. Aren't they?"

Kenna nodded. "Slightly." Even though the odor emitting from her soiled toes was much too familiar.

The driver jumped up into his place behind the brown Percherons and snapped the lines. "Let's go boys." The carriage lurched forward and merged into the traffic on the active street. Bicycle riders parted, other carriage drivers yielded their right of way. Kenna was a passenger in one of the nicest carriages available. Fringe dangled and jumped from the canopy edge as the carriage made its way down the busy street.

The driver turned, perched his arm on the back of his bench seat, and addressed his eight passengers. "Welcome to Mackinac Island, folks.

6

My name is Erik. As you can see there are many tourists that come to the island every year to get a glimpse of what it is like to go 'back in time.' The only motorized vehicles on the island are a fire truck, an ambulance, and a few utility trucks. They only run on certain roads. Other than that, the only other modes of transportation include horses, bicycles, carriages such as these, and of course the healthiest transportation...your walking shoes." The group of eight laughed. The driver smiled at Kenna. She scowled and dropped her glasses over her eyes.

Kenna could feel the brown goo hardening on her heel. Her toes tightened as the muck molded to them. She shook her head in disgust. Then she remembered her step. Her first step into her new life. On her own. Thoughts of her adventure dimmed, but she raised her chin in defiance.

The silliness of her misdirected foot placements subsided more as the large horses pulled the carriage up a side street and along the shore. Soon the water's edge disappeared behind her. But not before Kenna caught a glimpse of the Mackinaw Bridge expanding across the lakes beside the island. Like a postcard. The view was magnificent. Peace seemed to ooze off the whitecaps lapping up on the rock bedded shores.

The carriage lurched as the horses made their way up the steep side street. Soon old-fashioned white lamp posts lined their way. As Kenna glanced up the road to see the hotel she'd only dreamed about begin to emerge through the trees. The Grand Hotel's magnificent white porch stretched across the front of the hotel, outlined by American flags flapping majestically in the fresh, early summer breeze.

She'd heard about this island and the Grand Hotel from her father so many times. She thought she knew it better than he did. Especially after they watched the movie. Their famous movie. Kenna closed her eyes, imagining herself back in time, to the sweetest moments of her life, the first few times her father watched the movie with her.

"This is it, Alisha," he's said, "One of the greatest movies of all time." She opened her eyes. The comfort, of the short moment, now gone and left was the familiar ache left by her father's death. She fought back tears.

Kenna needed to find her own way, do her own thing. Perhaps in pursuit of an ideal life, she could meet a man. A man who might give her the attention she desired, just as her father had provided her since birth.

She glanced down at her foot. She had been certain that manure was in her past. Thankfully, she had all summer to give it her best try.

Chapter 2

"Alisha, are you up yet?" Silence from the bedroom assured Rita that her daughter must be out busy with chores. She opened the door to find the bed messed, but empty.

Rita picked up towels by the bathroom door and headed to the first floor of the farmhouse. Each stair creaked as she descended. She stopped to nudge a picture frame into place, perhaps brushed by one of her sons heading out to the barn that morning. As she adjusted the family portrait, she admired her husband seated next to her in the photo. He'd left such an empty hole in their family. The photo reminded her of not only the loss, but the fact that their family would never be whole again. The ache left by his death, refueled for yet another day. She sighed.

Her daughter-in-law, Claire, appeared to have breakfast started. As she entered the kitchen, a pot was brewing on the coffee maker.

"Claire, you beat me up again."

It was new to find someone working in the kitchen before her. But since the birth of her grandson just a few months before, it had become almost normal.

"Ah, coffee," Rita snatched her coffee mug from the cupboard and poured the steaming hot brew into it. Then she opened the door to the basement and threw the towels down to be washed.

"Good morning," Claire chirped.

"How was your night?" Rita asked the young woman cracking eggs into a bowl.

"He was better," Claire sighed, "Although I'm not so sure I want to break the record for lack of sleep." She smiled under the droopy eyelids. "It does get better, right?"

Rita laughed. "Well, it depends on the child. Samuel was a good sleeper. Right from the beginning. But Michael...not so much."

Claire giggled. "Of course. My hubby would be the difficult one. This new baby thing is not for wimps."

"It does get better, over time," Rita smiled. She remembered thinking that herself almost thirty years prior. "Eggs this morning?"

"Yeah. Could you start the hash browns?"

Rita went to the pantry for the potatoes. "Alisha's up early today. Talk about horrible sleepers."

"She is?" Claire stopped cracking eggs and looked back at her mother-in-law. "That's odd. I didn't hear her this morning and I've been up since four."

"Her bed is empty."

Claire shook her head, but returned to cracking eggs. "Hard to see how that could happen with our bedrooms so close."

"Knowing Alisha, she probably made it out just in time to help with the five a.m. milking." Rita set her coffee cup down on the counter and began shredding potatoes.

Just then the back door slammed and in walked Rita's second-to-oldest son, Samuel, covered in straw.

Rita turned to see him brushing himself off after entering the kitchen. "Samuel, for Pete's sake, brush off a little before heading into my kitchen with half a bale on your head." She pointed to the back door again as her son stopped and began wiping off his shoulders with his gloved hand. "Not here!" Rita pushed him back out onto the porch. She continued after the door was shut and she returned to the kitchen. "You'd think after nearly thirty years of farming, these boys would figure out where to brush off."

Samuel made his way back into the kitchen, "Breakfast ready yet?"

"Feet!" Rita again hollered at the boy who turned around and scuffed his feet on the door mat. "Is Alisha out there with you?"

"Not me," Samuel announced. "What's so important about today?"

"No importance," Rita cringed. "She's just not sleeping this morning. She must be out helping someone."

"Really? This is a special day." Samuel laughed as he washed his hands in the kitchen sink.

"Samuel Lee, not in the kitchen sink!" Rita pushed her son away from the sink and pointed to the bathroom just off the kitchen. "In there!"

"It's okay, Mother, I haven't cleaned in here yet today." Claire cracked the last egg and began to whisk them for cooking.

"Doesn't matter. Since these boys were little, they know the rules of morning breakfast eating. You'd think after having five of them, one would have caught on." Rita took a frying pan down hanging over the stove, and grabbed a spoonful of lard from the can by the sink.

"Some know the ritual well."

"Only," Rita added, "because his wife has reinforced it and somehow he listens to her much better than his own mother." The frying pan came to life with a hot morning sizzle as she added the fat to the pan then dumped in the potatoes.

Slowly, each son appeared in the doorway with much the same greeting as the others, except for Claire's husband, Michael. He stomped his feet by the back door and removed his light jacket, hanging it on a hook. "Breakfast smells great, Mom. Claire." Michael then bent down to kiss his wife by the stove as she fluffed eggs in the pan.

"Where's Alisha?" Rita asked Michael. Surely he would know where his younger sister was working that morning.

"Alisha? I'm assuming upstairs. Still sleeping?"

"She's not in the barn?" Rita turned from putting the prepared hot potatoes into a bowl.

"I haven't seen her." Michael sipped his coffee and sat down in his chair. "Boys?"

All the boys echoed the same sentiment, shaking their heads.

Rita knew that at least one of her five boys should have met their sister in one of the barns. "If I get my hands on that girl..., Where could she be so early?"

"Well one thing I think we've ruled out. She isn't doing her chores," joked Samuel.

Afternoon planting came to an abrupt halt when the search for their sister came up void. Every possible location turned up no sight of the soon-to-be nineteen-year-old youngest sibling.

Michael came into the house after searching every single part of the farm, even Alisha's childhood tree house. He found his mother wringing her hands at the kitchen table with the other boys. Each one looked ashen and yawning, afternoon cat naps given up to search. Claire greeted him at the door with their newborn son cuddled against her shoulder.

Michael kissed the baby's head and stroked it gently then bent over to kiss his wife's lips. "Any news?"

Claire shook her head, "Nothing."

Michael sighed and shifted his ball cap up from his face, "Anybody have other ideas of where she could be?"

Silence filled the room.

Claire said, "It's not like she was one to go very far in the past."

Everyone nodded and a few of the brothers murmured their agreement.

11

His mother stood from the table, went to the sink and looked out onto the back yard of the farm toward the milk barns. "I can't believe she's just left. I don't know what's happened to her, but one thing's for sure. Our looking will not get the wheat planted nor the eggs gathered. We've looked everywhere here. I'll go get dressed and head over to Erica's house. Those two are usually in trouble together."

Wiping her hands on a towel, Michael watched her methodically lay it over the handle of her stove. "Everyone needs to get back to work."

Michael met Claire's eyes. His mother hadn't been herself since last fall when she lost her husband and their father. Too many times she'd approached Michael for advice, which had never happened before his father's death. It made him nervous every time.

Each boy stood to leave the kitchen. Some quickly, others looked to Michael for direction. He only said, "Yeah go, I'll stay here and try and figure something else out." He hugged his wife and looked down into her eyes for support. This inherited authority part of his life now just made him miss his father more. Being the oldest, he knew it would descend on him, but he'd hoped it would be in the future. Long into the future.

"I'm gonna go and lay the baby down. I'll be back soon." Claire kissed Michael's cheek and left for their upstairs bedroom.

Michael stood at the door on the mat. "I think it will be raining by evening. If Samuel gets busy now, the main field will get seed before it hits."

His mother nodded, but didn't speak.

"I think I'll get out and see how that heifer is doing. She's due soon. Alisha was watching her."

His mother nodded again. That longing in her eyes frustrated him. No one seemed to know how to comfort his mother. Since his father's death, he'd been too busy to figure it out.

"You want me to go with you to Erica's house?"

His mother shook her head. "No. I'll go alone."

Michael adjusted his hat again and turned to leave.

"Michael?"

He turned back.

"I think she's run away."

Michael shook his head, "Why would she do that?"

Rita looked up at her son and Michael could see fear had now replaced the sorrow he'd been seeing for the past year. "Your father would know what to do."

Michael added, "Yeah." That remark made him angry. He should know as well. He should be replacing his father's presence on the farm in every way. Ask him how much feed was needed for each animal, he could tell you, to the ounce. Get his advice about how to help a cow give birth, he could solve the problem easily. But when it came to his sister, he had no clue. Claire was helping him understand women, but his sister? Their father had spoiled his sister. She'd been nothing but a pain in his backside the past few months.

"I'm sorry. I wish I had better solutions for you."

His mother nodded and patted him on the shoulder. "I know. It's okay. Go check that cow."

After Michael left, Rita felt her frustrations give way to anger. She'd had all she could take from this young female of her family. The boys could easily be tamed, but this girl had always been a Daddy's girl. Grant could talk to her, reason with her, much better than she. He'd been the quiet, listening type of man. It was what Rita saw in him, before she even dated him, thirty-two years ago. In the worst of situations, her husband could calm her angry reactions, look at her in just the right way causing her to stop talking in mid-sentence. She would watch in a bit of jealousy, as he did the same thing for Alisha. When all she wanted to do is discipline their daughter, Grant would take her aside and replace a nearing storm with sunshine and rainbows. Since his death, her relationship with their daughter had only grown worse.

She went to the back porch to put on a jacket. The coming rain had put a spring chill in the air. Slipping her farm jacket on, she pulled her purse strap over her shoulder.

She stopped, after walking outdoors, to think of places on the farm where she might find her daughter. There was one place she often found her, ever since she was a little girl, a place where she would hide when she'd been asked to clean her room or start a load of laundry. She also hid there when she'd been picked on at school and when one of their beloved dogs passed away.

As she went to Alisha's favorite spot, she gazed at the siding on their old farmhouse. It had seen better days. Her husband and she had discussed the need for new siding just last spring. They thought it could be replaced this spring, but the funds went instead to pay for her husband's funeral. The replacement of worn siding would have to wait until...who knew? The boys were working the farm now. They needed to use the farm profits for their futures, not her needs. Rita touched the siding and wiped a tear from her cheek.

She neared the side of the house. Standing at the back for a minute gave her the courage to look in the only spot left that she knew to look for Alisha. Many times, she'd find the small girl perched there with her Daddy, talking about all sorts of issues. She hesitated to look.

Finally, breathing in deeply, Rita gained enough courage to peer around the corner. The ache in her heart grew stronger when the only thing in Alisha's favorite hiding spot was a red-breasted robin poking the ground for a worm.

Chapter 3

Kenna leaned her luggage against a white picket fence bordering a path on the approach to the Grand Hotel. Standing at the fence gave her an encompassing view of the hotel, including the six hundred and sixty foot porch dotted with white rocking chairs and floral lawn furniture. The porch could be seen from as far as the mainland, nearly five miles to the south. The view of the porch drew visitors each year.

Smiling, she soaked in the view. It was as glorious as she expected. If only her father were here with her to see it.

"Quite a view, isn't it?"

Kenna jumped at the voice which came from behind her. Turning to him, she found the carriage driver. She lowered her sunglasses from her head to her face again and turned back to the view.

"I never get tired of the view," the driver approached the fence and stood beside her. "Sorry about your fancy shoe. Manure stinks."

Not wanting to reveal her true character, she instead gave him a look of disgust, "It better not happen again."

The young guy, not much older than herself, chuckled, "Better watch your step next time, Li'l miss fudgie."

"It was disgusting. You need to keep better track of how and where you let your team..." she wanted her words to help fuel her new-found rebellious image, and there was only one way of doing that. With an added swear word. She looked at the man over the top of her sunglasses. "And, what did you call me?"

"Whoa," the young man looked offended and backed away, "Sorry. I was just..."

"Just what?" Kenna stood her ground.

"Just tryin' to be friendly."

"By talking about crap?" Kenna cocked her head, put her sunglasses back on her head, and added the best disturbed look she could muster, And calling me a...what did you call me?"

"Sorry," he lifted both his hands into the air. "Didn't mean to upset you." He turned and began walking toward downtown. His riding boots and outfit detailed his slim waist and broad shoulders.

Kenna couldn't get over his eyes. As blue as the water surrounding the island. Maybe she'd been a little too hasty in cementing her image to this one. He might be fun to hang around with on her first night on the island. "Hey," she called after him, but he kept walking. "Can I ask you a question?"

He finally turned. "I don't know. Should probably be cleaning up piles of stuff down by the dock instead."

Kenna folded her arms, "Oh please, stop being dramatic."

The man turned on his heel and began walking away.

"How much is it to stay in the Grand for a night?"

"I don't know," the young man called over his shoulder, "I'm just a carriage driver." He turned around, "Where're you from anyway?"

"New York City," Kenna called after him. He really was trying to just be friendly. As he turned again to keep walking. Maybe she should stroke his ego a little. She called, "Has anyone ever told you that you're kinda cute in that get-up?"

"You're a little too late for that." He kept walking.

"Idiot." Kenna called him. He never turned around, he just shrugged his shoulders and waved his hand.

Kenna turned back to the fence and leaned against it again, she decided she needed to cement her New York City image in a somewhat different way. She fumbled in her purse for her lipstick and mirror, and applied the red stick to her lips. Smacking her lips she remembered she wanted to lure men to her, not push them away. No matter what impression they gave her in the beginning.

Turning with her luggage, Kenna headed back down sidewalk toward town. It wasn't a complete loss. This guy was way too young for her anyway. She wanted a mature man. One who would have never given her a second glance back in Iowa. Someone sexy and knowledgeable about how to treat a real woman. Nothing like the farm boys back home.

"Highway robbery...that's what this is," May Thomas took out a fifty dollar bill and handed it to the downtown baker. She motioned to him, "Be careful how you wrap up those goodies. I plan on serving after dinner."

The baker smiled, "As always, May, as always."

"Who's he, Bob?" May motioned to a young boy scraping recently baked cookies off a tray. "Is he new?"

"Never miss a new one, do you May?" Bob smiled, "Landon, meet May. She's an innkeeper here in town."

May dug into a large flowered bag, pulling out a pocket change purse in which to deposit her change. "London, that's quite the name. Very...England like."

"The name's *Laandon*, maam." The young boy set down his tray. "Landon with an *A* not an *O*."

"Landon?"

The young man nodded, "Yeah."

May clucked her tongue, "Names these days. What's wrong with names like John, George or even Tom or Ted?"

"Those, my dear May, are from our generation." The baker handed May her treats. He knew better than to hurry up one of his favorite customers. As much as she was a nuisance on a busy morning, he enjoyed her way of keeping an eye on his younger employees. She seemed to be passionate about finding out names of all of them each summer. Soon she would not only know their names, but would befriend them and offer a listening ear if they needed it.

"By the way Landon, I like your hair color." May shoved her money into the change purse and buttoned her jacket. "Very unique. Quite a chilly morning today, isn't it Bob?"

Bob, accustomed to May's particular sense of humor, understood her comment much differently than his new employee. "Yes May. Those hotter than blixen days of July will soon be upon us."

"Yes they will." May turned to leave the bakery, "Nice to meet you Landon."

The young helper motioned a hand wave, while holding a fresh tray of cookies, to the old woman as she walked away. "Who's that old lady?"

Bob smiled as May left his bakery, "She's one of the oldest residents on the island, Landon. She complains every single day about my prices. At first," Bob put some of the fresh baked cookies out on display, "you think she's just nosey, until you really get to know her."

"Nosey old women annoy me," the young worker, with the blue spiked hair, commented as he returned to the back room.

"She's not really as nosey as you think. She just pays attention to everything going on here on the island, especially all you young ones." He wondered how the young summer employees would respond to May's approach of influence. Each year it got harder and harder for her to relate to them.

Bob smiled again and then asked the next customer in line, "Can I help you?"

Back in high school, guys called girls like her one word. Erik refused to stoop that low, not wanting one chick's attitude to ruin his afternoon. Why couldn't all tourists visiting the upper Michigan island just be happy families on vacation?

She was kind of cute with her fancy shoes, stylish glasses and name brand purse. Yet, his first glimpse of her was quite different than what she portrayed, just minutes ago. He never knew a fancy girl to step completely into a manure pile without screaming her head off in disgust. But this girl, accepted it as a daily mishap. On top of that, she also wasn't afraid of his horses. She hadn't spent her whole life in a big city.

Erik looked across the street to see his friend Marty making his way down the sidewalk. He waved in his direction. "Marty. Hey, Marty!"

Marty looked up, waved, and made his way to Erik's side of the sidewalk. "I hate the Lilac Festival. Seems like every year the fudgies come out in full force." His friend held up a bag. "Gotta make a deposit downtown. Can I tag along with you?"

Erik nodded. "Sure can. Well, unless..."

Marty responded quickly. "What? Unless, what?"

"Oh nothing," Erik broke into a fit of laughter.

"What's so funny?" Marty appeared annoyed.

"No. It's not you." Erik put his hand on his friend's shoulder. "It's the little piece that just dumped me."

"Where?" Marty turned and looked back. "If she purposely dumped you, maybe she'd like me."

Erik slapped his buddy on the shoulder. "No, Marty. You don't want this one. She is a piece. Pretty, but she's got quite the little attitude. I wanted to be her hero, but no, she wanted no part of it."

Marty kept looking. "And the problem? How come she dumped you?"

Erik shrugged his shoulders, "I was just trying to be nice and before I knew it she turned on me like a poser."

"On you," Marty shook his head, "Whoa, bro."

"I know."

Marty laughed. "You fool. You know these fudgesicles are our bread and butter."

"I know. But I think I just did myself a favor."

"Really?"

"Positive."

"Well if you see her again." Marty pointed to his chest. "I wanna make my own mind up first. I like the challenging ones."

Both men laughed again. Erik looked over at his friend. "What type of girl do you picture liking me?"

"Not a piece, but a young, innocent thing would be your type. Prim, proper. Church-going type."

"That sounds pretty boring."

"No," Marty laughed. "She would be anything but boring. You see, she'd have to look a certain way too." Marty motioned an overall scan of Erik with his hand. "Just look at you. You my friend, are the piece-catcher type. Now me," motioning up and down himself with his hand, "I'm the demure, pleasantly plump, and happy type of fellow who knows without a doubt that any piece that is attracted to you, wouldn't give me the time of day."

"Don't be so sure," Erik laughed.

"Brother, I'm not only sure, I would bet this entire island on that one." Marty slapped his friend on the back. "Not only would I bet the entire island, I'd guarantee it. Your leftover pickings would be my..." Marty swooned, "...my dream come true."

"Why do girls do that anyway?"

"Do what?"

"Just look at the outward appearance?"

Marty's cell phone chirped. He dug into his pocket. "Chicks dig handsome, burley-type guys. Always have and always will. If one of us good guys were ever to pick one up," he fumbled the phone with one hand, but managed to get it to his ear. "Hello? Yup, on my way." He pushed the end call button, "It'd have to be 'cause we had something else to attract them. Like money or a fine car. You know it's true, man." He gave Erik a gentle shove. "You know it."

"Yeah, I guess. Hey, I gotta mosey on down this way." His friend crossed over to the other side of the road, calling over his back. "Have a good day, bro. Send that girl my way," Marty added, nearly tripping on the sidewalk in front of him, "I'll be waiting," pointing his thumb to his shoulder and then pointing back to Erik.

Erik knew the type of girl he wanted. He had always been attracted to the down home cowgirl. Someone who could milk a cow and hang up the laundry on a line to dry. Someone who wasn't afraid of horses or chickens. Someone just like Jenny.

Kenna wandered around the neighborhood for a few hours. Her toes grew numb. Her heel stuck hard to her right shoe. Her luggage grew heavier and heavier the longer she pulled it. The crowds were bustling around her. She needed to find a place to land and soon.

She knew she couldn't afford the Grand. Closer to downtown might be better anyway for all her plans of checking out the night life.

The wheels on one of her suitcases started to squeak. Every single step. Squeak. Step. Squeak. Step. Sweat rolled down her back and her stomach started to growl. She was in no mood to handle the situation. Maybe if she asked a few people, perhaps someone knew of a good place to stay.

"Excuse me," Kenna stopped an elderly couple. "Do you know of any vacancies around here?"

The older woman turned to her and asked, "What?"

"A place to stay. Anywhere?"

The woman shook her head. "We aren't from around here. Sorry."

Kenna rolled her eyes and kept walking. Squeak. Step. Squeak. Step. She felt the pads of her feet grow warmer and warmer. Her heel felt like it was rubbing against sandpaper.

"Excuse me." She approached a woman with a bag of groceries in her arms.

The woman turned around to her and smiled, "Yes?"

"I'm looking for an inexpensive place to stay. Are you from around here?"

The old woman shifted her grocery sack to her large hip, as her flowered purse bounced off her other hip. "Do you need a place to stay?"

Kenna grew impatient. She had her luggage, she must look a mess, and she even heard her stomach growl. "Duh?"

"Excuse me?"

"Yes, lady. A room. Food. A chair...Anything would do for now."

"As a matter of fact, I own a bed and breakfast in town."

Kenna sighed. "Do you have a vacancy for tonight?"

"Follow me." The woman began shuffling down the sidewalk. For some odd reason, Kenna felt like a duckling following behind its mother. But for now, it felt comforting to waddle behind.

The woman called out over her shoulder, "What's your name, dear?"

If Kenna hadn't been so desperate for a room, she might have walked away, but instead she answered, "Kenna."

"Kenna?" The old woman turned and stopped. She looked at Kenna as though she was trying to solve a puzzling question.

Kenna wasn't sure what the next question would be, but it seemed the old woman she now followed had a bit of senility. All she heard as the woman turned back around and kept walking was, "Okay, I know. I'm on it."

Chapter 4

Kenna leaned against the counter. She might as well get her first question answered before pulling out her money, "How much?"

"Seventy-five a night." Blue eyes twinkled from amidst the crinkles and folds of the woman's face. She radiated. Kenna wasn't sure from what, but she'd noticed it the first time she spoken to the woman on the sidewalk. It couldn't be perspiration because of the amount of rouge on the woman's cheeks and face. Her hair wasn't gray. The black and silver strands like salt and pepper. The woman pulled on a bright blue apron which covered her polyester, seam-down-the-front pants.

"Gonna make some cinnamon rolls. Do you like nuts?" The old woman took out a sheet of paper and handed it to Kenna. "How about raisins? Fill this out, honey."

"Nuts?" Kenna picked up the pen and began to fill in the information. Most of it all false. "Raisins?"

"In your sweet rolls." The woman smiled again causing Kenna's heart to skip a beat. There was something mesmerizing about this old woman.

"How much?"

"Oh, honey. They're free."

"What?"

"The sweet rolls. They're free." The woman handed Kenna another slip of paper to sign. "If you don't mind me saying, you look exhausted."

"Ya think?" Kenna wasn't sure if she was more tired than hungry.

The woman glanced at Kenna's registration, "New York City girl, eh?"

"Uh, yes." Kenna had tried to think up a perfect New York City address. Her heel, now sore from walking, made her jot something silly down.

"Thank you, dear. My name's May. If you need anything, holler."

Kenna smirked. "Sweet."

May took her time taking money and putting it away. "What's a New York City girl doing in a place like Mackinac Island? It's quiet here, except in July and August. We pride ourselves on peace, and the fresh air off the Great Lakes. In the winter, we are a small, quaint place. Far cry from taxi cabs and high falootin' restaurants."

"We've always wanted to come here."

"We?"

"No, I mean me." Kenna grew tired of her made-up game. "May, can I get to my room? I started early this mornin' and I'm whipped."

"Oh. Sure. Sure. Sorry. I like to get to know my customers. Follow me, sweetie. I'll take you up to your room."

May turned to Kenna as they ascended the stairs, "I'll put you in the Peony Palace."

Kenna knew she was tired but, "What palace?"

May turned and continued up the stairs. "Peony palace. I named all my rooms. Much better than just a number, don't you think?"

Kenna's exhaustion made the old woman's room naming somehow seem funny. "Whatever," Kenna laughed.

Kenna shut the door of her room and leaned against it in relief. Dropping her pink purse on the giant, queen-size bed she pulled her luggage up to rest at the footboard. Pink and purple pillows, edged with lace, were placed strategically against the dark stained headboard. She felt like the lavender Victorian room would swallow her in its peony-popping wallpaper. She wondered if she could sleep in all of this fluff.

The room screamed *princess* which made May's room name make perfect sense. As a ten-year-old she would have jumped on the bed amidst the pillows to bury herself in the old-fashioned surroundings. Instead she went for the bathroom to draw water into the claw-foot bathtub. She needed a warm bubble bath to not only clean the gunk off her heel, but to relax. Maybe she'd take a short nap before heading out for some food.

Her shoe stuck to the bottom of her foot. She winced as she pried it off her heel and set it by the sink. The smell made her stop, wondering if she could save the sling-backs. The memory of her morning made her think it might be worth a few bucks just to go buy a new pair and throw these in the closest trash can.

Soon she plunged her tired body into the mound of suds. The smell of lilacs wafted from the emerging bubbles. How appropriate. May thought of everything.

She sunk down into the warm water and laid her head on the back of the tub. Kenna smiled at the thought of tempting men. She'd have to use new tactics. She wanted to be a flirt, not a witch.

She was finished with other people ruling her life. She was free now. Free to be someone she'd never been allowed to be at home. Someone she'd wanted to be her whole life. Not her brothers' little sister. Not her mother's prim and proper, only daughter.

The only thing Kenna wanted her whole life was to be who her father always thought her to be: his baby princess. Kenna smiled at the room which fit her title, too. But without her father here any longer, she would have to do this, all by herself.

Chapter 5

For a moment, just a split second, she was back in her room at home. Her eyes were not yet open, and she knew her father would be wondering where she was to help milk the cows. Even though most of the job was mechanical, things still needed to be disinfected and cleaned. Being the daughter of a farmer was hard. A cow's schedule never took a vacation for birthdays, Thanksgiving or even Christmas morning. Trying her best to open her eyes, she knew her mother would be tapping on her door, telling her to pull on her muck boots and head out to the barn. Her father rarely scolded her. He'd just have that frustrated look on his face while he prepared the milking machines himself.

As her eyes opened fully, she catapulted through time and found herself not home, but in a room that looked like one of her pins on Pinterest. In the same instant, Kenna realized her father was gone and not waiting for her in the barn. Grief filled her heart just as it did every morning since he died.

Everyone had been so caring after her father died. Neighbors brought food, her father's farming associates stopped by to see if they could help, even friends at her school seemed extra attentive. One boy even asked her out on a date. She had been so excited to tell Claire, but knew she'd have issues when telling her mother that the banker's son asked her out. As she and Claire talked about purchasing a new dress, her mother entered the kitchen from gathering eggs.

"What are you two cackling about?" Mother had said, and she remembered giving Claire a knowing glance.

"Mother, I've been asked to the dance on Saturday night."

Wiping off the fresh eggs, her mother just snickered, "Um, I don't think so."

She got up her courage when Claire nudged her in the back, "Can't I go?"

Her mother's attitude said more than her words, "You know the rule."

"But I am close to eighteen."

"Close, sure, but you know the rule."

That had been the hardest day since her father died. Her mother would never allow her to do anything. Kenna slipped off the large bed

25

and walked to a nearby window. That was the moment she began to envision this adventure. Her father and she had discussed the age limit for dating just before he died. She'd turned seventeen a few short months before that, and another boy asked her out just after her birthday, but her mother refused to allow her to go. After talking to her father, she was pretty sure he would have allowed it. He'd said he would discuss it with her mother, but he died in the driveway just two days later.

Kenna pulled back the lacy white curtains to look out onto the street below her room. Bicyclists careened down a side street. A carriage strode by with a smiling couple at the reins. The scene enticed her to want more. Changing her life was now not only a priority, but a necessity.

Even on the second floor she peered across the street to a windowsill topped with pansies and petunias. A peony bush lush with large white flowers underneath. If her favorite spot at home could have had a large bush like this, even her father would have had a hard time finding her there. She didn't need another windowsill. She had an entire island to hide.

She went to her luggage and unzipped the case. Her new clothes were still in store bags. She wondered how long it would take her mother to realize her college savings account had been drained. She'd be furious when she found out.

Pulling a hot pink skirt out of a bag, Kenna held it up to her waist and looked into a full length mirror on the back of her bathroom door. She had never worn anything so cute and refreshing. The length of the skirt would have been the first shake of her mother's head if she would have asked her permission to buy it. That's what drew her to it in the first place.

She went to the bathroom for her white sling-back sandals and noticed they looked and smelled much better. She had managed to remove all the traces of Butch and his friends. Happily she removed her bathrobe and slipped into the new outfit.

Kenna tucked her fake ID card into her skirt pocket. Hoping the card would prove to be as valuable as her new name, she skipped down the steps of the quaint Victorian bed and breakfast. Not finding anyone in the front room pleased her. She imagined May to be the nosey type of hotel manager and she couldn't risk getting involved, or worse, discovered.

Finding some available men was a little harder than she expected as she strutted down the sidewalk. A family approached her on the sidewalk, walking in the opposite direction. The mother appeared frustrated by the yanking arms of her two young children. "Sammy. Stop pulling away from me." The mother jerked a little harder on the hand of a young blonde boy closest to the road. "You have to hold onto Momma's hand, especially by the road."

Kenna smirked as the little boy insisted to his perplexed mother, "Mommy, there aren't cars on these roads." The mother stopped and looked down at the child. "There might not be cars, but Sammy, there are horses and bikes. They can hurt little boys just as much as a car."

Behind the three was a stroller pushed by a man loaded down with a backpack. He looked more like a pack horse than a father. As the mother passed by Kenna she continued hollering orders to her children.

In the stroller sat a chubby little girl, with a pink bonnet and white shoes, pointing at a dog walking on the other side of the street. "Woof, woof!" She exclaimed.

The father reacted with, "Yup, that's a dog," and at the same time his eyes became transfixed on Kenna as she approached him. Kenna thought about smiling at the man who appeared bored with the family walk. But then she decided to do even more, especially since the wife had already passed her by. She lowered her sunglasses at the man and winked and then pushed them back into place. The moment was fleeting, but she watched the man trip over absolutely nothing on the sidewalk.

As she passed him, she lightly brushed his shoulder and then turned again, "Oh, I'm so sorry." Lowering her sunglasses, she hoped to give the weary husband a glimpse of her backside much like the dockhands that morning. The adventure was gradually emerging into fun. If she could get a middle-aged man to turn for a second look, she could find others. She was sure of it.

She chuckled to herself as she heard a voice crescendo with each call. "Tom. Tom! *Tom!*" She knew the man had stopped to check her out, because the stroller wheels stopped squeaking for a few seconds. As she walked away from the family, the squeaking continued. Standing a little taller, confidence penetrated Kenna's independence.

Steep hills down toward the island's main street caused Kenna to slip off a heel once or twice, then glance around to see if anyone saw her. No one seemed to notice her blunders, especially anyone who mattered.

Quaint shops with lilac-adorned windows lined the street to the main thoroughfare. Kenna paused a few times to glance into the windows. Erica would have loved to peruse through each shop trying to discover the most unique find. Kenna sighed as she gazed into one shop window full of gifts. She'd have to do it alone.

Downtown was swamped with tourists. Kenna stopped at another store window and watched a man with a giant paddle scoop out the contents of a large brass pot onto a marble table. Soon another employee began to quickly lap up the edges of the deep, dark colored fudge. Scooting around the table, he lapped up the liquid candy. Fold after fold turned it into a long log of fudge. Other tables contained the finished product ready to cut into slices for waiting customers. The smell drifting through the air caused Kenna to stop long enough to watch the entire process from start to finish. After getting some lunch, she'd have to satisfy her taste buds now watering with delight.

Customers came out of the candy store carrying small white boxes. Many sat right down on the curb to open their boxes and sample their purchases. Kenna's stomach growled in protest. A corner pub grabbed her attention. Her mother would be furious to know she was going into a bar, but courage surged through Kenna as she looked down at her short skirt and high-heeled shoes. She smiled as she opened the door of the pub and found the closest stool at the bar.

Placing her purse on the bar, she twirled her chair to glance at the other customers. Waitresses set plates in front of customers and poured drinks for others. Kenna was perched at the end of a long marble counter strewn with all kinds of people. She was hungry, but a cool drink would be just as fun to celebrate her new freedom. The first item, on her agenda, was to see if she could order an alcoholic drink. Her next agenda cross-off was to attract someone. He needed to be older, attractive and someone Kenna could see as a bigger adventure than just running away from home.

Although she felt out of place, she inched her skirt up a little higher and crossed her legs off to one side and smiled. Soon a bartender approached her. "What can I get you, sweetheart?" The man with gray temples smiled as he leaned toward her.

This was it. The moment she feared and had longed for at the same time. She pulled the identification card out of her pocket and slapped it on the counter. "I have a feeling you're gonna ask for this anyway, so let's get it out of the way before I melt on this chair." The bartender grinned and glanced at the card. "You're right. I would have asked."

Glancing from the card to Kenna he gave her a quick once over. "You're new here. I also find it a bit hard to believe you are twenty-one."

"Of course I'm twenty-one. Granted," Kenna winked at the man, "my birthday was just last week. But this is my first day on the island. Can't a girl celebrate her twenty-first in a big way? And what can you give me so I won't leave a puddle on your floor." She could feel herself glow as the new sexy flirt she'd always dreamed she could be.

"Well, newbie, some girls do appear much younger than they really are." The bartender smiled as he handed her card back. Kenna swore it glimmered gold as she slipped it back into her pocket. Erica assured her the card would be valid. She thought about her old school friend back at home and hoped her family wasn't giving her too much grief over her absence. Erica could be trusted.

Kenna put her elbow on the bar and leaned her chin into her hand. "Hmmm. I can't decide. Why don't you pick something fun out for me." She tilted her head and flashed the older man one of her fake smiles.

"Well our specials for this weekend are the pink margaritas. How does that sound?"

Kenna flashed a genuine smile. "Perfect!"

"Comin' right up. Want anything to eat with that, ma'am?"

"How about a menu?"

Kenna peered into the menu, so full, it made it hard for her to decide quickly what she wanted. What would a girl from New York City order? She settled on a side salad with dressing on the side but soon changed her mind. Hunger caused her to order a burger to go with the salad.

Her salad arrived shortly after her drink. Both tasted divine. Hunger stopped her from looking around too much but she noticed a few men noticing her. They were young though. She'd flirt with them to get her bearings, but what she really wanted to do was find a challenge. Someone much older. A man guaranteed to be out of her league. Experienced. She smiled at her boldness.

Just as she did, she turned her chair and saw a man eyeing her from a back corner of the restaurant. Alone. Hesitating, she turned and dug her fork deeper into her salad.

How could she pull this off without appearing inadequate? She had never attracted an older man. Especially like this guy. What could a little teasing and flirting do? She'd have to gain an art for doing it sooner or later.

Looking up at the man, she lifted her drink and held it up as if to toast him. Now that was bold. She felt energized. He stared back at her. She turned back to the bar. He hadn't responded either way. No smile. No responding toast with his own drink. She questioned looking again, but she knew she needed to continue the game. As she turned she found him no longer seated at his table. Kenna looked off toward the far room, and then as she turned to look toward the door she felt a warm touch on her left shoulder. The man now stood beside her. A shiver ran up her spine.

"Hey." His voice was deep, low, and she prayed her deodorant would stand this test.

She smiled and answered, "Hello," accidentally tipping her glass toward him.

A splash of her drink must have escaped the edge because, before she knew it, he had taken her napkin from her lap and was wiping off his shoe. Kenna just sat frozen. Before she could right her glass, he grabbed it and righted it for her. "Now is that a way to treat a guy?" He smiled at her.

Kenna shuddered. How could she keep making huge blunders like this? Someone was going to notice soon that she really wasn't the girl she appeared to be. Quickly she decided she could right this one. "Oh sir. I'm so sorrreee! I guess…" she giggled a little, "I guess I've had a little too much alreadddee." Then she squeaked out a tiny burp. "*Excuuse* me."

The man smiled again and leaned onto the bar next to her. He smelled amazing, like fresh hay with a hint of lavender. The smell intoxicated her more than her drink, but her ruse seemed to have worked. Those days in high school drama class now seemed more beneficial than the reality show examples she'd been watching for the last six months.

"Here for the parade?" The man asked.

"Naw," Kenna tilted her head. "Just lunch."

The bartender approached the couple. "Hey Brock. How are ya?"

"Fine now. Once this little lady came into the bar."

"Wanna refill?"

"Sure. Fill her up." The man sat his own drink down on the counter.

Kenna picked up her drink again and carefully sipped this time. She'd have to be careful. She didn't know her limits or what would happen if she had too much to drink. Soon she motioned for the bartender to fill up her drink.

"Where'ya from?" Asked the man who now leaned closer to her.

"New York City." Kenna nodded in affirmation.

"Wow. City girl, huh?"

"Absolutely. I work...uh, *worked* for an advertising agency there."

The man nodded. "I dabble a little in marketing. What firm?"

Great. The first one Kenna could get was someone to catch her in a good lie. "Oh. Uh," Kenna took another long drink to give her a little more time to think of a good line. "I work for myself."

"Hmmm. Self-employed. I like those kind of women."

Kenna grew warm, a little lightheaded as answers seemed to grow foggy. She would need to fix this. Build up her resistance so she could handle liquor better. Could that happen?

"Can I sit?" The beyond imagination, deliciously attractive man sat down right beside Kenna. He held out his hand to her. "Brock Mitchum."

Kenna held out her hand for him to take. His hand was soft and warm. Hers must have felt sweaty. "Kenna."

"It's very nice to meet you, Kenna. That's a pretty name."

"Thanks. My father's choice."

"Are you a resident here or a fudgie?"

Kenna laughed. "A what? What is it with you people here? Why do all of you keep calling people fudgies?"

The man picked up his glass and laughed. "A fudgie? That's what we call tourists around here. Because they all like to eat the famous island's fudge."

The bartender sat Kenna's burger right down in front of her. She looked up at the bartender. If she accepted, what appeared to be a most delicious burger in front of her, what would her new friend say? She needed to think quickly. "I didn't order this."

The bartender gave her a questioning look. "You didn't? I thought you ordered a..."

Before he could throw out the name Super Burger, Kenna stopped him. "No. Don't you remember?" She implored him with her eyes. The bartender's eyes widened and he gave her another questionable glance, but took the plate. "Oh, okay. What did you order?"

Kenna blurted out, "A turkey club." She relaxed with her much more appropriate selection, but looked longingly after the burger as the bartender took it away.

"How long you here for?" The man didn't seem to notice her order mix-up. His eyes were as blue as today's Michigan sky. His black polo lined his muscled body. He was even a bit gray at the temples.

"Oh," Kenna said, "who knows? At least for the summer."

"I'm the manager of a gallery down the street," Brock said. "I hope you'll come down and see it sometime."

"What do you sell?"

"Artwork from the locals. Many residents make things throughout the winter and I help them by selling it during the summer while I'm here. I'm just a summer fudgie, too."

Kenna laughed again. "A summer fudgie. I got to see someone make fudge down the street just now. It looked almost sinful."

Brock laughed. "Yes, you don't look like you have had much of a chance to sample any of the famous island fudge yet though."

"Oh I did," Kenna laughed remembering her misstep of the morning. "But I'm over it now." She moved her heel in her shoe.

Brock shook his head and laughed. "What?"

Kenna waved her hand. "Never mind. Long story."

"Well, Kenna." Brock brushed his hand on the outside of her leg sending shivers through parts of her body she never thought would react to a stranger. "Please stop by soon. I gotta get back to the shop." He stood to leave and dropped a couple of twenties on the bar.

The bartender quickly came back for them and also delivered Kenna's new order. He picked up the money and gave Kenna a skeptical look. She winked at him and he smiled.

"For both me and the cute, little, summer fudgie here." Before Kenna could do anything Brock picked up her hand and lightly kissed the top of it and then walked out of the bar.

Kenna turned on her bar stool and looked at the bartender. "I didn't order this. I ordered a burger."

The bartender put both hands on the bar and eyed Kenna with disgust.

"No problem," Kenna waved him off, "I'll eat this." As the bartender walked away, Kenna began to devour her sandwich. Surely that was all the flirting she could muster for an entire day without falling to pieces. Her first official act of being the new Kenna had even earned her a free lunch. Her new lifestyle could be profitable as well as indescribably, desirable, fun.

With the last load of hotel passengers delivered, Erik wanted to get away early to take Jenny and the kids to the parade.

Getting the horses traversed down Main Street was harder than ever. The crowds were huge. He would be glad when the festival was over and he could get back to the normal summer crowds again. They were big enough.

Looking up, he saw her again. She had changed from her outfit and now wore a short pink skirt, with a matching skimpy top to match the same high heels of the morning. She donned the same white sunglasses and was coming out of the corner bar.

Before she could get her purse on her shoulder and her white sunglasses off her head and into place on her face, she looked up at Erik. He smiled and tipped his cap. She blushed, but immediately lowered her sunglasses into place and pranced away. The pink princess now looked a little on the sloshed order and she slipped off one of her heels as she walked away.

Erik maneuvered his competent pulling team down the street. The girl seemed to have only one purpose. She might be cute, but at that moment Erik knew that he needed to concentrate more on his duties, his job, and Jenny and the kids. He'd had enough of girls like her, but he couldn't seem to help himself from looking at her as she walked away. Girls like this frustrated him. They could be so alluring, tantalizing even. His older brother Tom had warned him of the ways of women. His advice rang true in the case of this city girl now strutting down Main Street.

Brock returned to the bar just minutes after he'd left. He'd forgotten his lighter at his table.

"Lose something Brock?"

Brock turned and saw Carl, the bartender, talking to him from behind the bar counter, "My lighter."

He found his lighter under a napkin, put it in his pocket and turned to leave.

"Brock," the bartender put both hands on his hips, "what are you doing?"

"Returning for my lighter." Brock pulled the lighter back out of his pocket, went to the counter and flicked it on for the bartender.

"No, I mean, the girl."

"Who? Kenna?"

"That girl is only twenty-one," the bartender smirked, "if that." He shook his head. "Leave her alone."

"Can't a guy have a little fun around here?" Brock looked down his nose at the guy plaguing him day and night. "I give you enough business around here. Lay off."

"If you want to hit on women in my bar, they need to be old enough to know your ways."

"My ways?" Brock grinned. "I'm just having a little fun with a new girl in town."

The bartender wiped off the counter where Kenna had been sitting. "Yeah, she isn't old enough nor smart enough to see through your fake attention. Leave her alone."

Brock leaned over the counter and looked the bartender in the eye. "Carl, what do you got against me? Leave me alone." Brock turned and walked toward the door. "I have every right to hit on anyone I want. It's a free country...last time I knew."

That guy was a complete annoyance.

After watching Brock leave the bar, Carl turned to the nearest customer at the counter. "That guy is after just one thing. But...," he added as he handed the man his drink, "it's not gonna be off my sailboat."

Chapter 6

Erica once told Kenna that getting drunk felt as though you were escaping reality in exchange for a special place you've always wanted to visit but could never afford. It also resembled gambling with the enticement of always wanting more.

The stress of Kenna's day almost melted away. She thought of the manure step and started to giggle. Leaving the bar, she almost wanted to skip down the street, even though her new heels could cause an even worse misstep than just one foot in a nearby horse pile. Instead she smiled and swung her purse until she realized she'd hit a few people. The island surged with tourists. The quaint atmosphere now replaced with a type of hurried frenzy. She stopped and looked around, wondering if an emergency had happened.

An older man bumped into her almost sending her to the ground. Kenna righted herself after stumbling. "What's going on?"

The man pulled off his ball cap and nodded to Kenna. Soon she saw a woman pulling him in the opposite direction like a two-year-old leaving a candy store. "We're gonna miss the parade, Fred."

Kenna giggled. A long tugboat drone infiltrated the air around her. Then a gun fired from the nearby Michilamackinac Fort. "Whoa!" Kenna jumped.

Within a short distance, she spotted a freshly mowed grass-covered slope, dotted with blankets. Families, intimate couples, and senior citizens all awaited what must be the annual island's Lilac Festival parade. May had told her about it when she registered that morning. Glancing up the hill were the tall, white-washed walls of the fort.

Kenna weaved her way through groups of bystanders and families as she inched her way through the crowds. She belched a couple of times, and hiccups followed. Stopping, she held her hand to her mouth. Her stomach felt queasy. The hot sun added to her discomfort. She needed to sit down.

Passing a small group of young men, she noticed every single one stopped sipping their drinks to eye her. One even whistled. She turned away, afraid she might make a fool of herself, but so flattered at the attention. She'd never had so much male attention in one day. Attention from these dudes was not what she really desired, but a little practice couldn't hurt.

She sat down beside the group. Just as though they'd asked her to join them.

"Hey, boys."

They all laughed and moved around her closer.

A particularly cute guy nudged through the crowd and planted himself directly next to Kenna. "Hey there, gorgeous."

Kenna smiled. "Hey back."

"Come to watch the parade?"

Kenna was blown away by the amount of liquor on his breath. Beer bottles were strewn on the grass around them. Kenna fought for control of her emotions and her stomach. "Sure," was her only response.

"Kinda lame. Alcohol helps."

Another guy slapped the cute guy on his shoulder, "You should know."

The cute guy nudged back hard, causing the other guy to grimace and yell, "Ow! Hey, watch it bro!"

The cute guy must have won because soon he turned back to Kenna and asked, "Got a name, beautiful?"

"Al--" Kenna slipped, "Allison."

"Are you sure?" The boy laughed.

Kenna smiled, "Yes." She was also happy she'd chosen a different name. She wasn't sure if these boys should know her real name. Her real fake name. She giggled to herself.

"What's so funny?" The boy took a swig from his can.

"Nothing. What's yours?"

"Um...Paul." All the other boys surrounding Paul began to laugh.

"Okay, *Paul.*" Kenna knew what had just happened.

"Where you from?"

Kenna tossed her hair behind her shoulder. "New York City."

"Whoa. Really? Do you know anyone famous?"

Answering this would take a little ingenuity. "Not personally."

"Have you seen any?"

"Of course, what do you think? It's New York City."

Silence came over the group for a moment and Paul grabbed up his can again. "Wanna swig?"

Kenna really wanted to say no. Her stomach churned and she felt like one more sip would send a wrong message to these dudes. She knew if she didn't, it might give them another wrong impression of who she was trying hard to be. So she grabbed the can and took a swig.

Paul smiled.

The beer tasted bitter and acidy. Now the sun felt like it could melt her right here on the grass. She handed the guy back his can and got up to leave.

"Hey, where're you going?"

Kenna couldn't talk. She couldn't breathe. All she could think of was finding the closest trash can.

She came back to the parade after losing her lunch. The crowds were so thick, only a few people passing seemed to notice. One woman stopped and ask her if she was okay. She'd answered with a, "duh." The woman kept walking. Kenna found a tissue in her purse and wiped off her mouth, then found a small patch of grass in which to rest for a while.

Just as she felt an urge to leave and find the closest restroom, she looked up to see her carriage driver from the morning on a nearby blanket. What looked to be his wife and children surrounded him. He looked happy as he tousled with a tiny boy, pinning him to the blanket and tickling him. Kenna could hear the boy's shrieks of laughter from where she sat.

She hadn't noticed how handsome the young man was until now. His dark hair matched his suntanned skin. He wore a dark blue polo with blue jeans. His broad shoulders slimmed to his waist. As he tickled the little boy on the blanket, he turned his face to her and she noticed a dimple on his right cheek and a strong jaw. She had been so busy cleaning her shoe she'd missed how attractive her driver was. He sat close to the woman next to him. He was married.

Why should she care? He'd been rude. Opinionated. At that moment he turned and stopped playing as he caught sight of her just a few feet from him. Not wanting his attention, Kenna rummaged through her purse for her sunglasses.

She needed a restroom even worse than a few minutes before. She stood up, brushed off her backside and placed her purse over her shoulder. Confidence surged through her again as her balance had returned, and she wanted to prove it to everyone still seated around her. That was, until her heel slipped off her shoe and she stumbled to right herself.

So many tourists on the island, Erik couldn't believe he caught sight of the city girl again. He watched the manure-stepping piece as she replaced her sour look with an arrogant one, then stumble out of sight. He chuckled to himself, and reached out for Taylor's hand. "Ready group?" The little girl grabbed on tight to his hand. The crowds were crazy, the child's mother just ahead of him.

"Do you need me to carry him?" he asked his sister-in-law.

"Erik, this isn't my first day of carrying this child." Jenny shifted the baby to her other hip, "You could carry him," Jenny handed the boy to Erik. As Erik took him she added, "He really needs a diaper change."

Erik laughed as the whiffs now came from his nephew's shorts. "Thanks, so..." shifting the baby to another hip and trying to endure the smell, "...much."

Laughing, Jenny added, "Blake couldn't stop admiring the soldiers."

"I like the band," announced Taylor. She lifted her knees high in the air as she marched beside Erik. "They march like this."

"Yes. Very good," Erik smiled down at the little girl beside him.

Blake babbled over his shoulder, "*Blla, phelb, poo.*"

Erik giggled, "You're right, buddy."

He looked away from his sister-in-law to see what appeared to be every tourist from the island heading to the boat docks to leave for the mainland.

"It'll be quieter soon." Jenny acknowledged the direction of his look just as Taylor slipped and fell. A scream erupted. Jenny motioned for Erik to hand Blake back to her. "Here, let me take him. I'm used to the smell. Can you carry Taylor? She's getting tired."

Erik picked up his niece, brushing off her leg. "Are you okay, munchkin?" Taylor whimpered for a little attention and then touched Erik's chin and turned it toward her face. "You look like my Daddy."

"I do?" Erik could feel his face flush. The comment taking him completely off guard.

"Yes. Are you my Daddy?"

"Taylor. We've talked about this before. Remember?" Jenny turned to her daughter, but didn't stop walking. "Erik isn't Daddy, he's Erik. Uncle Erik."

Taylor grinned. "Can you be my Daddy?"

Erik shook his head. "No precious, just Uncle Erik."

The little girl rested her head on his shoulder.

Jenny turned, mouthing, "Sorry," to him.

Erik shook his head. It was okay. A little girl needed her daddy. Erik was just a substitute, for now. That was okay.

As Jenny's house came into view, Erik couldn't help but wonder how other people perceived Jenny and his relationship. Not everyone knew about Tom or even why Erik now took his place in Jenny's house. Most of the residents knew of the situation, but many didn't. Erik never wanted to put his brother's wife's reputation in jeopardy. Jenny wasn't his wife. These children were not his children. But for the few weeks after his brother's death, Jenny needed someone. Her parents were no longer alive. She had a sister, but she lived in Alaska. Days turned into weeks and soon Erik found himself enjoying the friendship of his sister-in-law. He loved his niece and nephew. It seemed right for him to be here to support them.

He knew the discussion about his support would come up in conversation. Jenny would soon need to stand on her own again. That she could do. She proved that when his brother was gone so much on deployment. Yet leaving her seemed wrong to Erik. His brother would want him to be here...but for how long? Neither he nor Jenny had discussed that issue at length. Erik wasn't even sure he wanted to bring it up. He was enjoying being on the island.

Erik had been alone since his brother left for Afghanistan. Helping to care for Jenny and the kids had been a good change. He felt like a family again. Even though he knew it wouldn't last long, he loved the feeling.

As Jenny put the kids down for their naps, Erik determined what he would say to her.

"Want coffee, Erik?" Jenny asked as she came into the room.

Erik laughed. "Sure."

As the two sat down at the kitchen table, Erik decided to get right to the point. Cut and dry as it was, it needed to be said, "Jenny, I've been thinking."

Jenny held up her hand as she sipped her coffee. "No, Erik. I know what you're going to say and I agree."

Erik set his cup down and smiled, "What?"

"I think it's time you move out."

"Are you sure?"

"Yes." Jenny smiled at him with tears starting to brim her eyes. "I think."

39

"Now, Jenny. I won't leave until you think it's okay. I promised you..."

She sipped her coffee and added, "Erik. I know what you promised me and you have lived up to it in a wonderful way. I couldn't thank you enough for staying with me through these weeks. You have been my hero."

Erik smiled. He would never tire of being someone's hero.

"Since Tom's death you have been the rock beneath me. I would have never imagined you in that role, but you have done everything in your power to ease my grief. I will be eternally grateful to you for that. But the island is small and people have begun to talk. I don't want Tom's reputation tarnished by my loneliness. It's time for you to leave."

Erik nodded as he took another sip of his coffee. "Are you sure, Jenn?"

"I guess when I heard Taylor's words on the way home, that solidified it for me. She needs to realize that it's just us now. She needs to know that her Daddy will never be coming home from the war, and you aren't here to replace him."

Erik nodded again.

"But there is one more thing you could do. I know you have a life back home waiting for you. But would you mind staying on the island for a few more weeks. I know the kids would be thrilled and I would appreciate the help until I can figure out what my next step will be."

Continuing to nod, Erik added. "I promised you the summer. Remember?"

"I hate being by myself. With Tom being away for the past seven months, I should be used to this by now. But before..." The tears began to flow freely down Jenny's cheeks, "I always hoped that he would come back. And now..."

"It's okay Jenny. You'll get that strength back again. I'm sure of it. But until then, I'll be here for you."

The couple sipped their coffee. Jenny got up for a tissue and wiped her tears. "Maybe I could get a boarder. That would help with expenses and give me," she blew her nose, "some company as well."

"That'd be cool," Erik added. "Lots of kids need a nice place like this to stay.

Jenny set down her cup and smiled at Erik. "I'll get through this."

Erik smiled and nodded, "Yes you will," even though his heart ached for the life his brother was now missing.

Chapter 7

"Jenny, she just can't stay with me much longer," commented May. "She can't afford to pay me the normal fee for every single night she's with me. She's told me she wants to live on the island all summer. I have reservations almost every weekend from now until Labor Day."

"Where did she come from?" Jenny never found May so upset by a customer before.

"She doesn't talk much. I never find her in her room." May clucked her tongue. "I don't like it. She's too young to be out late by herself." Jenny's elderly friend propped her grocery bag on the other hip and adjusted her broad brimmed hat. Jenny was almost sure the windy afternoon would take it sailing down the street. "Well someone has to help the poor thing. She comes home drunk every night and sleeps until noon. There's just something very odd about her. I can't put my finger on it, but..."

"Like what?" Jenny reached down to tie Taylor's shoes.

"I don't think she's exactly who she's portraying to be."

"Portraying to be?"

"Yes. Jenny, you know me. God shows me hurting hearts with some of these summer resident teens. This one seems out of place. Out of character." May pulled her hat down firmly again. "She has manners. I know that shouldn't be a big sign, but teenagers these days are rarely kind, let alone say please or thank you. She calls me ma'am occasionally. Then, her clothes. She moves in them awkwardly, like she has never been taught to sit in a tight, short skirt. Maybe it's just my old age talkin'."

May did know people well. When Jenny first met her, she smiled and held her hand out to her. "If I can ever help you with anything, sweetie, you just give me a call," she'd said.

"Didn't you say she was a city girl?"

May winked, "She's not a city girl, Jenny. I would bank on it. But one thing is for sure, she needs help. She needs guidance."

May turned to Jenny and smiled. "What about you?"

Jenny finished tying Taylor's shoes and stood up. "What about me, May?"

"It's about time that Erik moves out, don't you think?" May edged closer.

Jenny smiled. "We were just talking about that yesterday, May. But how did you?"

"Doesn't matter. I agree. Doesn't look good and the children are thankfully too young to understand, but Mabel has begun to talk. Once Mabel starts telling others around this place..." May clucked her tongue again and shook her head. "It's bad. Just plain wrong." May's sentences sometime flooded together like creeks on the island in the spring. "You'll have a spare room. Especially if Erik moves out." May smiled at Jenny. "Am I right?"

Jenny nodded.

"She can probably pay you a little rent. She doesn't appear to be too poor with her high-falooting sunglasses and clothes."

"What are you saying?"

"I'll send her over this afternoon. Then you can meet her."

"Oh, May. I don't know."

"You'll like her. And if she gets too out of line, you can always ship her off again. But I just think," May sighed and tightened her hat once more, "I think we need to keep an eye on this one."

Jenny learned many years ago not to deny May her wishes. She'd been a very good friend. Why not see what kind of girl May was all worried about?

Kenna counted her money on her bed. She counted the hundreds and then the twenties stacking them in piles. "Three thousand, five hundred." She bit her lip. It seemed to be dwindling fast. From bus tickets to her new clothes, what seemed to be a huge amount of savings when she drew it out of the bank, now seemed to be nothing in light of her latest expenses.

She needed a new plan. She stood up, pacing in front of the window. She crossed her arms. Why did she have to drop her cell phone in the trash can in Lansing? She probably should have kept it. If she had, she would have called Erica right now. Her best friend had helped her plan this whole adventure. She had given her advice and talked her into so many of the things she only dreamed about during the last few months.

Quickly she dressed, adjusting her skimpy denim shorts and halter top in the mirror. Why did she always see her mother's face when she saw her reflection? She turned away, grabbed her purse, and dashed for the hotel door.

Prancing down to the lobby of her temporary home, she got to the bottom of the stairs to find May coming in with a grocery bag. Her first instinct was to grab the bag and help the woman to the kitchen, but she had a new mission today: to find a cheaper place to stay, and avoid interaction with this meddling old woman.

She pushed past May and made a beeline for the door.

"Kenna, watch out, sweetie." May nearly dropped the bag, but only a few cans tumbled out. Kenna couldn't help herself. She turned just in time to grab the bag before it all fell to the floor. She wanted to apologize and help the woman, but knew a city girl wouldn't care. May's hat hit the floor instead of the grocery bag.

"Kenna. Can you please help me with these things?"

Grabbing the loose cans, Kenna sighed and followed May into the kitchen. If she didn't know any better, she'd have sworn the old woman dropped some of the groceries on purpose.

They walked into the kitchen and May placed the half bag of groceries on the counter and pointed to Kenna. "Take those things over to that counter, would you dear?"

Kenna sighed again. The other counter was on the far side of the kitchen. When she set down the cans and turned to leave, she found May right in her face. Kenna jumped.

"Dear, I don't mean to pry. Really I don't, but are you planning to stay here all summer with me?"

Kenna shook her head, unable to get around the woman to leave. "No. That's where I was going. To find another place."

May nodded and then crossed her arms. "Where did you plan to look?"

Kenna needed fortitude with this woman and to keep her guessing. "I truly don't believe that is any of your business." Kenna cringed inside when she thought of how cold her words sounded, but kept going. "I'm just your customer."

"I'm sorry dear, but I have an establishment to run here. I need to know how long you plan on staying in the room. You've been paying me every afternoon for days now. Now I'm thankful for that, I truly am, but I have guests coming in for the weekend and they have had your room booked since April."

"I'll be gone by tomorrow. I promise." Kenna pushed past the nosey old woman.

"Kenna. Can I suggest something to you?"

Kenna turned on her heel to look back into the room at May.

"Be careful, dear. There are many people out there that would love to take advantage of you. If you need advice, find someone you can trust." She said something else, but Kenna didn't hear it. She was already headed out the door.

Kenna huffed as she turned down the street. "Trust," she uttered out loud. "I don't need anyone." She slung her purse on her shoulder and headed out to find a different place to stay. There was only one person in the whole world she could trust, and he was dead.

"You know what I just had to do?" Michael slammed his keys down on the top of a dresser startling little Nathan. A small whimper turned into a mighty scream for a moment.

"Michael, calm down. I just got him to sleep."

Michael went over and sat on the edge of the bed, watching his wife pat Nathan's back as the screaming turned to whimpers again. "I'm sorry, but *sheesh* Claire! How did I have to turn into Father so fast?"

Claire shook her head, "What now?" She adjusted Nathan to her other shoulder.

"Phillip! I'm comin' in from the barn and what do you think he's doin' in the driveway?"

Claire stopped patting. "What?"

"Him and that Blaire girl are makin' out in his pickup. If I hadn't of broke 'em up, we'd have had two screaming babies in this house soon." Michael threw his ball cap on the floor and put his head in his hands. "This responsible older brother thing is killing me." He stood up, with both hands in the air. "I'm just their brother, not their father!"

Claire smiled, adding a little smirk with her right cheek dimple, "Do you remember when we used to do that?"

Michael sat down on the bed and eyed her.

"Well?"

"Yeah, and look where it got us." Michael grinned and pointed to baby Nathan. "You'd never let me do anything like that until after..." he pointed to the ring on his left hand.

"Just the way God planned it, that's all. It wouldn't have been perfect any other way. Sex is a sin and wrong if done out of wedlock. You know what I think about it."

"I know. It's one thing to have to stop yourself from going too far, but why do I have to be in charge of my younger brothers? It was hard enough for me to follow the rules."

"You just are." Claire rocked again as baby Nathan cuddled deeper into her shoulder. "It'll be okay, Michael. God will help you be a good big brother to all these young ones."

"Well, if these last few weeks are any indication of how I'm doing, I'm in big trouble."

Claire stood up and handed Nathan to her husband. The baby looked up at his daddy and smiled and cooed. "I think you're just getting started."

Michael looked down into the face of his son and said, "No necking in the driveway. Got it, boy!" The little baby looked up into his father's eyes.

"I have a feeling I know why Kenna left." Michael looked at his wife, "Mother can be really controlling. She's made Alisha pretty miserable since Dad died."

"She has always had a forceful hand on Alisha, but yeah, I agree."

"She would never let Alisha have her own life. It seemed like she couldn't wait for me to grow up, but Alisha..."

"She's a girl, Michael. It's different."

"Well, I better never catch her out in the driveway in some boy's truck." Michael leaned back on his elbows on the bed and lowered his baby to the space beside him. "Ugh."

Claire laughed.

"Maybe God has you helping these boys so you are good and prepared when you sit Nathan down to explain the birds and the bees to him." Claire came over and stroked the baby's head and then settled her hand on her husband's shoulder. "You're gonna be a great dad if this new role is any indication. I know this is a huge burden on your shoulders right now. The farm, the boys..." Claire knelt down by his chair, "...our own new baby, and now Alisha."

"I thought God doesn't give us more than we can handle."

"Sometimes," Claire smiled at her husband, "He wants us to trust Him and watch Him handle our frustrations. It's big lessons which mold us to be more like Him."

Michael looked up into the eyes of his wife. He had always been astounded by her love and affirmation of him. He was still amazed that she had became his wife and that in the bargain, she loved him. He looked again at their son, lowered himself to kiss his soft cheek. "I'm a slow learner."

Claire sat down on his lap and put an arm around the back of his neck, "He's an extremely patient God."

Kenna checked through three bed and breakfasts and around five hotels. All charged over seventy-five dollars a night. She decided to check one more, and entered The Hotel Iroquois lobby. Adjusting her sunglasses on her head, she approached the front desk. "How much a night?"

A young man looked up from the computer. "Need a room, ma'am?"

"Single bed. I'm alone."

"Well, the only thing we have available tonight is a suite at one hundred and forty dollars."

Kenna rolled her eyes and rubbed her forehead. She thanked the man and turned to walk out. "Miss, I'd be happy to look on the computer for another room for you. We can surf and maybe find something cheaper."

Kenna turned back to the desk and walked up to the clerk. His name tag read 'Marty.' "Uh, *Marty*, that would be great." She purposely didn't thank him.

"Okay. Let's see here." Marty looked up from his computer and smiled, but his fingers kept tapping the keys. "Where you from?"

"Uh..." Kenna began to grow tired of today's inquisitions. She needed to be discreet, but keep her story straight. "New York City."

"Oh, you must be the new girl in town I've heard about."

Kenna shook her head. "You've heard about me?"

Marty stopped a moment, "Word gets around the island. Guys keep tabs on the new girls in town. The ones who stay longer than a day, that is."

Kenna grew frustrated as the clerk looked back to his computer, "Girls like me don't need guys like you spreading it around that we're in town. We're cute enough to cause our own waves."

Marty nodded. "I can see that. Yes, I can." Marty blushed, "There is a room at the Windemere Hotel for eighty-two dollars. How does that sound?"

Kenna shook her head and turned to leave. "Thanks, but no thanks." She waved Marty off as he tried to call out another price to her. It was useless.

As she walked out onto the street, she felt her demeanor sink to a real low. She didn't want to pretend to be someone else right now. She cringed to think of having to leave the island. Somehow the island made her feel close to her father. She could almost hear him cheering her on to be independent.

She walked to the closest bench and sat down opposite the most gorgeous view from the island. Waves lapped up on the beach just feet away from her. The grass around her appeared to glow green, and pansies danced in the breeze from their beds amidst tufts of grass. She couldn't leave this place.

Independence was fun, invigorating. Defiance grew in her heart whenever she thought about having to go home. That wasn't an option. She loved partying every night and gaining the attention of older men, especially Brock. She breathed in a big gulp of the cool Michigan breeze to try and gain composure. She didn't want to cry, but she did. For the first time since leaving home. It wasn't because she was sad, but frustrated. And angry. If she had to sleep out on this bench and become a homeless tourist, that's what she'd do.

Erik drew up behind the park bench. He pulled back on the reins for the horses to stop. "Stay boys," he commanded as he got off his carriage.

He leaned up against the carriage. With arms crossed, he watched her blonde hair softly fall around her face as she turned to look out at a boat sailing toward the island. Did her face glisten just then?

Marty had seen her at the hotel earlier that afternoon. She had been trying to find a place to stay. He questioned his motives. Why would he want to help this poser? She was rude and full of herself. He was a sucker for needy women, but crying ones made him melt into submission.

He stepped away from the carriage and approached her from behind. She wiped her face with a tissue and then blew her nose. Even though she probably didn't know he was behind her, she was using the tactic to lure someone. He felt the bait in his mouth.

He stood a foot behind the bench and almost decided to turn and walk away, but something drew him to her like a magnet to a refrigerator. He stepped closer to the bench and crossed his arms. What would he say? This girl's issues really weren't any of his business. Were they?

She must have sensed someone close as she abruptly turned to look at him. His easy escape was gone, he now had no choice but to speak. "Hi." It was lame, but he was caught unprepared.

She looked away. "What do you want?"

47

"I was just giving the horses a break and happened to see you sitting out here."

"Can't a woman sit on a bench?" She turned back and looked away from him. "Look at the view?"

"Absolutely." Erik almost turned to leave. Her attitude was still in place since their last encounter. "Call me stupid, but I'm a sucker for a crying woman." He wasn't sure why he had to tell her that.

"What does that make you? My guidance counselor? A hero?" She looked back at him again in annoyance. "Why do you care? You don't even know me."

Erik resisted the urge to get back on his carriage and drive away, even though that's exactly what he really wanted to do. He stepped closer to the bench. "Can I sit down?"

Kenna shook her head. "No. Just leave me alone."

Erik held his tongue and growing irritation. He turned to leave, but stopped dead in his tracks. He remembered some of the young kids from the shelter where he used to volunteer, and he knew that her comment was a cover-up. A veil. One thing he was very good at, and that was reading people. He turned back. "I know we didn't start our..." he grasped for a good word. Relationship? Encounter? He decided to not finish the sentence and stood to the side of the bench looking down on the small, very young-looking girl.

As a gentle breeze blew off of the lake, the scent of her perfume drifted through the air. It was a familiar smell and unfortunately for him, one of his favorites. He bent closer. "Please?"

Kenna looked up, "Why?"

Erik put his hands in his pockets. "I have this insatiable appetite to help people. Kinda like...,"

"A super hero?"

Erik shifted to the other foot. "Maybe."

Kenna shook her head. "I don't need your super powers, or your help."

Erik sat down beside her as she edged her way down to the opposite end of the bench. He laughed. "I don't bite." Women never slid away from him like that. For some reason, it made him want to try harder. "Why are you crying?" She was silent. Erik held out his hand. "By the way, I'm Erik."

This wasn't in the plan. She didn't want this man's help. Her whole reason for leaving home was to be rid of people wanting to protect her.

Shield her. How could any girl have her own life or ever enjoy it, if everyone around her wanted to protect her?

Above all, what would his wife think of her? "I need to go." She'd managed to see their little family several times in the last few days. She wanted to disappear on the island as a flirt and a city girl, not a home wrecker.

Erik caught her arm and pulled her back down on the bench.

She turned to glare at him, but he was smiling.

"Leave me alone," she demanded.

"Okay." Erik raised both hands in the air. "Can I ask you your name? I gave you mine."

"Kenna."

"Well, I would say it was nice to meet you, but I'm not sure that would be anything you want to hear from me." Kenna thought he wanted to say something else, but he stopped himself.

She kept quiet. Not because she really wanted to, but because she knew, down deep, that was probably the wisest thing to do.

"Okay then. Sorry to bother you. Maybe you can find someone else to stop and ask if they can do anything to help." He stood to leave.

Kenna knew his statement was true. All the men at the bars wanted one thing, and it wasn't to help her. Even though she knew that to be true, she had to keep up her image. If she didn't, she might be found.

"You don't know me. I know you think you can help me, but I'm here to find myself, make a life for myself without others trying to tell me what my life should be." Kenna cringed at telling him even this much information.

"I understand, Kenna. I've been there myself."

Kenna blinked back tears and looked off toward the lighthouse at the far end of the island. Her city girl image began to crumble.

"You wouldn't understand." Kenna looked around, trying to see who might be watching them. "Where's your wife?" She purposefully needed to change the subject.

"My wife?"

"Yeah, and your kids?"

Erik laughed.

Kenna turned to him. "Why are you laughing?"

"They're not who you think they are."

Kenna stood up and crossed her arms. "Oh, I see. You're that kind of man."

Erik stood and put his hands up like he was about to be arrested. "No. Now wait."

Kenna pointed to Erik's chest. "No. You wait. Go back to your wife and stop trying to flirt with other girls." She turned on her heel and walked away.

She could hear Erik laughing from behind her. Before she got out of earshot she heard him say, "You have the looks of a New York City girl, but you have a Nebraska temper."

She turned her head and sneered at him.

He laughed that much harder.

Fury surged through Kenna. The more she thought about a man like that flirting with her, the more her blood boiled. It was one thing to be doing what she was doing, pretending to be someone else, escaping from her old life, but cheating on your wife was despicable in her eyes. He probably did it a lot. He was very attractive. If he produced lines like he just did with her, many women would succumb to a hero. A rescuer. A man trying to be a friend.

She shook her head as she walked down the sidewalk. Well, not her. She wouldn't fall for this kind of man. Even someone as handsome as he. No way. Her mother might have caused her to only want to rebel, but her father managed to instill in her morals, and one of them was not to date a married man.

Above all, how did he know she wasn't from New York City? She needed to be much more careful from now on, especially where Erik was concerned. Maybe she needed to cement her image a little more. The only way she knew to do that now was to solidify her relationship with Brock. She'd been dying to know what it was like to kiss a man, especially someone like Brock. She headed right for the bar where she usually found him around this time each day.

Kenna found Brock at the corner of the restaurant, at his usual table. She headed right over and sat with him.

"Kenna." Brock smiled as he looked up from his plate.

"Brock, I have a question for you."

Brock set down his fork, picked up his napkin and wiped off his mouth. "Shoot." He smiled.

"Am I pretty?"

"Kenna," Brock looked down at the table, "That's quite the question."

"I know, I know," Kenna shifted in her seat, scooted her chair back and crossed her legs so Brock could see them.

His eyebrows raised. "Why, Kenna. Yes," he nodded, "yes you are."

"Attractive to you?"

Brock scooted his chair closer to Kenna. "Absolutely." Kenna watched as he looked down at her legs as though he would give anything to touch her right now.

"Good." Kenna scooted her chair closer to him. "What are you drinking?"

Brock knew Kenna was younger than most of the women he usually hung out with, but he just couldn't help being attracted to her. Especially because of her age. Most women his age knew his wiles and wouldn't last longer than a few drinks and a free dinner. Kenna seemed to adore him, fueling his fire to spend more and more time with her. She stroked his ego. He smiled at her.

"Kenna?"

The girl turned to him and smiled, "What?"

"Can I kiss you?"

Surely this was her first kiss. He pulled her close as he pressed his lips to hers. She tasted heavenly, with a scent of rum on her breath. It was a sweet kiss, and as he pulled away, he was positive his premonition was dead right.

This young thing looking at him with longing in her eyes had never been kissed.

He prided himself on getting older, more mature, lovers. Somehow Kenna made him feel young again. Renewed. He'd teach her how to kiss and hopefully, much, much more.

Carl watched the two in the corner and shook his head. That girl had no idea what kind of trouble she could be getting herself into. He saw her bend down, kiss Brock on the lips, and leave the restaurant.

Brock finished his lunch and headed toward the door, tossed a twenty dollar bill onto the counter. He smiled at him.

"Eating out of my hand," he grinned and pounded the counter in triumph.

Carl handed a drink to the man at the other end of the bar.

"Who was that?"

"His name is Brock. He's a man whore."

"Whoa. Seriously?"

Carl nodded. "That girl is playing with fire."

Marty nodded. "I've heard all about her."

"I wish I knew her real age." Carl picked up a cup and began shining it with his towel. "I'd get him in trouble for sure if I only knew her age. I guarantee one thing...she's a minor. They come in here all the time wanting liquor with those fake IDs. One day, maybe I'll get a back-bone and tell them no."

Chapter 8

Kenna paced in her room that afternoon. She couldn't spend another night in a place costing seventy-five dollars. In forty-five days she'd be out of money, and that didn't include food and eating out. Even though today, she'd gotten a free lunch from Brock.

She decided to begin packing to avoid chewing her lip. Pulling her pink luggage from where it sat in her closet, she unzipped the flaps. One by one every outfit Kenna owned came out of her closet, as she placed them into her suitcases.

Maybe she could stay out tonight. All night. Then she wouldn't have to worry about another hotel fee. But where? The bars would close around two. The evenings were usually cool on the island. And where could she put all her stuff?

What about Brock? Maybe he'd keep her luggage at his place. Would that be too forward? Would he think of it as her way of saying, "I'd like to spend the night?" After this afternoon's flirt session, she tended to believe she might have gone a little too far. But she didn't care. She loved kissing him more than even flirting.

She quickly folded more clothes and stuffed them in a duffel bag. It might work. She could tell him she was transitioning into a place of her own and it wouldn't be ready until tomorrow. Scanning the room, she made sure she had everything. She left a small tip on the dresser. Then, thinking of May, she stuffed the money back into her pocket.

Throwing her duffel bag over her shoulder, she dragged everything to the door. She pulled open the door, and listened for any sound of May. She'd need to leave unnoticed. May would pry. The old woman had been nice to her, but knowing all her business just wasn't an option.

Hearing no noise outside her room, she descended slowly. Quietly. Tiptoeing down the stairs, Kenna came to the bottom just as another guest turned from the dining room to go to his room. Kenna jumped and gasped.

"Oh, I'm sorry, did I scare you?" The man touched Kenna's arm.

"Sorry, I'm just a bit jumpy I guess."

The man apologized again, then proceeded up the stairs.

Kenna opened the door and found herself walking the streets of the island, without a place to stay.

Chapter 9

Claire glanced at each of Alisha's brothers as they put all the evidence gathered over the past week onto the kitchen table for everyone to see. Her mother-in-law took away their dinner dishes, placing them into a sink full of suds. Soon she began stacking clean ones in the kitchen strainer to the right of the sink.

"Have you tried tracking her cell phone?" Phillip asked as he took another bite of his dessert.

Michael sifted through the stack of papers in front of him to find the cell phone bill. "The cell phone company said it's expensive. Her calls stopped on the fifteenth, a day after she disappeared. I think she ditched it."

John spooned some sugar into his coffee and stirred, "Officer Dan said she's of legal age. If there is substantial evidence that she has run away, they really can't do anything about it."

Samuel shook his head and leaned back into his chair, folding his arms. "When I get my hands on that girl I think I'll..."

"We aren't going to talk that way. None of us are really sure why she left or even wanted to leave," Michael rubbed his forehead. "But one thing's for sure, she planned the whole thing."

"Have you talked to Erica yet?" John added.

Rita wiped her hands on a towel and sat down to join the boys. "I talked to her mother yesterday. She's not talking."

"I'll make her talk," Samuel sat forward and rested his elbows on the table.

"I think she knows something, but Alisha's sworn her to secrecy. I guarantee it. They are best friends, for Pete's sake. Girls can shut their mouths tighter than a drum or prattle on until you want them to stop and they won't." John threw the police report back down.

A baby cry erupted from the other side of the table. Claire shifted the baby up on her shoulder and put her finger to her lips. "Don't raise your voice, John. You're scaring Nathan."

"It's hard not being angry at Alisha." Every son stopped their drinking or talking to look at their mother. "She has chosen to run away. She's old enough to know better. Your father and I raised her to know better. If she feels this is how she should treat us, then we should let her have her way."

Silence reigned.

Rita left the room. The stairs creaked under her footsteps. Claire knew at that moment, her mother-in-law had given up.

"Getting mad isn't going to help this situation," Claire stood and began jiggling the fussy baby in her arms.

"I'm sorry," John responded. "I don't mean to get her so upset, but I'm with Samuel. When we finally figure out where that girl is, I'm gonna let her have all of this frustration that has built up in me."

"Maybe that's the problem," Claire leaned closer into the table and every brother stopped to look at her. "Listen to all of you. You've been so eager to get to her so you can do what? Beat her? C'mon. Could that be why she left? You boys can be so protective of her at times."

Michael touched his wife's shoulder.

"I don't mean to hurt anyone's feelings. I know how much all of you love her, but sometimes she would tell me how she felt so stifled around here. She's grown up now. Maybe you boys need to start treating her as thought she is grown, instead of always your baby sister."

The brothers all shifted uncomfortably in their chairs.

"I didn't listen as carefully to her as I should, but sometimes you guys strangle her with good intentions. I know you want her safe, but she's just nineteen. A nineteen-year-old wants some freedom. Do you give her any?" Claire shifted the baby to her other shoulder. "I don't mean to be disrespectful, but your mother hasn't helped. She has smothered Alisha ever since your father died. I'm not sure why, but we've all been caught up in the moment of everything changing around here." Claire sat as the baby settled down. "Guys, she ran away from home to get away from here. For a reason."

Silence now replaced agitated discussion.

"But why now? Dad's death was hard on all of us. She hasn't thought of anybody but herself." Samuel added.

"What time would have been a good time to go out on her own, you guys? When could she have approached any of you and said anything about leaving home? Someone here raise your hand if you ever encouraged her to think about doing anything but staying here. On the farm."

"She's great here. She took good care of the books. She's a miracle with the calves, and knows exactly when a birthing cow needs attention. She was amazing at listening to the nightly monitor from the birthing barn."

Claire sat back in her chair. "There you go. This farm is your life. Maybe that's not exactly what Alisha wants for her life."

"Did she tell you she wanted to leave home, Claire?" Michael took the baby from his wife's arms.

"Not in those words, but all the signs were there. You were just all too busy to see them. Look what I found up in her room yesterday. I didn't dare let Mother see these."

Claire got up from the table and went to the kitchen counter. She grabbed some DVDs from behind the toaster and put them on the table for the brothers to see.

"What are these?" Samuel spoke as he picked up a video and looked it over.

"They're some reality show DVDs. These are just three I found, but there are many more. Probably ten or fifteen stuffed under her bed."

"Mom never allowed Alisha to watch things like that. How'd she get them?" John picked up the videos and grimaced.

"Who knows? But they have to be a link to what she's been wanting to do for a while. We just need to find things like this and figure out how they link together."

Chairs scooted across the floor as two of Alisha's brothers got up and left the table, going up the stairs to their rooms.

John sat back in his chair, tipping it on the back two legs. "We need to tell Mom if you really think this is a tip to where Alisha went. Do you?"

"I don't know. Maybe. I truly believe that she didn't want the farm life to be her life. She'd often tell me how she wanted to see places. Far away. She wanted to travel. To see the world."

The baby started to cry again. "I need to feed Nathan, but I would stop arguing and start looking for her. We know Alisha better than anyone else. We can find her, we just need to get our heads together and figure it out. But I'm warning you. If we find her and she has run away, she just might not want to come home."

***

57

Erik saw Marty coming down the sidewalk. He held up his hand to catch his friend's attention.

"Erik, my man." Marty gave him a hug and patted his back. "How's life on the ranch?"

Erik laughed. "Great. What's up?"

"Just heading home from lunch. Hey, you know that chick?"

Caught off guard, Erik shook his head. "Who?"

"That girl. From New York City."

"Kenna?"

"Yeah, her!" Marty look puzzled, "How'd you know her name?"

"What about her?" Erik had no intention of going into a lengthy conversation about the girl.

"Well, I was just having some lunch and I got to talkin' to the bartender."

Erik wasn't sure what this had to do with Kenna, but he let Marty continue.

"It's a guy. At the bar. The bartender said he's a player. Your girl has been hanging out with him."

Erik shook his head. "Marty, she isn't *my* girl. Why would I care?"

"'Cause. You're a good guy. You care about people."

Erik laughed. "Okay, I do care about people."

"Of course you do." Marty hit his shoulder.

Erik folded his arms. "But what does that matter?"

"She's got this old guy hitting on her," Marty pointed to the bar behind him, "in there."

"How old?"

"Well, not hearing aid or cane kind of old guy, but a much older guy. Too old for that chick."

"So, what's that got to do with me?" Erik raised his hands in defiance.

"If the bartender is worried about it, shouldn't you be?"

"Whatever bro!" Erik headed toward the hotel. "Catch you later." Erik turned from his friend and headed in the opposite direction. He really didn't think this guy would be a huge problem for Kenna. On the other hand, Kenna might be a handful for him.

Marty called from behind him, "I just thought you'd care, that's all." It was evident that the guy didn't know Kenna very well, but soon he'd learn the truth about her. Erik knew at least one thing for sure, it wasn't Kenna he was most worried about.

Kenna stood at the gallery door. She knew it wasn't the best of ideas, but there wasn't a place available on the island that didn't make her spend her savings or sit homeless. She started to turn around just as the door swung open. "Kenna! How are you? You've finally come to see the gallery. Good for you!" Brock gestured for her to come inside.

He had been fun company for her at the bars on most nights. It kept the really wild, drinking boys away to have him at her table. They'd often shared evening meals.

"Come to stay for a while?" Brock commented as Kenna pulled her luggage over the door's threshold.

"I'm sorry, Brock, but I have a bit of a problem. I've rented a room on the far side, by the stores," she added off the top of her head, "but it won't be ready until tomorrow."

Brock smiled. "You wanna stay here?"

Kenna felt sweat drip down her back. It was a hot day, but the perspiration wasn't all from being warm. She knew she had to keep up her image. So she smiled. Charmingly. "Just for tonight. I promise. I'll be gone in the morning."

Brock brushed his hand across her cheek. "I couldn't be more happy to share my place. C'mon in."

Soon he was leading Kenna up the stairs to his apartment. She cringed as she realized there was probably only one bedroom, but maybe a couch. She'd do her best to make it very clear, that was where she'd be sleeping.

"I'll just set my things here." She found a couch just under Brock's front window.

"Wherever you are comfortable, my dear." He picked up a coffee cup off his kitchen bar. "Coffee?"

Kenna nodded as she set her duffel bag on the couch. "I'd love some. My head hurts from last night." She giggled.

"Was good last night, wasn't it?"

"I'm a sucker for champagne. Always have been."

She went to sit at the bar as he finished putting water in the coffee maker.

"I really appreciate this, Brock. I like the island, but I really don't want to spend the night out on a bench."

"No biggie. We'll have fun." He smiled as he handed her a mug. "This coffee will be ready in just a minute."

Kenna slid the mug across the counter from one hand to another. She knew the key to making this work was to keep him out as late as possible. "Let's hit the Pink Flamingo tonight. Want to?"

"She needs a place to stay." Jenny told Erik that afternoon. "May has a guest at her place."

Erik knew this day would come. It was time to leave Jenny and the kids. Not off the island, but just out of her house.

"Isn't that May's business? She does run a bed and breakfast." Erik sat down in the chair he'd miss the most after leaving Jenny. It had been his brother's chair, and he loved sitting in it while watching the kids play at his feet each night. He reached down to unzip his boots.

"This girl appears to have run away or something. You know May. She hates to see anyone in trouble. She says she stays out almost every night. Late. She says she's too young to be doing that."

Erik shook his head. "May needs to mind her own business."

"Erik, that's cold."

He knew it and sighed. "I'm sorry. I've just had my fill of trying to help people lately."

Jenny looked at him with surprise on her face. "You're ready to leave us. Aren't you?"

Erik cringed. "That's not what I meant."

Jenny walked into the kitchen. He reached down and pulled off his work boots. She misunderstood. Women were starting to really annoy him.

"Jenny," he walked into the kitchen and came up behind her. "I didn't mean you and the kids. The day I leave you and the kids here alone will not be a *prize winning* day."

He turned her around to talk to her. "In fact. I'm already regretting it." She was crying.

He did what he knew to help her. He enveloped his arms around her shoulders and hugged her tight. "I'm sorry, Jenny. I didn't mean you at all."

"Then what did you mean?"

Erik held out a tissue box to his sister-in-law. "There's a girl on the island. I keep running into her."

Jenny pulled away, nodded, and wiped her eyes.

Erik sighed. "She's very pretty. I met her about a week ago when she arrived." He waited a moment.

"Yes? Continue."

"She just..." Erik looked at the ceiling trying to get the description of Kenna, "Drives me nuts."

Jenny grinned. "Why?"

Erik shook his head. "No." She raised her eyebrows. "No, Jenny. I'm not interested."

"Okay. If you say so."

"See, now you are annoying me." Erik laughed and pulled her close again. "May wouldn't send you anyone who wouldn't be a good boarder. Why not go for it?"

"You sure?"

"Unfortunately, yes."

Chapter 10

Brock moved in closer to Kenna at the bar that night. He hinted more than once that they should be heading for home. Something made her hesitate to think of sleeping with him, even though there had been nights when his alluring personality made it hard to head home to her own place.

He'd dropped passes more than once, but never as forcefully as tonight. Yet tonight, she was the one flirting with danger. She'd prided herself on how alluring she could be, never really following through with how far she would go with a man.

"So Kenna, how about a little stroll by the water tonight?" The man leaned into Kenna and brushed his hand against her shirt, so gently that Kenna almost didn't notice it.

"Ummm," after experimenting with all the drinks, Kenna now had a better grip of what she could handle without running out of the bar and vomiting into the nearest trash can. She also knew to keep her senses intact for nights exactly like this one. Especially tonight. She needed to think of a new plan. Her belongings were safe in Brock's apartment, but she wasn't sure she was ready to spend the night. Just yet. She knew he wouldn't allow her to just sleep on his couch. "I need to use the restroom. Can you excuse me?"

She let her hand linger on the art man's shoulder as she walked around him. Nothing like leaving him wanting for more. When she reached the bathroom she went into a stall and sat down on the lid of the toilet. "What now, Kenna, what now?" She fumbled with the handle of her purse and then looked up above her head. A large window opened to let the island breeze filter in. Standing up, she stepped up on the toilet's lid and reached out to pull down the window a little more. She could do this. Escape through a window in the bathroom. What a concept. She'd done it many times out her own window at home.

She stepped up on the back of the toilet's tank and then pulled with her hands to get her first foot on the windowsill. It proved to be a stretch, but she'd rather escape this way than have to go back through that bar and back to Brock's apartment.

She pulled herself up, and managed to get both feet onto the windowsill. Sitting in a squatting position, she looked down. A trash can perched just below the window. It was overflowing, with the lid askew, but Kenna was able to turn around and plant one foot on it. She tested it first before putting all of her weight on the lid. It seemed doable. She gripped the windowsill and lowered her second foot.

Before she knew it, the trash can had gained a life of its own and wheeled away from under her feet. She hung from the windowsill for seconds, contemplating whether the drop of approximately six feet would cause bodily harm.

That's when she heard it. Loud and clear.

"Need a little help?"

She looked over her right shoulder to see Erik standing behind her on the curb. She felt her hands grow numb from the sharp edge of the windowsill. "If you wouldn't mind."

Erik secured her calves, supporting all of her weight, and Kenna released one hand from the windowsill. As she did, she looked down to see him not looking up her skirt, but facing the wall instead.

"Let go, Kenna. I've got you."

She released her second hand and grabbed the top of his head. He lowered her to the sidewalk. Kenna wiped off the front of her dress. She knew her face revealed the embarrassment of the moment. Wincing in pain, she felt the blood rush back into her fingers as she flexed them.

Erik stood in front of her and crossed his arms. "May I ask?"

Before he could say more, Kenna offered, "Looks pretty silly, huh?"

"Well, silly or..." Erik smiled. "Maybe you like hanging from bathroom windows."

Kenna giggled, "Kinda like that."

"You okay now?" Erik strode over to his bicycle on the sidewalk.

Kenna nodded.

"See you around." He jumped onto his bicycle and began to peddle down the street.

There was only one thing for her to do. He was her last hope. Brock would soon catch on that she was no longer in the bathroom, and she knew he wouldn't allow her to just walk away tonight.

"Erik?" She called after the man.

He stopped his bicycle and turned around. "Yes?"

"Uh. I think I might need your help after all."

Erik got off his bicycle, turned it around and walked it over to her.

"Kenna, it's not any of my business why you were escaping out of a bar window," he sighed, "But how can I help you?"

"There is someone in the bar that..." Kenna knew that everything she revealed now would be not only embarrassing but very uncomfortable. So she decided to just get to the point. "I really need to find a place to stay tonight."

Erik nodded. He put his bike in a rack close by and motioned for Kenna to follow him. "C'mon."

Chapter 11

Kenna inspected the room Erik offered her, finding it comfortable. It had a bed, dresser, a desk and two windows, complete with fluffy white curtains, looking out over Main Street. All of it reminded her of her old room back home.

She sighed and perched herself on the edge of the bed. She smoothed down the pink and mint green quilt. Her mother made quilts. Kenna usually cut out the squares for her log-cabin and around-the-world designs. She fingered the edge of the quilt and looked at the mitered corners. They matched at the corners. Whoever made the quilt knew how to sew.

Standing up, Kenna made her way to the window and pushed up the window pane. A cool breeze fluttered the curtains. Relief filled her heart like the fresh air now blowing her hair. Did she really think she could just spend the night with Brock without having to sleep with him?

Kenna raised both hands to her face. She rubbed the sides as a headache began to form. She'd never had so many headaches. Perhaps it was the drinking.

She enjoyed getting drunk. It helped her escape the thought of how she would manage to stay on the island all summer with the finances she had left. Somehow it relieved her pain, and the loneliness left in her father's wake. The headaches and a few vomiting sessions were the only bad part.

A soft knock made her jump. "Yes?" she answered.

"Hi," The woman held out her hand. "I'm Jenny."

Kenna shook her hand. "I'm Kenna."

The woman smiled. "Hi, Kenna. Erik told me you needed a place to stay tonight."

Kenna nodded.

"Well you are welcome here. I just wanted to make sure you didn't need anything before I go back to bed," she added.

Kenna shook her head.

Jenny turned to leave. "Well, if I can get you anything, just let me know. My room is just down the hallway. The last one on the left. There are towels here in this closet," she opened up a closet behind her. "The bathroom is between your bedroom and mine. The first door on the right."

Kenna got her voice back. "Thank you."

Jenny smiled. "You're welcome." She went to the door and opened it to leave. Before leaving she turned back to Kenna, "Where have you been staying, if I may ask?"

Kenna didn't feel like the woman was being nosey, so she answered, "A bed and breakfast a few streets over." Before she thought it through she added, "I needed to leave it. A nosey old woman wouldn't leave me alone. I need my space."

Jenny nodded, "Well, sleep well."

As soon as the door shut, Kenna laid her head down on the soft, plush pillow. May's rooms were nice, but her pillows were a little hard and the beds had seen better days. This bed felt, not only soft, but familiar. And very comfortable. She looked out the bedroom window. One of her most familiar and happy places to hide was under a windowsill at her house back home. Jenny's room made her feel safe, too.

Jenny came down the stairs picking up toys off the staircase as she descended. She found Erik waiting at the bottom. "I think she's comfortable."

Erik nodded. "Thanks for doing this. She looked pretty scared tonight. She must have been in a pretty bad situation to be crawling out a bar window."

Jenny nodded and put the toys in a nearby playpen. "I think she's May's tenant, the one she's been telling me about. Kenna just told me that she's been staying at a bed and breakfast with a meddling old woman." Jenny smiled.

"Yeah, that would be May." Erik added.

"Why do you think she is on the island?"

"I don't know," Erik answered. "I found her on a bench a few days ago. Crying."

Jenny scowled. "She seems awfully young to be on her own. The older I get, the younger the island college kids seem. But I think you're right. There's something different about this one."

"Marty said a guy in the bar was hitting on her. Maybe we can help."

Jenny nodded. "Maybe she can stay here for a while."

Erik shook his head. "Not unless she straightens her act up. I've seen her drunk and running the streets late at night. That isn't an influence I want around my niece and nephew."

"I agree. But reaching out to her for a few nights wouldn't hurt. If she did want to stay, I would need to talk to her about all of that."

"Yeah. Big time. A little bit of big brother Erik wouldn't hurt her either."

Laughing, Jenny pushed his chest. "Oh yeah, you're so big and tough."

"What?" Erik laughed. "I'm important back home. Everyone's scared of me." He strutted a little and puffed his chest out for his sister-in-law to see.

Jenny laughed harder. "Erik, the only thing tough in you is your denial that you see something in her that interests you."

"Sheesh," Erik harrumphed, "Why does everyone keep saying that? No way. I'm done with girls like her. Girls like Kenna are trouble with a capital T."

"Whatever you say," Jenny motioned up the stairs. "I'm going to bed."

––––––––––––––

"What's the matter, Brock?" Carl grinned at the patron. "Lose your date?"

Brock sneered. "She's probably passed out in the bathroom. Wanna send someone in to check on her?"

He called one of his waitresses over and whispered in her ear.

"Tell her to bring her out. I'll take care of her."

"Oh yeah. We'll do that for sure," he eyed the creep. "You know, she's a minor."

"Oh really?" Brock crossed his arms.

"I could get you in trouble for soliciting a minor."

Brock laughed and uncrossed his arms. He leaned into the counter, "I'm not the one serving her drinks."

The waitress came out. "No one there."

"Are you sure, Deb?" Carl was about as surprised as Brock looked.

"You're lying," Brock said.

"See for yourself," Deb motioned toward the bathroom. Brock stormed out without checking for himself.

"That guy's a jerk," Deb waved the angry man off.

"Yeah, I know," Carl picked up another glass and began wiping it.

"If he wasn't so blasted hot, more women would figure it out sooner and not get involved with him in the first place."

"He's not so hot." He flexed his muscles for Deb.

Deb laughed, as she added more beer to the cup she was filling, "Yup, you right, hotness right here. Who needs men like Brock?"

Carl smiled and nodded.

Chapter 12

"How was your morning?" Erik stomped into his sister-in-law's house after work, trying hard to get a bit of straw off his boots before entering.

"Quiet," Jenny giggled, "Well, as quiet as it can be with a four-year-old and a toddler."

"Where's Kenna?"

"Still sleeping, I guess." Jenny bent down to pick up a toy on the living room floor.

Erik dropped into a chair, "Sleeping? Are you sure?"

"She hasn't come downstairs all day."

"Lazy child," Erik scowled and crossed his arms.

"Erik, be kind." Jenny sat on the couch across from her brother-in-law.

"She's a piece." He slumped forward, and got right to the point. "Jenny, I want to take her with me to unhitch the horses."

"Why?"

"We need to talk."

"About...?" Jenny crossed her arms. "Erik, I know you don't trust this girl. I'm not really sure who she is, but there is one thing you need to remember..."

At that moment, a door creaked at the stop of the stairs and then shut.

Kenna felt a chill as she descended into the living room. She rubbed her arms and stopped when she saw Erik, in his carriage outfit, and Jenny talking in the room. She knew she needed to leave. She'd managed to pull her hair up into a ponytail so it wasn't so messy, and yesterday's make-up had long been wiped away. She grew more uncomfortable thinking about her appearance.

"Kenna. Did you sleep well?" Jenny smiled up at her.

"Uh, yes," Kenna almost stumbled on the last step. "What time is it?"

"Three o'clock." Erik stood from his chair.

Kenna blinked. "In the afternoon?"

Both Jenny and Erik nodded.

Erik approached her, "We need to talk. Do you want to take a ride with me?"

Jenny stood up, too. "Erik, maybe Kenna would like some breakfast or something to eat." Jenny pushed past Erik and went to Kenna.

Kenna was famished. She'd awakened to a grumbling stomach, yet the drinks from the night before also left her with a headache and upset stomach. It had been easier to just fall back to sleep in the comfortable bed, than to face questions and accusations from Erik. Last night had been the first time she'd begun to see him in a different light, but she knew morning would be different. "I am a bit hungry, but I can head into town now and get myself something to eat."

"Nonsense. The kids are taking their naps. I have some leftovers from our lunch. C'mon and stay here," Jenny motioned toward the kitchen.

"Oh, I don't know. You've been so kind to let me stay here overnight, I couldn't impose," Kenna was shocked to hear manners come out of her mouth, and so easily.

Jenny smiled and held out a hand, "I insist. C'mon. How about a turkey sandwich?"

Kenna ate in silence as Jenny and Erik grabbed some glasses of iced tea and sat at the table with her. They chatted about various things, but Erik still seemed annoyed that she had stayed for some lunch. She tried to finish quickly, so she could escape his accusing eyes.

She pushed the empty plate away and began to thank Jenny for the food, but before she could, Erik started in.

"May I ask why you were hanging from a bar window last night?"

"Erik, let her finish her lunch." Jenny took the plate. "Would you like a cookie or something for dessert?"

Kenna shook her head, "No. Thank you." More manners. Jenny was so nice, Kenna had a hard time being her ornery, sassy self.

The thank you must have shut up Erik, because now he just sat back in his chair.

"So, I was thinking," Jenny sat down beside the girl, blocking Erik's stare.

Kenna listened as the woman told her she'd been looking for a roommate and was wondering if Kenna was interested. Kenna wasn't sure how to process this. Erik would surely not want Kenna in his path, especially not in his own house. She looked past Jenny to Erik who was now on his feet and pacing.

"Jenny, we need to talk," he said.

"Erik," Jenny turned to him. "I think it's a great idea. I've been looking for a roommate. Kenna obviously needs a place to stay."

Kenna could no longer keep quiet. She stuffed the manners that seemed to be oozing out of her and stood, "Why would you need a roommate with a husband and two kids living with you?"

"Oh, Erik?" Jenny laughed, "He isn't my husband."

Erik looked at Kenna and crossed his arms, appearing more alarmed and annoyed.

"Erik is my brother-in-law." Jenny pulled on Kenna's arm. "Please sit down. We need to tell you a little more about ourselves."

Kenna sat, but eyed Erik. Just like he was eyeing her.

Jenny continued, "My husband was recently killed in Afghanistan. He was in the Army."

Kenna's stare now shifted uncomfortably to Jenny. "I'm sorry," she mumbled automatically, knowing her words would bring little comfort. She couldn't believe what she was being told.

"Erik is his little brother. Since Tom's death, Erik has been here to help me. I don't know what I would have done without him."

Erik turned and walked out of the room. He seemed just as angry as before Jenny told Kenna her story. "I'm sorry. I really did think you two were married."

"I know. Many people didn't know Tom. It's okay. I miss my husband desperately." Tears began to form in Jenny's eyes. "It's been a rough few months, but every single day something happens that I know helps me to get through all the hard times. Erik has been so great. To me and the kids. We cherish the time he has been here, but you know, the relationship is now getting confusing to those who see us together. We need to make other arrangements. A few days ago Erik and I were talking about me getting a roommate, and then he would move out. The income I could get from a renter could help me meet expenses and also give me the company I need until I figure out where and when my next step will be."

Kenna looked at the sweet woman across from her. She would give anything to be able to stay with her. She was kind and Kenna found the room upstairs not only comfortable, but familiar and warm. Before she could respond, Erik came back into the kitchen.

_____

He sat down at the table and faced Kenna. "Now, we need to talk."

"Erik," Jenny turned to him. "Can't this wait?"

"No," Erik motioned for Kenna. "We need to go for a ride, so we can talk."

"Erik, I'm not kidding."

"Neither am I. Kenna, c'mon."

"Whatever you have to say to Kenna, I can hear. This involves me, too." Jenny sat back and folded her arms.

"Not this time."

Kenna knew by the tone of Erik's voice, he meant business. She could just get up and walk out, but somehow she'd lost her voice. She knew she needed to hear Erik out, or the opportunity of this great new place to stay would be gone forever. She stood, "Jenny, it's okay. I'll go with him."

Jenny stood. "Erik, you really have no say in this whole matter."

Erik shook his head. "I have a responsibility to keep you and the kids safe."

"What does this have to do with?" Jenny started to interject, but Erik brushed past her.

"We'll be back," Erik took Kenna's elbow as he maneuvered her through the kitchen and out the front door.

Jenny walked behind them, but Erik kept guiding Kenna out to his carriage waiting at the curb.

Kenna heard just two words from Jenny as she scooted up onto the carriage bench. "Be nice." Kenna wasn't so sure which was more afraid of: Brock, or the man now calling the large horses to move down the street.

Before long, Kenna knew she needed to say something to get herself out of this little conversation about to take place with Erik. If he hadn't been so kind to her the night before, and been a bit of a rescuer, she'd not have been so obliging to go with him just now. As the horses picked up speed, she knew jumping off the carriage would not be an option. So she began with the only ammunition she had in defending herself against men. "Erik?"

Erik looked over at her, but continued to move the horses on faster and faster.

Kenna grabbed hold of the seat a little tighter. "You have no right..."

"Did you stay in Jenny's house last night? Did we not rescue you from whatever was scaring you out of that bar last night?"

Kenna shut her mouth. She wouldn't be able to reason with this man. After the carriage left a main road, she began a braver attempt, "Where are you taking me?"

"Oh, don't sweat Kenna. Just back to the stables. I need to unhitch the horses for the day and it's a place where we can talk."

Kenna knew that when the carriage stopped, she'd have a way of escape. She relaxed a bit on the seat. "What are we going to talk about?"

Erik pulled back on the reins as he entered a stable behind the Grand Hotel. "Whoa boys, whoa."

Kenna thought to run away while his hands were busy, but curiosity made her hesitate and stay in her seat.

Erik jumped down and began unhitching the horses from the carriage. Kenna looked back as other carriages came into the stables behind them. She might as well face her fate and listen to what Erik had to tell her.

"I need you to get off the carriage now," Erik called up to her. Kenna climbed down the side. For once, she wished she had on her farm boots and overalls. She looked down and saw a rein flopping around the hoof of one of the horses. She reached down and untangled it from his leg.

She looked up and saw Erik watching her. He nodded his thanks. Kenna tossed him the lead.

"Follow me," Erik took hold of the team and began leading them into a nearby barn. Kenna looked around, but all the men in the barns were busy taking care of other horses or sweeping barn straw. She decided to follow Erik. The barn's familiar smells matched Jenny's comfortable bedroom, each giving Kenna a sense of nostalgic relief.

As Erik grabbed a brush from the side of a stall and began brushing down his team, he asked Kenna, "Why don't you carry a cell phone?"

Kenna stopped in her tracks. "Is that why you brought me here? To ask about a cell phone?" She couldn't stop the irritation in her voice. This man was so confusing.

"No. I want to talk about other things. I was just curious about the phone. Kenna..."

Kenna knew this couldn't be the real reason he'd brought her here. "What?"

"I love Jenny. I love Taylor and Blake, too. They mean the world to me. They're about the only family I have left in the whole world. Since Tom's death, we have grown closer."

Kenna sat down on a bale of straw closest to the team. "I'm sorry about your brother."

"He was a great guy. He had everything in this world that I only dream of having someday. Since coming to the island this past spring, after he died, I thought I could be the one to help his wife get over his death. I thought, for some insane reason, that I could replace him." Erik unleashed more of the reins off the big horses. "Can you hand me those lines?"

Kenna rose, went to the side of the stable, and took down the lines Erik had asked for. "I couldn't replace him. I tried. Oh I tried hard, but I wasn't Tom." He started brushing again. "I will never be Tom."

Kenna sensed a bit of frustration in Erik's voice. She reached up on the wall and grabbed another brush and began brushing down the horse closest to her. Erik stopped talking and looked at her, but soon went back to his own brushing.

Finding her voice again, Kenna asked, "Why did you want to be someone you aren't?"

Erik stopped and looked at Kenna and smiled. "Hmmm, good question." His brushing continued, "I guess, if I have to admit the truth, I have always been jealous of my big brother. He always seemed to have it all together. Then when he married Jenny, I vowed I would have someone as wonderful as her someday."

"Why are you telling me this?" Kenna stopped her brushing and looked at Erik.

"I don't know. I guess I'm finally admitting something to myself. I'm not Tom and I know that now. I can't replace him."

Kenna nodded. The whole conversation reminded her of Michael and Claire. She had often envied their relationship as well. How easy it had been for them to meet in high school and fall in love. Her parents never questioned how Michael's life would be for him. They knew it would include Claire and caring for the farm. To have that much confidence in what was to be your future, would take away many of her own frustrations with life.

"I just need you to know one thing," Erik put down the brush and walked over to Kenna. Looking her directly in the eyes, he said, "You'd better not hurt either Jenny or those kids."

Kenna stepped back and put the brush she'd been using behind her back.

"I had better never hear that you came home drunk or was a horrible influence on those kids." Erik pointed a finger in her direction. "Do you understand?"

"What?" Kenna dropped the brush and looked to a nearby door. She wasn't quite sure what this man was capable of doing. She grew rigid and immediately the new Kenna returned, "How dare you?"

"I'm serious, Kenna. If you hurt any of them, if you don't pay your rent, or if you even eat something in that house that isn't yours, I'll put you on a ferry right back to wherever you came from. Do you understand?"

"You have no right!" Kenna began to walk for the closest door. "How dare you?"

"Kenna," Erik called after her. "You better know that if you stay in that house, you'll have me to deal with. If you do any of those things..."

Those were the last of Erik's words that Kenna could understand as she quickly walked out of the stable door.

A light rain began to fall as Kenna made her way back downtown. As she sat on a covered bench outside a downtown restaurant, it began to pour. Thankfully, the night before, she'd stuck her debit card in her pocket. Teeth chattering, she ducked into a nearby tourist shop and bought a sweatshirt and a cup of coffee.

Outside the store, she sat on a bench and pulled the shirt over her. It felt like a warm blanket on a winter night. She stopped shivering for a while, and sipped the warm drink. She did her best to come up with a good lie that Brock might believe.

Looking out over the water, dark clouds on the horizon alerted her that the rain wasn't going to let up. She needed her things. After drinking the coffee, she bravely headed toward Brock's art gallery. Despite the cold and rain, she needed to drum up the best flirty Kenna she could.

Lying to Brock was now her only alternative, but it was becoming easier and a bit fun. When she returned to the gallery, disheveled and wet, Kenna giggled and flirted, and told Brock that she'd passed out in the bathroom floor, and once she woke up, he was already gone. He seemed to believe her lie. And she easily got her luggage back after telling him that her apartment was finally ready.

She pulled out a little more charm. He seemed busy and would possibly let her go with just a kiss on her cheek. But he pulled her closer just before she left and whispered in her ear, "Someday I'll kiss you like a real man should."

She giggled as shivers ran up her spine. Brock had a way of making her know she shouldn't want more of his attention. But she did. If he wasn't so tantalizing, his actions would be scaring her. Even though he was a little forceful at times, she never encountered a man quite like him. Who was she fooling? She'd never had a real man like him give her attention before. He made her feel mature. Worth something. She admitted it to herself, he made her feel desired. She liked that feeling.

The night grew colder and the rain came down harder. Kenna was cold, hungry again, and weary. Even though she'd slept until the early afternoon, she felt as though she hadn't slept in days. She didn't want the suspicions of May. She knew there was only one place for her to go. Jenny was the only friendly one. Could she deal with Erik and his anger? She wasn't sure, but as she gazed down the empty streets of the town, she knew she couldn't sleep out on a bench tonight.

She made her way up a side street to Jenny's house. Pulling her luggage up onto the front porch, she sat down in one of the white wicker rockers, and took in the warmth of this woman's front porch. Pastel-covered cushions and pillows were arranged neatly on the furniture. Bright flowers spilled from the pots now soaking in the rain. As she sat back in the chair, Erik came out the front door.

"What are you doing out here?" he asked.

Kenna stood up. "I'm sorry. I know you don't want me here. But it's raining. I'm cold. I..." Kenna fought back tears. "I have no other place to go."

"I don't want you to misinterpret what I'm about to say, but I want to get something off my chest."

Kenna sat back down in the chair. "What?" She knew she had no other place to go. She had to listen or be out in the rain again.

Erik sat down and moved his chair up closer to Kenna. "You left me at the stable before I could communicate further my intentions. Like I said, Jenny and the kids are really important. They mean everything to me. I worry about them constantly. I'm always trying to protect them from absolutely anything and everything that could make their life harder." He smiled at Kenna. "I want them to be comfortable. Happy."

Kenna nodded. "I can see that."

"Well good. I don't want anything to make them worry. So I need to ask you a favor."

Kenna agreed. This was a bit easier than his earlier demands.

"Your lifestyle needs to change a bit."

"Like what?" Kenna suddenly felt the constraining life of home begin to emerge again. She grew rigid.

"It's your business if you want to drink, but it becomes my business when you arrive home drunk. I don't want my niece and nephew to see you in that kind of condition. I don't want Jenny to have to lie awake at night and wonder if you are coming home or not."

"Why should she care?"

Erik darted an angry look her way, "Because she will. She cares about others. She worries."

"Sounds like my mother." It came out of Kenna's mouth before she could stop it. She had to think quickly. What could she say to get out of this comment? Before she could say anything, Erik started again.

"I worry about Jenny. She misses my brother very much. She doesn't need stress. Any stress. Do you understand?"

Kenna's back stiffened. Even though she wanted to walk off the porch and out into the rain, she knew better. Instead, she said, "I understand."

Erik rose, too. "And, if you do anything to cause her stress, anything at all, I'll march you right out to the boat dock and send you back where you came from."

Kenna couldn't believe her ears. But she had no place to go, nowhere to stay as nice as Jenny's guest room. So she agreed. This had to be a temporary situation. She hadn't left home to be thrown into another jail.

Jenny came out the front door with Blake on her hip, "Kenna, what are you doing out here?"

Before she could answer her, Jenny was pushing her into the house and asking her if she was hungry again, and asking Erik to bring her things in behind them.

Rita sat down at the edge of her daughter's bed and looked around the room for any clues as to where her daughter might be hiding. They'd asked everyone they knew and no one had heard from or seen Alisha. The family had run out of answers.

Rage continued to build in Rita's mind. This child was only making things difficult, as usual. It wasn't that she didn't love her daughter and long for a meaningful relationship with her, but she knew what it took to keep an attractive girl like Alisha free from anything that might harm not only her reputation, but also her innocence.

At times, Rita wished she could have at least better communication with Alisha. She would watch Alisha talking with her father and wonder what it would be like to have a meaningful talk with her daughter. Jealousy would erupt in her heart whenever Alisha ran to her father, instead of her for answers or even a quick hug. Rita didn't have that kind of relationship with her own mother, and she knew it would probably never happen between Alisha and her. Not after this, especially.

Grant took time out of his life for each of his children. If he wasn't stopping by to assist one of the boys hoist a straw bale, or thread a worm on a hook, he was putting Alisha on his lap on a winter evening to rock her to sleep. He seemed to have a perfect relationship with each one of their children. And with her. For just a moment, she let herself remember the feel of his nuzzle in the morning, the look of laughter in his eyes, his voice saying her name, even the gentle way he scolded her for a harsh tone in her voice.

Rita shook her head and refocused. It was up to her to keep the family safe now. She understood what happened to young girls, Alisha's age, and she couldn't afford a situation where her daughter's reputation could hurt their business or their name. Not now. She needed her daughter's life to be exemplary and clean.

She hated thinking of Alisha watching those lascivious videos. She wondered what else could be found in this room which would hinder her own reputation with even her daughter-in-law? Rita stood and began rummaging through Alisha's drawers and under her bed.

She'd always been the disciplinarian; her husband was the softy. They came to her to confess their crimes. He always made her do the punishment, bring out the paddle. This was no different. Now she had to be the one to find out what Alisha was really up to.

Rita sat back on the bed and sighed. There was nothing in here to even hint at where Alisha might be. Alisha had disappeared so fully, that even after they reported it to the police, every avenue had come up empty. Just then, Rita then noticed a red light flashing on Alisha's DVD player. Alisha must have been watching this the last time she was in her room. She stood up and pushed the button to eject the DVD.

Rita looked at the title of the movie.

Michael rushed into the house. His mother sounded so sure on the phone that she had found a clue to his sister's whereabouts. He expected to find her and Claire sitting in the kitchen awaiting his arrival. What he found was them sitting in the living room, they seemed transfixed by a movie. He stared for a moment, then said, "Didn't you call me with a...?"

"Shush, Michael. Sit down." His wife pointed to the couch beside her.

He stood beside her instead. "Claire, I left Samuel alone with a birthing calf. I don't have time to watch..."

His wife pulled him down beside her on the couch and pointed to the television.

The scene of the movie showed a young man trying to find a suit to purchase in an antique store. Although the movie's setting looked to be in the nineteen seventies, the man was trying to find a suit from the eighteen hundreds.

"What the...?"

"Michael," his mother announced, "I think this might be a clue to where your sister has run off to. I found it in Alisha's DVD player upstairs."

Michael watched the movie for a few more seconds and grinned. He turned to his smiling wife burping his son over her shoulder. "Mackinac Island?"

Claire nodded. "Why wouldn't she go there? That's where your father always said he dreamed of going. Remember?"

He remembered. He chided his father and sister for watching this movie until they had to go out and purchase a new DVD because they had worn out the previous disk. His mother and Claire just might be on to something.

A smile appear on his mother's face. "Go find her, son." She stood up, and patted him on the back as she left to go upstairs.

Relief flooded her heart as Rita sat back down on Alisha's bed. This had to be the location, but how would they find Alisha? Would her reputation be intact? What if her daughter was doing things that would bring grief and heartache to her family and their reputation? Somehow, all of that grew dim against the hope of getting her daughter back.

Maybe Claire was right about stifling Alisha. She was now a maturing young woman. Rita had taught her right and wrong since she was a little girl. Why did she believe Alisha would stray from that now as she grew older? Perhaps she had been a little too harsh whenever Alisha brought up the fact she wanted a new hairstyle or fun, more stylish, clothes.

She was the mother of five sons. Alisha was not only her only daughter, but her youngest child. Perhaps she needed to change her domineering ways a bit. She admitted to God many times her frustrations over her daughter. Rita decided that if God allowed Michael to find her, she would do her best to be more of a friend to her daughter, instead of just a mother. Maybe, in a tiny way, they could have a relationship she only dreamed of having with her own mother.

Chapter 13

Erik stumbled upon a two-day weekend off. He whistled as he walked home that Friday night after wiping down the horses and putting them into their stalls. The roar of the daily crowd had settled to a dull hum, odd for a cool night in early July. A gull squawked overhead and sailed skillfully down on the path in front of him. As Erik grew closer, the bird danced out of his way and into the street.

"I've got nothin', pal." Erik opened his palms, displayed them to the curious bird, and continued his journey home. Crossing the street, he found Kenna directly in front of him. She wore a cute outfit, which seemed to be more appropriate for her age. Picking up his pace, trying to catch up to her, he saw her stop at a local vendor displaying flowers outside a store. He slowed as he watched her pick up a bouquet of lilacs and press them to her nose. The island's bushes had burst open thousands of them during the past day or two.

Kenna pushed her blonde hair back off her face and behind her ear. Her earlobe sparkled with a tiny diamond stud earring. He marveled at how pretty she was. Her tiny nose and prominent chin showed tanned skin and rosy cheeks. Her wild side sometimes contrasted with her image.

He couldn't get out of his head how comfortable she seemed in the stable with him just last week. She knew to pick up the line around the horse's hoof and she wasn't afraid to do it. This girl had been around horses before. It became truly evident when he asked for a special halter and she'd reached for the exact one he'd asked for. No New York City girl could know that draft horses always used lines instead of reins.

As he approached her, he pulled out his wallet. Kenna rummaged through her purse with her left hand, while still holding the bouquet in her right. He snatched the flowers out of her hand and held a ten dollar bill out to the clerk standing behind the flower display.

"Allow me."

Kenna gasped and jumped. "Erik. I didn't see you."

The clerk handed him back two dollars. Erik pressed the flowers to his nose. "Don't they smell absolutely delicious?" He handed them back to Kenna.

She smirked and took them from him, "Thank you."

"No problem. Pretty girls should have flowers every once in awhile."

Kenna blushed as she pressed the flowers to her nose again.

They looked into each other's eyes for a few seconds. Kenna blinked and then turned away. "I gotta get home."

"Funny. That's where I was headed." Erik put his hand out motioning to continue down the sidewalk. "Can I walk with you?"

Kenna pulled her purse onto her shoulder tighter and mumbled what sounded like a reluctant, "Free country."

They walked in silence for the rest of the block. Erik sensed her tension as she reached up again to pull back an escaped tendril of blonde hair and finger it behind her ear. She cleared her throat.

"Nice night tonight, isn't it?"

Kenna nodded.

"I love nights like this on the island. The sharp breeze of the afternoon replaced by the calm wind of a beginning night." Erik smiled at Kenna. "So refreshing."

Kenna grinned again and looked down at the sidewalk. "Another reason why I love this island."

"Especially on nights like tonight."

"My father always told me that. He said that this island held deep, dark secrets just waiting to be explored." Erik heard that loud and clear.

"Do you have family?"

Kenna cleared her throat again as if she were choking on something. "No. I have no family."

"But you just mentioned your father."

"He's gone." Kenna placed her sunglasses back on her nose. "He died."

Sympathy oozed out of every fiber of Erik's being by the sharp finality of her words. Her attitude reflected a deep loss, just as he recently experienced with his brother, Tom.

"I'd tell you I'm very sorry for your loss, but those words suddenly seem so empty to me. I've heard them over and over during the last few weeks, and they truly are just hollow. I didn't know your father. I don't know how much he meant to you. So how could I truly be sorry for your loss?"

Kenna nodded. "So many people come to the house after he died. They brought food, cards, and said those same words. I think funerals are a waste."

Erik looked at the young woman beside him. Pain etched her face now and she raised the flowers to her nose. "Some people need them," he said.

"Not me. When I saw my father lying dead in the grass beside our house, it was closure enough for me. When the paramedics put his body in the ambulance, that's when I knew it was forever. That was closure for me."

Their pace had slowed to almost a standstill. Erik desired to reach out and take her hand, let her know that she wasn't alone. But just as he thought she might let him, she stepped up her pace. "I gotta get home," she said. "I agreed to meet a friend tonight and I need to change." She picked up her pace and moved ahead of him. "See you at home." Without a moment's hesitation she started running.

Erik stood back and folded his arms. Home was within viewing distance, but he was still wearing his knee-high riding boots. He watched her run out of sight and around the next corner. He shook his head and kept walking. The girl kept him guessing almost continually. So, she was also grieving. Puzzle pieces connected in Erik's mind.

"Did you find a good photo?" Michael picked up the one his mother set on the table in front of him.

"This is just after Easter in May. Remember she was out in the field among a patch of wild flowers? Claire had just French-braided her hair. She looked so pretty that day."

Michael peered at the photo of his little sister, with her long, brown hair and glasses. If she were to really take care of herself better, she would be a very pretty girl. But their mother kept a close tab and kept her in "modest" clothes.

"Claire sewed the buttons on this dress for her. I always thought it was sweet on her."

"It's a good photo of her. Now are you sure the boys can handle the farm while I'm gone?"

"Yes, Michael. It's about time they learned the ropes, just as you have had to do this past year. You don't have to do it alone around here."

Michael picked up his computer case and slipped the photo of Alisha into it. He zipped up the case and turned to see his wife enter the kitchen, pulling his suitcase behind her.

"Claire. I told you I would come back up for that."

"I'm not pregnant anymore, Michael. I can lift a silly suitcase." She smiled up at him and kissed his cheek. "Let me do something for you once in a while."

He turned to give her a bigger kiss but his mother still stood on the other side of the table. She smiled and walked out of the kitchen.

As soon as his mother left the room he pulled his soft, short wife into his arms and planted a kiss on her lips letting his mouth really feel hers for a few seconds.

"I'm not so sure I'm going to let you go now," smiling Claire looked up into his eyes. He lowered himself so she could wrap her arms around his neck.

"Are you sure you'll be all right here for a few days?"

"Michael. We'll be fine." She kissed his lips one more time. "It's not like there isn't anyone else around here that can adequately take care of your new baby and wife, if we need any help." She let her hands fall to his waist and pulled him in tighter to her body. "But they can't make me feel as good as you can."

Michael smiled down into her face. He wished they lived alone on mornings like this. The cows would wait for their morning feed.

He let go and cursed his sister's name. "That child makes me so mad! If I do find her on the island I think I'll..."

"No Michael. Do you want to drive her farther away from us?" His wife put her hands on her hips. "Be patient with her. There will be plenty of time to sit her down and give her a good talkin' to, once you get her home."

"Can I spank her though?" he teased.

Claire shook her head. "Just be careful. Bring me back something sweet." She then pulled his face down onto her lips again and kissed his cheek. "I love you, Michael."

"I love you, too, Claire."

Jenny, the children, and Erik ran into May as she marched down the sidewalk in front of their house the next morning. Taylor bumped into her, started to cry and held her lip. Jenny bent down to see the damage.

Erik laid his hand on May's arm, "May, what's wrong?"

"She's on the streets, Erik." With her hands in the air, May spoke with a voice that sounded as if tears would escape at any moment.

"Who?"

May gave Erik such a look.

Erik looked to their upstairs window. "Kenna?"

"On a park bench," May motioned toward the closest shore. "Out cold."

Jenny stood up to hear the conversation better as Taylor's cry dimmed to a mumbled pout and added, "I thought she was upstairs still sleeping."

"Nope, she's warming the park bench in front of the elementary school." May shook her head. "I thought living with you two would keep her under wraps. But no..."

"We're not in charge of Kenna, May. You know that," Erik's response revealed his frustration.

May adjusted her hat on her head and began trudging up the hill past Jenny's house. "Well, someone needs to keep an eye on that baby or she's just gonna get into a heap a trouble."

Erik bent over and picked up Taylor who whimpered, "I wanna go to the park, Uncle Erik."

"I know, sweetie." Erik examined Taylor's face, like a father would. "You okay?"

"That big lady almost ran me over," Taylor pointed to May who, thankfully, now had gotten twenty feet away from them.

Erik pressed Taylor's head to his shoulder, "I'm sorry." Jenny tried to suppress laughing out loud as she got a glimpse of Erik's frustrated expression. She began pushing Blake's stroller.

Erik's tone grew intense. "What's up with that? Did you hear her come home last night?"

"What do you mean? I didn't even hear her leave. She spent the entire evening up in her room. I assumed she was still there when I went to bed."

"Let's get the kids down to the park and I'll see what that girl is up to now."

Jenny couldn't help but realize how much older Erik acted than other young men his age.

_____

"Kenna, wake up."

Alisha could feel herself being shaken, but couldn't seem to respond or find the words to tell her mother to leave her alone.

It didn't appear through foggy vision to be her mother. Why was the person calling her Kenna?

"Kenna. Sit up." She felt herself being lifted, and she reached out to hit the person who now looked more like her brother.

"Stop it, Michael, let me sleep."

"You gotta wake up." Someone propped her up in a sitting position, and asked, "Who's Michael?"

She continued to fight the fog until she heard a seagull squawking at her side.

"Go on, get out of here," the person waking her seemed to be swatting at the bird.

"Yeah, bird. Go away." She swatted at the air. She wondered how a bird had gotten into her bedroom.

"Kenna. Look at me."

Alisha tried her best to squint through the fog by shaking her head and breathing in deeply. "Where am I?"

"On a park bench."

That's all it took. She then realized who was talking to her, but not where she was. "Erik?"

"Yes, Kenna. It's me, Erik. What are you doing out here?"

She felt herself lean against Erik, who now sat beside her. That's right. She was Kenna now. "What are we doing out here?"

Erik shook his head at her. "I just asked you that question."

Kenna rubbed her eyes and looked out over the sparkling water in front of her, blue skies and sunshine doing their best to creep into her senses. Rubbing her forehead, she finally came to. "How in the world did I get out here?"

"I think you fell asleep out here."

Kenna stood up and stretched. "It appears that way."

"Why?"

Kenna turned to Erik and noticed the bottles littering the ground around her. Slowly she bent over and picked up one, "Did I drink all of these?" pointing to the six other bottles around the bench. As she did, her head began to throb. She moaned.

"Not sure," Erik commented, leaning back with his elbows on the top of the bench.

"My head feels like I could have." Kenna swayed a bit and nearly sat right down on Erik's lap.

He stood and held out his arm, which she used for support. "I need to go home," she said.

"Where is that, Kenna?"

Kenna looked up into Erik's face. "What?"

"You're not going back to Jenny's like this."

Kenna slurred out, "Why not?"

Taylor called out to them from her swing at the park across the street. "Hi Kenna."

Erik waved at her and then pointed to Taylor. "That's why. Now let's go."

"Where are you taking me? Where are we going? My head hurts."

Erik grabbed Kenna's arm and maneuvered her around the park bench and out onto the sidewalk. "This way."

Kenna winced at Erik's grip on her forearm. Alertness crept into her senses. "Stop, Erik. Who do you think you are? You're hurting me."

Erik didn't stop, but held on to her arm as he continued to lead her down the street.

"What did I tell you, Kenna?"

"About what, Erik?" She began to realize that this man wasn't going to stop or take her back to Jenny's house. He wouldn't be her hero today. She jerked her arm free, "I don't want to go."

"I told you I'd do this, didn't I?"

A shudder went through Kenna's senses and she felt her morning daze disappear. He wouldn't. He couldn't. But despite what she thought, Erik grabbed her elbow again, and leading her directly toward the ferry docks. "Where are we going?"

"I told you, didn't I? I told you that you weren't going to be a bad influence on my family. And I meant it."

"You have no right to put me on a ferry. Do you understand me?"

I have every right to call the police, and have them look into who you really are and where you came from. Would you rather I do that?"

Kenna's heart skipped a beat at the thought of being discovered, "Why are you doing this?"

Erik stopped dead in his tracks, looked right into her eyes, and said, "Because I told you I would. That's why."

Erik pulled her through the Saturday morning crowds of visitors, past the fudge shops, candy stores, and through the mass of visitors finding carriage rides or bicycle rental shops.

They arrived at a ferry ticket booth. He pulled out his wallet. "Two tickets to the mainland, please."

Panic began setting into Kenna. She couldn't leave the island, and she couldn't have anyone looking into where she came from. She needed to buy some time.

She knew only one way to make a man stop, and she poured it on with all her might. "Erik, please, stop! I can't leave the island," her crying escalated into sobbing, but Erik continued to pull her in the direction of the waiting ferry.

She cried harder. "I promise, I won't do it again. I didn't realize what I was doing."

Erik finally stopped and faced Kenna. He glared into her eyes like her brothers did when they caught her lying to them about doing her chores or being home at a certain time each night.

"Let me get this straight. Are you being for real now?"

Kenna looked into his deep brown eyes and knew her life on the island could soon end. Her tears weren't fake. His look, resembling her mother's, sent a panic through her that melted her resolve. "Oh, Erik. Please don't make me get on that boat. I promise I won't drink like this again. It was just..."

One of the dockhands now approached Erik from behind. Kenna saw him and knew she could put on a magnificent show and get Erik in trouble. She hesitated for a second, and then knew if she did, her secret would be discovered. Erik would see to it. So she chose another option.

"Just what?" Erik breathed on her, and for once she saw not angry eyes, but caring ones. "Our talk yesterday. About Daddy. I miss him so much."

The deckhand reached them. "Hey, what's going on here?"

Erik turned and said, "My wife..." he pointed to Kenna. "She just hates to leave the island."

The deckhand looked at Kenna, "You okay, ma'am?"

Kenna evaluated her options as if they were on speed dial. "Yeah, I'm okay. Thanks."

Erik stepped back as the deckhand walked away to untie the churning ferry. He folded his arms, "I want you to promise that you'll stop being a stupid, little party girl around the kids."

Kenna could only look down at her feet. She knew if she looked back up at Erik she would lose all her resolve and her secret would come spilling out. He could bring it out. Maybe it was the way he helped her out of the window that night at the bar or maybe how he had bought her flowers. Something about this man seemed so much different from her brothers or her father. She knew she needed to keep her secret image and, right now, there was only one way to do that, "I promise, Erik."

She also knew she wouldn't find a cheaper place to stay anywhere on the island. She needed to keep Erik happy and abide by his wishes.

She'd figure out a way. She had to. "Just please, don't make me leave. I need to stay at Jenny's house. I can't afford anywhere else."

Erik stepped closer to her and tipped her chin up with his finger. She looked away. She couldn't look into those eyes and still hold her resolve.

"Kenna, look at me."

She knew if she didn't, they would board the ferry beside them, which was just about ready to depart. She looked at him.

"Don't ever believe I won't make you do this in the future. Do you understand?"

Kenna nodded as real tears formed in her eyes. As angry as he appeared, his eyes spoke volumes differently. They were kind, soft, and seemed to tell her this conversation was important.

"Can I go now?"

He nodded.

She turned quickly to get away before he changed his mind. She hated feeling like a child again, yet the look in Erik's eyes didn't resemble a scolding. It was almost as if he were pleading for her to stop. Turning to look over her shoulder, she saw Erik standing on the dock talking to the deckhand again. She watched as he put the tickets in his wallet.

Kenna reached home and bounded up the steps in Jenny's house. She entered her room and immediately began shedding the clothes she wore the whole night and pulled on a robe. The quietness of the house disturbed her, but she needed a shower. Once down the hallway and into the bathroom she shut and locked the door.

She turned to look into the mirror behind her and was shocked at how she looked. Deep circles under her eyes couldn't be masked by yesterday's mascara smudges. Her hair ruffled around her face. She looked horrible. As she tried to comb the tangles out of her hair, tears again spilled down her cheeks. The night before had been a nightmare. She'd never gotten that drunk before. She wondered how she got out onto the bench. The mystery behind it all put fear into her heart. She'd never wanted to be so wasted that she didn't have control of herself or her situation. Running away was one thing, but she really didn't want to cause something to happen she'd regret for the rest of her life.

If she were to get into trouble with the police, they could try to find out who she really was, and her whole story might come flowing out. She turned to flip on the shower and shed her robe. Her crying now turned to sobs. She sat on the edge of the bathtub and cried harder than she had since leaving home.

She knew now that Erik meant what he said and she never wanted to get that close to him forcing her leave. As she stepped into the shower she knew she didn't need more late nights. Her reputation as a drunk and frivolous single girl now intact would keep her hidden from anyone who might come looking for her.

As water flowed through her hair and down her body, she sensed another emotion entering her heart and starting to pry away at her hidden darkness. It was the look of Erik's eyes on the deck. She hadn't seen that look in many months. She thought she'd never see it again the day her father died.

Chapter 14

Deb gave Brock the last of his order and asked if he needed anything else.

"One more thing," he said, as he reached down to take a bite of his sandwich, "Have you seen Kenna?"

"Who?" She knew good and well about the young girl keeping Brock company these days. She knew Brock could tell she was acting dumb by his expression as he took another large bite from his sandwich.

"No, I haven't seen her in a few days."

"Hmm, that's odd." Brock took another bite of his sandwich as she topped off his water glass.

"Let me know if you need anything," she added before leaving Brock to his meal.

She went to the counter to put up another order as Carl leaned over. "Did he ask about her?"

Deb nodded.

"Keep it quiet."

She nodded again, "That guy gives me the creeps."

"The less that guy knows about her, the better I'll be able to sleep at night," Carl left her to help another customer.

Kenna had spent nearly a week in her bedroom. She grew bored of just sitting, occasionally looking out the window for some sign of something to do. Maybe she should finally get a job. Looking for one would be a pain. Nearly everyone on the island had gotten their jobs before arriving.

Growing bored, she remembered that Jenny had a bicycle she might be able to borrow. Perhaps she could take a bike ride around the island. The cement path around the perimeter of the island was a favorite excursion for summer guests. She had yet to complete it all the way around.

She found Jenny in the living room reading to Taylor cuddled up on her lap. Both looked up as Kenna came down the stairs.

Kenna didn't want to talk about her experience with Erik on the dock, especially, not with Jenny, so she immediately made her request.

Jenny smiled and told her where she kept the key to her shed. As Kenna left the room, Jenny called after her, "Have a good time."

Jenny's generosity and kindness was a blessing. She didn't deserve dealing with Kenna and her partying ways. She felt guilty asking for another favor, but surely it would be good to get out of her bedroom.

Soon she found Jenny's bike and headed out to the east path around the island. The day was a brilliant, sunny, not-a-cloud in-the-sky, kind of Michigan day. Kenna felt the wind in her hair and soon she was cruising down the path and feeling free again.

Kenna found a large rock off to the side of the path, jutting out of the water. It looked warm as the water splashed around it. Its large round top seemed to be inviting someone to come sit on it and enjoy the view of the Mackinac Straits. Slipping off her shoes, Kenna tiptoed out to the rock. The cold water made her inhale deeply.

The clear water revealed rocks of all sizes and colors. She gathered a handful, and began throwing them one by one into the water. Never before had she seen such rocks, almost as beautiful as the view of the islands around her.

Soon she got lost in the process of trying to find flat rocks to skip across the water. That was, until she heard someone splashing up to the rock from behind her. Turning quickly, she began to slip off the rock and almost fell into the water below.

Erik grabbed her arm before she did and righted her on the rock. Kenna gasped, saw who it was, and jerked her arm back.

"Come to take me back to the dock?"

Erik reached down to pull up his pant leg which had been wadded up by his knee and now was dangling in the water. "No."

"What do you want?" Kenna sat down, pulled her legs up, and grabbed her knees, lowering her chin onto her knees.

"I saw you out here. I was biking around the island. We should probably talk."

"About what?" Kenna wouldn't look at him.

"Well, you know. I want you to know my word is true, but I think I scared you. I have a tendency to do that to people."

Kenna shrugged her shoulders. She didn't know what to say.

"I just needed you to get the message about Jenny and the kids. Do you understand my concern for them?"

Kenna nodded, "Yes."

"Isn't it great here? I love this place. The water is so clear. You can see every rock." The water continued to gradually lap up on all the bright colored rocks surrounding her make-shift chair.

She wasn't sure she wanted to talk to this man. Now or ever. But he continued and she really didn't have much of a choice. He didn't appear to be leaving anytime soon.

"Just breathe." Erik breathed in deep and then exhaled. "Never clearer or fresher."

"Yeah. I noticed that the first time I stepped onto the island."

Erik chuckled, "Yeah, that was a great first step, don't you think?"

Kenna finally looked over at Erik. He had on a dark blue polo shirt tucked into his blue jeans. One leg of his jeans was soaked at the bottom, but still tucked up to his knee. The other one scooted down his leg. His hair fluffed in the wind.

Erik gave her a big smile. "Well, if you really want to know, you aren't the first one to step in manure on your first walk on Mackinac Island." Erik nodded. "I've seen much worse. Have you ever seen an overweight man get plastered on Main Street when he stepped in front of a family on bicycles?"

Kenna could just imagine it, "What?"

"Yeah, it was sad. The poor man never saw what was coming. A toddler on a bike was the last to run him over just after the family on bikes before him."

Kenna couldn't help but smile.

"Yeah. It wasn't pretty."

Erik leaned on the left of her rock with his back to her. "Don't hate me," he said.

Kenna wasn't sure what to talk about now. Erik was close enough for her to smell his cologne. It was a fresh and clean smell, much different than Brock's.

She was the first to break the silence, "Don't you have to work today?"

Erik turned toward her. "No. Just out for a bike ride."

"Wanna go with me?" She wasn't sure what made her ask him, but she knew if she didn't get off this rock and onto her bicycle again, she might have to answer more questions.

Erik grinned at her, "Sure, let's go."

Erik determined to show Kenna his favorite spot, as the couple ventured farther inland from the bicycle path. He'd found it soon after his arrival on the island. He needed to go to it many times in the past few weeks to get his bearings and to feel refreshed with a little time in prayer, alone and somehow closer to God.

Climbing to the top of the island, Kenna needed to stop more often than Erik. He teased her, and then she pedaled faster and harder. Soon they reached Sugar Loaf Rock jutting ahead of them on their path.

Erik stopped just ahead of Kenna on the road and leaned his bike against a tree. She followed his example. He motioned for her to come closer to him. He then proceeded to be her travel guide.

"This rock is a limestone formation created when the waters of Lake Huron receded in the beginning of the island," Erik orated, just like the carriage speech he recited day after day. Kenna smiled, so he continued, pointing upward. "It rises seventy-nine feet above the ground at its base. According to Native American mythology, Sugar Loaf was the wigwam of the Great Spirit, Manabozho. Another legend refers to swarms of bees which once inhabited the rock, filling every single nook with sweet honey."

"You are a wealth of information, aren't you?"

Erik shrugged his shoulders. "Part of my job."

He pointed to the left.

"The large island over there is Bois Blanc. It means 'white wood.' Everyone here calls it *Bob-Lo*. I've heard the fishing is great."

Kenna shielded her eyes from the sun as she looked at the island. "How do you get there?"

"Ferries take you there from the mainland town of Cheboygan. I've been wanting to do it, but haven't had the time yet." Erik pointed, "See that lighthouse over there?"

Kenna looked in the direction of Erik's gesture. "That's Round Island."

"I know that lighthouse. It's in the movie."

Erik smiled, "What movie?"

Kenna looked at him as though she'd just heard a horrible pronouncement of doom. *Somewhere in Time.*

"I'd like to say I have seen that movie, but…"

Kenna turned to him with an angry expression. "What? You can't be serious."

He raised his hands as if in trouble with the police. "Guilty."

"Aww, Erik! We need to change that," She grinned at him, "Quickly."

"It's just a movie, Kenna."

Putting her hands on her hips, she glared at him, "Are you kidding me? Just a movie?" She started back to her bike. "You're hopeless."

Erik followed her to his own bike and got on. "Are you one of those hopeless romantic types?"

"Hopeless," she got on her bike and took off down the road and over her shoulder she said, "and romantic."

Erik would have stopped to take a drink from his water bottle, but decided if he did, he'd lose her completely as she disappeared out of sight.

Chapter 15

All May could think about was the delicious casserole dish she would make for the guests that night with the fresh asparagus she'd found at the market this morning. Wiping the sweat off her forehead, she rushed down the crowded street toward her resort.

She nearly bumped into a man standing on the sidewalk looking perplexed and totally not like the ordinary island visitors. What looked to be a small computer bag in one hand contrasted with his work boots and John Deere ball cap. He kept glancing at a map of the island in the other hand.

He started into one store and then stopped as if he wasn't sure if he wanted to shop or not. He approached it again and May watched him go directly to the checkout counter.

She paused at the door watching him. He took something out of his pocket, and showed it to the clerk. The clerk shook her head and pointed in the opposite direction.

May continued to stand outside the door as the man came back out of the store. She always commended herself for knowing happenings about the island, even during the summer. This was odd behavior for a fudgie.

As he came out the door he again looked at the map in his hand and turned to walk in the opposite direction. Perhaps she should follow him to see what he would do next, but then the hot sun would mold her sour cream for sure if she didn't get her groceries home.

Sergeant Fetter glanced at the photo, of the demure girl. "Can't say I've seen her around these parts, but sir, you have to understand, there are hundreds of visitors on this island every day. If she's here on the island, I might not recognize her during the summer months."

"Do you have a clue where I could ask about her? A place where someone would know just about everyone?" The man took off his John Deere hat, and wrung it like a dishrag.

"Well, let me think." Fetter clenched his jaw and stroked his chin. "Uh. It'd probably need to be somebody that stayed on the island year round. Do you have any clue when she may have arrived here?"

"I'm not even sure she is here, but if she did come it would have been the first or second week in June."

"Hmmm. That'd be early enough in the summer to maybe miss most of the crowds, except that's our festival time. Tons of people on the island that week. Is she missing?"

"Well, yeah." The man deposited the photo back into his back pocket.

"Runaway."

He bowed his head. "Probably."

"I'm sorry. You just have to know that I don't know everyone that visits. I barely see them unless they get in some kind of trouble."

"I see. Well, thank you." The man turned to leave.

Fetter spoke up. "Hey. Try the bed and breakfast up on Turkey Hill Road. Go down here to the east and take a left at Marquette Park. It'll be your first street on the left. Ask for a lady named May. She'll probably know something about her."

"Thank you." As the man turned to leave, Fetter could only find sympathy for his search. Faces like hers would easily get lost in the sea of mainland passengers visiting his island every day.

The bicyclists made their way to the top of the island. Kenna loved the spot Erik just pointed out to her, a grassy patch between rocks and pine trees. Patting the ground for her to join him, he sat down on the grass. She felt like she could drop her "city girl" act, like somehow it didn't matter here. Or maybe it didn't matter because she was having so much fun with Erik. She found he possessed a sweet sense of humor. The look in his eyes made her catch her breath more than once.

Even though she hated the protection of her mother and brothers, she longed again for the steady guidance of her father. Erik had shown her the brother kind of protection on the dock, but she knew that was more to protect Jenny and the kids. She felt a bit ashamed at how she had been acting around Jenny and the kids. They'd only been kind to her.

They sat side-by-side in silence for a time, overlooking the view of the majestically blue Lake Huron, the surrounding islands, and five mile expanse of the Mackinaw Bridge. The sky cast shadows of various colors of aqua over the water.

Kenna was the first to speak. "It is pretty out there, isn't it?"

"You should see Lake Superior. It's even more beautiful than this lake."

Kenna had wanted to ask Erik about his brother, more than once. She hesitated for a moment, scrutinizing how best to ask the question without revealing too much of her life at home. Yet she couldn't help but ask, "How are you handling losing your brother?"

Erik looked surprised, but answered, "Grief is a weird thing. Everyone handles it differently."

Kenna nodded.

"I've decided that God must have had a very important reason why He called Tom home so early."

"How old was he?"

"Twenty-eight."

"Wow. Leaving behind Taylor and Blake, they're so little."

Erik nodded.

"How is Jenny handling it? She seems so confident and sure of herself."

"She is. I've never seen a woman with so much strength before. But, she has no other family to come and be with her. Her parents are gone. She has a sister in Alaska with a large family of her own."

"Did the military come right to her door to tell her?"

"Actually Tom put my name on the next of kin to be notified list. If anything happened to him, he didn't want Jenny alone to hear the news. They came to my house and told me first and then I came up here to break it to her."

"That must have been horrible."

"It felt like my duty somehow. Tom wouldn't have wanted anyone to do it but me. Once I arrived unannounced, she knew before I even got on her front porch. She saw me walking up the sidewalk and seemed to just know why I was there."

Kenna looked off into space and decided no answer could show her grief for Jenny or Erik. That must have been a horrible time for all of them.

"How about you?"

"What?" Kenna hadn't considered the prospect of Erik asking about her father.

"Where were you when your father died?"

She needed to consider carefully her answer before speaking. Revealing too much could put her identity into jeopardy. She hadn't really talked about her father's death to anyone else before.

She looked at Erik, "My father and I had just finished lunch. All I did was hear a worker yell for someone to call 911. My father had many people working for him. I ran for the phone and grabbed it on the way out the door. When I got to my father, someone had already rolled him over on the driveway. His face was bloody and dirty. He died of a massive heart attack before the paramedics could even get to him." Kenna hesitated for a moment, but felt relief to be telling the incident to another person, for the first time. "It was a horrible day. I called 911, but Michael told me it was too late." As soon as the words left her mouth, she worried she had said too much.

"Who's Michael?"

"Uh, a worker. He's always on the property." Kenna sighed in relief as Erik didn't seem to react suspiciously of her honest recollection.

"So, boom!" Erik snapped his fingers. "Without your father, you had no one left."

Kenna nodded. "I guess you could say that."

Erik put his hand on top of hers. His hand was strong and firm. Jenny must have felt comforted having him around since her husband's death.

"So did they have a military funeral for Tom? Is he buried here?"

"Yes to the funeral. He's buried in a cemetery near Detroit. Jenny wasn't sure if she would stay on the island, and she wanted to be closer to his grave so that she and the kids could visit it. We had to decide quickly. I'm not sure if she regrets her decision now."

"Do you think she'll stay? Here? On the island?"

Erik shook his head. "Who knows? It is beautiful here, but the winters are brutal. You often feel alone having to be inside all the time."

"So you won't be here this winter?"

"No." Erik looked off to the side as a family of bicyclists made their way toward them. He seemed to want to tell her why, but hesitated.

The family struggled with two little ones tagging along on bikes with training wheels. The father looked frustrated and the mother tired.

As they passed by, Kenna thought of Jenny's children. "Do you like Jenny?"

"Of course. She's my sister-in-law."

"No. I mean," somehow Kenna needed to know this answer. "You seem to like the children so much. I just wondered."

Erik adamantly shook his head. "I couldn't do that. I'm not their daddy. I don't want to replace Tom. I just want to help right now. Somehow I just don't think that would be right."

"Why is that?" Kenna pulled the strands of hair away from her eyes.

"Even though Tom is gone I just somehow would feel like I was betraying him."

Kenna admired this man sitting next to her. She thought of his sacrifice, his ambition to help his brother's family. So unlike her family, they only thought about the farm and cows.

"I'm not even sure she would be interested."

"Have you asked her?"

"No."

"Then how do you know for sure?"

Erik shrugged his shoulders.

"Maybe she needs you more than you think."

Kenna looked at her watch. "I need to get back."

"What's the hurry?"

"Summer's wastin' away." Kenna jumped on her bike, leaving Erik standing by the side of the road. Kenna wondered when Erik would realize he was really in love with Jenny.

Michael's feet were tired, he hadn't had a good meal in twenty-four-hours and he had found only tourists since he arrived on the island. He'd ask people all along the street, and each one claimed they didn't live on the island or were just employed there for the summer. It was hard trying to find someone that resided on the island year round. Would they even be able to pick Alisha out of the floods of tourists that came every day? Finally he decided to take the police officer's advice. Before he left the post, he'd given the officer his name and number just in case he saw Alisha.

Soon he stood in the doorway of a bed and breakfast hotel. Michael cleared his throat as he made his way to the empty counter. A bell had gone off as he entered but as of yet no one came to wait on him.

"Hello?" He called.

"Just a minute, taking something out of the oven," cried a voice from the next room. "I'll be with you in a minute."

Michael looked around the room wondering if he should take a room here tonight. He imagined the astronomical cost, planning to get back to the mainland on the last ferry of the day.

Soon a large, but pleasant lady approached him from the other room, wiping her hands on a towel. "Sorry sir, I just had to get that casserole out of the oven."

"It smells delicious."

"It should. It took me all day to make. What can I do for you? Need a room?"

"Well, maybe, but the police officer told me to talk to you."

The woman smiled. "Of course. I remember you. You were downtown this morning."

Michael nodded. "I guess. Yes, I was."

"What are you doing on the island today? Doesn't look like you're here for a vacation."

"Well, no. I'm not. I've been asking around to see if anyone has seen this girl." Michael held the photo of Alisha up to the woman and she took it from him.

"Oh dear," she cried. "My glasses are upstairs. But wait…" she held the photo up to a light on the counter.

"No, she doesn't look familiar." The woman squinted at the photo. "Is she Amish?"

"No." Michael cringed. His sister didn't look Amish.

"Well, I'm sorry. With the dress, long braided hair…"

"We're not Amish. Just farmers."

"Oh. I like farmers." The woman handed the photo back to him. "I wish I had my glasses."

"It's okay. Do you know anyone else that might be on the island all summer that might know this girl?"

"Are you sure she's here?"

"No. We're just grasping at straws."

The woman stared at him until he added. "She ran away from home."

"How old is she?"

"Nineteen."

"That's scary and so young."

Michael nodded, tucked the photo away and turned to leave. "Thanks for your time."

"I do hope you find her," the woman called after him. "I truly do."

Just as Michael was about to shut the door behind him the woman yelled out, "Sir, is this girl related to you?"

Michael turned with his hand on the doorknob. "She's my sister."

"What's her name?"

Michael shook his head. "Why?"

"I like keeping track of the young ones on the island. Some can get carried away with being adults…wanting to act like them, but not facing

101

up to the consequences required of one. I'll add her to my prayer list, perhaps looking around for her."

Michael entered the little inn again and told the woman, "Her name's Alisha and we appreciate it."

Chapter 16

Erik found May down at the local bakery the next morning. She happily recited her order to the baker, "Two dozen rolls, four bagels, and six sweet rolls, please."

Erik came up from behind and stood beside her at the counter.

She looked up from fumbling in her purse for change. "Erik. How are you this wonderful morning?"

"Just fine, May. How 'bout you?"

"Delightful. Isn't it a beautiful day? The weather this summer has been unbeatable."

Erik nodded as, the baker, handed May her order.

"That'll be twenty-two fifty."

"Twenty-two fifty? Bob, I'm not raising your children."

"It's still twenty-two fifty, May." Bob laughed and shook his head. "Why do we have to do this every morning?"

"It's not every morning. I only need your rolls and baked goods once or twice a week."

Bob held out his palm over the counter, "Twenty-two fifty, May."

Erik chuckled at the exchange.

"What can I get you, Erik?" The baker asked as he headed to the cash register with May's twenty and a five.

"I'll take one of those cinnamon rolls right here." Erik pointed to the glazed roll seeming to want to be a part of his life behind the enclosed glass display.

"Did you see the farmer in town yesterday?" May asked Erik as she took her change and put it in her purse.

"What farmer?" Erik could easily be annoyed by May's comments. Thousands of tourists visited the island each day.

"The one who lost his sister."

"Kenna and I took a bike ride to the top of the island yesterday. I wasn't around."

"Kenna!"

"Yes," Erik nodded, although his answer was with trepidation. He didn't want others to know all his business, especially May.

"Did you set her straight, young man?" May looked up at him as if he were the Doctor Phil of the island.

"She has issues."

"What did she tell you?"

"May!" Bob looked over the counter at them both. "You guys are blocking the customers wanting to see my baked goods."

May turned to the baker. "Oh, please. They'll get one look at your prices and leave anyway!"

Erik grabbed May's elbow, leading her through the crowd of other patrons to the door.

"His sister ran away from home." May added when they got out onto the sidewalk.

"Who's sister?" Erik tried to remember what they'd been talking about in the store, but was grateful the subject had changed from him and Kenna.

"The farmer."

"That could be almost anyone on the island." How many college students are on the island that probably didn't give their parents a clue as to their whereabouts this summer?

"She looked Amish in her photo."

Erik laughed and put his change into his wallet. "May, you have a vivid imagination."

The two walked down the street.

"Imagination! Ha!" May strutted off down the street just before raising her hand and giving Erik a wave. "Be good today, Erik."

Erik chuckled as he waved at May down the street. "I'll do my best."

Michael lay back on the bed in a hot sweat with not a thing on but a smile. Claire leaned over him with a giggle and kissed him full on the lips again. "How was that welcome home?"

Michael closed his eyes and felt the naked shoulders of his wife as she kissed him deep and hard. He felt her slim, soft body as she pulled herself on top of him and laid her head on his chest. "That was an amazing welcome home."

He could lay here like this for hours, but dawn would soon be brightening their bedroom window and with it came the rigorous morning chores of the dairy farm.

Claire picked her head up and looked into his eyes, "Did you sleep in while you were away?"

Michael scowled, "Course not. Get a farmer away from his duties and the latest he can sleep in is six."

Claire smoothed his hair back with her hand and kissed his nose. "Now you know how us new mothers feel," Claire smiled. "Although," she circled his mouth with her finger, "making those babies is just about the most fun of the whole motherhood adventure."

They kissed long and hard again and enjoyed a few moments of intimate talk and tickling.

Claire rolled away from him and snatched her robe from the bedpost. "Speaking of that, I better get breakfast started or soon we'll have more little ones bothering us each morning."

Putting a hand behind his head Michael longed to pull his wife back in bed and stay there the whole day. It would keep his mind off Alisha and his inability to find her. "Claire?"

Claire turned toward him as she tied her robe. "What, sweetie?"

"Are you disappointed in me?"

Claire sat on the edge of the bed and looked at him with concern written all over her face.

"I would never be disappointed in you. What are you talking about?"

"Alisha." Michael rubbed his eyes. "I didn't find her."

Claire shook her head and lay back down beside him. "Michael, you did your best. I'm sure of it." She rolled to her side, smiled and looked into his eyes. "She'll come home. I know she will."

"How do you know?"

"Because. There's too much love here for her to forget us completely."

"Maybe just not the type of love Alisha wanted."

"Why do you say that?"

"Girls like attention. Don't they?"

Claire nodded.

"Alisha probably wanted attention from a boy. She's never had that. In fact, her only true love was Dad. When he died, it was over. Maybe she felt like she needed to fill that void. We couldn't do that, we're just her brothers. I didn't see it."

"I loved my father's attention."

"Absolutely. Girls need that kind of love. Don't they?"

Claire agreed.

"Could be she just has gone to find it. With Dad gone, maybe she's trying to replace his love. His attention."

Claire added, "I just hope she finds the right kind of love."

"Me, too." Michael sighed.

Chapter 17

Kenna grew bored in her room. As the afternoon lingered, she caught herself gazing out her bedroom window. The view of the water and the Round House Lighthouse distracted her.

She hadn't seen Brock in over two weeks. Despite how he made her uncomfortable at times, sometimes the thought of seeing him again brought unexplained thrills. What would it feel like to really be loved as he said he could love her? She felt her face blush at the thought.

She'd heard from someone on a walk yesterday that Brock had been asking about her. The thought gave her chills of excitement. Never before had a guy asked about her.

Everyone was gone from Jenny's house. She could sneak out tonight for just another late night with Brock. He was intriguing. He made her feel older. More mature. His attention made her feel important. She couldn't deny that she loved that part of him. And as Erica would say, "He is so hot!"

She went to her closet, found her shortest skirt, and held it up to her waist. Looking into the mirror she saw instant sparkle come into her eyes. One night of fun couldn't hurt. Just one more round of drinks with Brock and his friends.

Before she could change her mind, she whipped off her t-shirt and jean shorts and pulled on the skirt and a skimpy top. Kenna ran to the bathroom to fix her face.

When she reached the corner bar, she hesitated for a moment before going in. She peeked in the window to see Brock sitting at the bar with a friend. The day was hot and humid. She felt her emotions boiling over like her mother's pan of potatoes cooking on the stove. Opening the door she felt the coolness of the air-conditioned bar hit her, cooling her emotions.

Brock looked up as she came in and a slight smile emerged. He completely ignored the friend talking to him to turn his stool in her direction. Kenna sauntered directly for him, like a bee to a flower.

"Hey beautiful. Where have you been?" Brock took her hand and kissed the back of it. She knew she was blushing, but there was really nothing she could do about it.

"I've been around," she answered. She gave the older man a sweet smile.

"Not around me," Brock led her to a nearby table leaving his friend alone at the bar.

"What about...?" Kenna pointed to his friend.

"I am particular about who I talk to and, honey, you are now my highest priority."

They sat at their favorite table on a dark side of the room, even in the middle of the afternoon.

"What can I get you?" Brock motioned to a waiter walking by.

"Um," Kenna giggled. "You choose something for me." Her current thoughts were not food related, nor did she have a clue of how to answer him.

"Give us two scotches," Brock placed a twenty in the waiter's hand.

"Coming right up, sir."

Brock appeared to now give her his full attention. Exactly how she wanted it. She smiled again.

"Where *have* you been, my beautiful Kenna?"

"Around."

"And now," Brock caressed her hand with his index finger, "you decided to come see me."

Kenna nodded.

The waiter placed their drinks on the table and Brock raised his glass, "To Kenna."

Kenna smiled and picked up her glass.

"Kenna, come home with me?" Brock scooted his chair closer to her.

Kenna blushed. As Brock moved in closer she could smell his aftershave. What would it hurt? Just to go to his home. Perhaps they could watch some television. But who was she lying to now? That wasn't quite what she had in mind.

She did like to kiss Brock. She liked how he tantalized her every single time they were together. It wasn't like she would let him get any farther than that.

Before she could think clearly, which was a little tough after the hard liquor they had consumed, she answered, "Okay."

Brock smiled and stood to leave. He seemed to not want to waste any time. He threw three dollars on the table and took her hand and led her out of the bar.

The bartender asked Kenna if she needed a ride home, almost as if he was disregarding Brock right beside her. Brock went back and muttered something to him. He shut up and turned away.

Evening had descended on the island. The night was warm and still humid. Kenna followed Brock down the sidewalk. This couldn't be happening. She wished beyond wishes that Erica were here to see it. A handsome man wanted to take her home. A part of her was giddy with excitement, but a tiny bit of her started to wonder if she could really stop Brock if she wanted to. She was glad they had stopped drinking earlier than usual.

"Where's Kenna?" Erik picked up Blake from his playpen and kissed him on the cheek.

Jenny got up from her chair in the living room, and went into the kitchen. "I think upstairs. Want some dinner?"

Erik answered, "Absolutely, I'm starving." He hugged his nephew and planted another kiss on his head before putting him back into his playpen. The baby started to cry as Erik left him. "Buddy, what's wrong?" Erik returned to the playpen to pick him up again.

Jenny called from the kitchen, "He's been like that all day. I wonder if he is teething. He's drooling like crazy."

Erik felt the baby's forehead. "Does he feel warm to you?"

"I don't think so," Jenny called again, "It's so hot today, I can't tell. Maybe I should check to see if he has a temperature. "

Erik wasn't quite sure what a baby with a temperature felt like. But Jenny was right, everyone was hot today. Blake put his head on Erik's shoulder and cuddled into him. "Aw, poor li'l guy." Erik carried the toddler into the kitchen where his sister-in-law was dishing out something out of a crock pot.

"I love crock pots on hot days like this. It doesn't heat up the kitchen."

"What did you make me?" Erik sniffed the plate coming at him.

"Chicken ala king."

"Yum."

"Give me that boy." Jenny took the child from his arms and he sat down to eat his dinner.

"Has she been up there all day?"

Jenny nodded as she sat down with Blake. "I think so. I've been gone all afternoon. "Taylor is playing at a friend's house."

"Wow, that's nice."

"Yes. Especially with Blake fussing all afternoon."

Erik finished his dinner and headed up the stairs. "I'm gonna check on Kenna." He saw Jenny smile at him.

"What?"

"Oh nothing," Jenny giggled as she cuddled her son, his head resting on her shoulder.

Erik went up the stairs and knocked on Kenna's door. Only stillness penetrated the air. He knocked a little louder, as if she wouldn't have heard his first knock. He hesitated but then opened her door. "Kenna?" He spoke into the room. The bed wasn't made and Erik found the room completely empty.

Kenna grew warm. Brock's apartment was small. He didn't waste much time in kissing her full and hard on the lips. Kissing was new, but her insides grew fluttery and her breath caught every time Brock's soft lips touched hers. Surely she could stop this anytime she wanted, but at this exact moment, why would she want to? Brock caressed her knee and without much hesitation, just above her knee. She pulled away.

"Brock, let's not get out of control here."

Brock sat back on the couch. "Well, that's gonna be a little tough."

"Why?" Sometimes Kenna's own naivety sounded stupid even to herself.

"Cause," Brock came toward her again. "You are too beautiful to not taste." Another long kiss caused Kenna to even forget to breath. Brock touched the front of her shirt. As she took a deep breath, his cologne penetrated her senses, making her swoon even more. He tasted of scotch, but his smell was even better. Cologne mixed with a bit of cigar smoke.

She couldn't believe what she was doing. She wanted to stop. She really knew she should, but her whole body trembled with excitement. How far could she go before she would get into trouble and not be able to stop Brock or even herself? As another kiss followed, she sensed stopping wouldn't be as easy as she thought.

Brock's kisses got more intense, Kenna couldn't believe how her body was feeling. She began to sweat, her breathing short. As Brock's lips left her mouth, they found their way down her neck and around by her ears. It felt heavenly. "Oh, Brock," she moaned. Brock continued to nibble on one of her ear lobes and she removed her dangling earring. "Do that some more." She could feel his tongue twirling around her ear, and then his kisses went down her neck.

Suddenly a little fear took over her senses. When could she stop him without upsetting him? She felt as intoxicated by his kisses and caresses as she did with a few too many beers. Her bearings were off. As Brock stroked her back and then pulled her close she melted into his arms.

Everything went a little dim. The music playing in the background faded until all she could hear was Brock's heavy breathing. She felt him pull her shirt out from under her belt and she didn't seem to have the means to stop him. She let him reach up under it. When he touched her undergarment, she let him.

"Oh Brock."

Brock said something about what he wanted to do to her, and even that made her senses grow numb. He began to undress her and Kenna knew it was time to call it off. To stop him. *Get up*, her senses screamed. *You gotta leave*, she told herself. But for some reason, as soon as he touched her, she knew she may not have the strength to do it.

———————

Kenna sat on the park bench out on the shore. The ache in her heart wanted to consume her as the darkness now surrounded her. Why couldn't her father have taken her here? Why did he have to die before they could share the joy of Mackinac Island together?

Being on the island and alone didn't seem to ease her grief. It just made her miss him all the more.

And now this. A night she wanted to forget. It had seemed so innocent and fun when it started out. Now she regretted every single moment. Moments she couldn't take back. Things she had done she never knew she was capable of doing. She had given herself to a man almost completely, until finally her senses had come to, and she realized that if she didn't stop it, the next moment she wouldn't be a virgin anymore.

"Alisha, these things are hard to stop," She could hear her sister-in-law's voice in her thoughts. "Once you get started, by that time, it's too late."

"I think you can stop anytime you want," she had sneered back.

Claire sat on the edge of her bed. "Yeah, I once thought that. But something crazy in your head kinda swoons you into doing things you would swear, seconds earlier, you'd never do. You get swept up in the moment. Emotions run high."

111

"Is it great?" She asked the question of the only woman in her life that would give her a straight answer.

"Yeah," Claire smiled. "Sex was created by God. Anything created by God is a good thing."

"Seriously, Claire. What's it like?"

"You'll find out soon enough." Her sister-in-law stood to leave the bedroom. "But promise me one thing, Alisha."

"What?"

"Be sure he is your husband. That's the only time that sex is good, pure and perfect. With any other person, it only makes you feel violated."

That conversation had flooded her thoughts just at the right time. She had stopped Brock. Just in time.

Brock was mad. He was furious. But the fear in her heart went beyond his anger. She stood up and ran to a bathroom to try and get herself together. Splashing water on her face made her come to her senses even more. She buttoned her shirt and tucked it back into her skirt wanting to escape, this time not out a window, but out the front door. Brock needed to know that she didn't want to sleep with him. Not now, probably not ever. She didn't need a baby on top of all the rest of her issues. Protection hadn't even been brought up.

Her courage strong, she left the bathroom and told Brock she had had a fun time, but she didn't want to go that far yet. He wasn't happy, but let her leave. How had she let it get so far? She played with fire, she'd been burned even, but she wasn't about to let it consume her.

Kenna wiped the tears from her face with her hands.

Whether she wanted to accept it or run away from it, she realized one important thing while sitting alone on the beach this mid-July night: being careful was underrated. Having sex with someone was a place she wasn't prepared to go. The intense guilt penetrating her heart was almost too much to bear, and she hadn't even gone all the way. The consequences of this night felt like they would haunt her forever. She rubbed her arms for warmth and wished she hadn't left home without a jacket or something. For the first time since leaving home, she longed to be back. Back in Iowa. The only real safe place she knew.

She remembered the day well. It had been a scorching hot day on the farm. They'd all been sent out to the far field to help their father with the haying. Bale after bale of hay had to be hauled and stacked onto trailers behind the tractor Samuel was driving. They were all hot, and tempers rose as high as the afternoon sun. Samuel had stopped the tractor without warning. John didn't realize it had stopped, and he and his quad ran into the back. Alisha heard the crash of metal and wood. Her brother fell off the quad and laid motionless on the ground. Their father had seen it all and had come running across the field.

She was only six years old at the time. Hearing her brother moan and her father and brothers shouting scared her. She ran across the field all alone. She wanted to hide, find somewhere safe to block out the sounds of the ambulance coming for John. She'd put her hands over her ears and found the place below the windowsill to sit. It felt safe there. John had badly broken both legs, but he survived the crash. From that point on, she ran to her safe spot whenever something frightened her. Her father always knew where to find her. Under the windowsill.

John's accident from long ago didn't scare her as bad as she felt right now. As tears streamed down her face, she realized even though she had kept her virginity intact, her loss of innocence left a deep hole. Claire had tried to explain to her how she might feel if she allowed a boy to get too close to her. She never imagined it would make her feel so cheap and used.

Chapter 18

Erik had been out most of the night trying to find Kenna. He hadn't been able to find her in the bars or any of her usual places. The next day, Marty hailed him down just before lunch, to get a ride to the bank.

"I saw her out by the water last night," Marty commented.

"You did?"

"Yeah. Was gonna try and hit on her, but she was crying." Marty zipped and unzipped the money bag he was carrying.

"Crying?" Erik almost stopped the horses. "You tried to hit on a girl while she was crying? You do realize that was pretty crazy, right?"

Marty laughed, "Of course, and I didn't hit on her."

"Did you bother to ask her what was wrong?"

Marty shook his head.

Erik slapped him on the knee. "Fool!"

"Fool?" Marty slapped him back. "I don't like crying women. They make me nervous."

Erik turned back to the horses and maneuvered around fudgies trying to cross the street. Tipping his hat to a family, he said, "Yeah, you're right. Cryin' women are scary."

For a few moments the only sound was the clopping horseshoes as they slapped the pavement on Main Street.

Marty nudged Erik with his elbow. "You're surrounded by women, bro, how do you handle it?"

Shrugging, Erik grinned, "I might be surrounded by them, but understanding them..." Erik shook his head, "I think only women understand," he coughed, "other women."

"Well, then, that's it," Marty sighed and sat back on the seat of the carriage. "We aren't super heroes."

"It's not the first time she's been out there. And I am still," Erik emphasized the *I* and grinned, "a super hero."

Marty sat forward. "She's been out on the bench before?"

"Yup, too often." Erik clucked to the horses. "Whoa, boys."

"What'd you do then?"

"I calmed her down. I talked to her."

Marty laughed, "See, you do understand them. I concede, you are a super hero."

Erik shook his head, "Of course not. I just listen."

"Do you answer their questions?"

"No. Who do you think I am? But," Erik maneuvered the horses around bicycles blocking the trail, "God tells us to treasure women. You are lucky to have one if she loves God and wants to help you do the same."

"Ah, more Bible crap."

"No, really. The more you treasure a woman, the more you realize what kind of gift she is to a man. And I've found that the more you make them feel special and worthy, amazingly, they make you feel the same way back."

"Well, I don't know anything about that. But you are pretty cool with the ladies." Marty jumped down from the carriage.

Erik laughed. "Get out of here."

Marty tipped his head back and laughed. "Hey bro, have a good day."

Carl heard and saw him coming before he even entered the bar that night. Brock stormed in and didn't even look at anyone as he perched himself on a chair at the bar. He already reeked of alcohol. One of the waitresses asked him what he wanted and he almost reached over the counter to grab her arm when she struggled to hear him to write down his order.

He'd seen Brock like this before. When the guy set his mind on pursuing a woman, he wouldn't let up until he possessed her. Every time the waitress got close, Brock tried and grab her. After about the third attempt, Carl had enough.

Picking up his cell phone he called Sherriff Fetter. "Yeah, he's at it again. Send a guy."

After closing his phone, he knew the only way to keep Brock cool and calm was to keep the drinks flowing, so he motioned to the waitress and told her, "Whatever you do, keep his glass full."

Carl placed his towel on the bar and went over to where Brock was sitting. "Can I sit for awhile?"

Brock motioned to the chair, "Be my guest." Carl sat down, Brock took another long swig of his drink. "What'd you need?"

"Nothing. Just thought I'd ask about your upcoming art show. I wanted to ask you about a deal we could work out." Brock eyed him with a turned-up brow.

"Deal?"

"Yeah. Maybe you could bring some of your artwork to the bar here. We'd display it for you and give a coupon or something to lure more folks to your gallery." The bartender was doing his best to think up the conversation as he went.

"If there is a gallery after today."

"What?"

"Nothing, I mean sure," Brock hesitated, but continued, "We can work something out."

Soon two police officers made their way into the bar. They talked a bit to the waitress and then headed over to Brock's table. Carl knew he needed to get away before they arrived. He'd done his job to distract him until they arrived.

"Hey Brock!" The officers stood on each side. "Let's take a walk."

Brock shook his head, "Great. That's all I need today."

Carl made his way back to the bar and then heard Brock shout across the room, "Sure, you want to help my gallery."

The officers picked Brock up by both arms. "Can't a man just have an afternoon drink, officers? I'm not bothering anyone."

"Okay, whatever you say. Let's just go and sleep this one off."

The officers escorted the drunken man out the door, but not before he hollered back through the door. "You're gonna regret this."

Carl shook his head and rung up an order at the cash register.

Erik found Kenna sitting on the stairs of Jenny's house that evening. He stopped just down the sidewalk from her. She sat with her head in her hands as he came closer, she didn't move. "Hey, Kenna," he said.

Her head jerked up, as if he startled her. "Erik," She gasped, "You scared me."

"Sorry." He sat down beside her on the stairs.

Kenna continued to look down at the sidewalk, neither one said anything until she looked up at him. "What do you want?"

Erik shrugged his shoulders and shook his head.

"I think your dinner is getting cold." Kenna motioned toward the front door.

"Do you need anything?"

Kenna shook her head.

"Have you eaten?"

Kenna repeated the same answer.

"Well," Erik stood up. "Okay then."

"See Kenna on your way in?" Jenny said, as Erik came into the kitchen.

"Yeah. She's not talking."

Jenny stood wiping dishes, "Is she drunk?"

Erik shook his head. "I didn't smell anything."

"What's wrong now, do you think?"

"If you knew, then we'd both know." Erik took a towel off the cupboard, began wiping a cup and put it away.

"She's one mixed-up little girl. I knew something was wrong. She wouldn't answer Taylor this afternoon. Some days she just gets in a mood, but usually she responds to Taylor." Jenny went back to washing more dishes.

"Did that upset Taylor?"

"No, she's fine." Jenny smiled, "I just told her Kenna didn't hear her."

"Some days she seems so lost." Erik stacked more cups in the cupboard.

"You're right."

Jenny placed washed plates into the dish strainer for Erik to dry. "Erik, are you liking this girl?"

"*Phhht*, no. Why would you ask me that?"

"You're awfully concerned."

"Course I am. She's young and can't seem to find her way in life."

Jenny giggled, "She's not that young."

"Yes, she is. A mere baby. Isn't she only like," Erik grabbed a potato chip out of a nearby bag open on the counter and popped the chip into his mouth, "nineteen?"

Jenny nodded. "That's how old I was when Tom and I started dating."

Erik set down his towel and leaned into the counter. "Nineteen? My brother, the cradle robber!"

Jenny nudged her brother-in-law. "He was not. He was only twenty."

Erik raised both hands in the air. "Way too young." He grabbed back the towel and began wiping the plates. "Dad taught us, from the time we were little," he stood up tall, and tried to sound like a father, "Women are special and should be treated with their best interests in mind."

117

"Tom always treated me well," Jenny said softly. "Perhaps," she changed the subject, "Kenna thinks I'm in love with you."

"Why would she think that?" Erik stopped wiping dishes and looked at his sister-in-law.

"Well, sometimes we act like we're married."

"Jenny, we need to talk about this. Are we giving other people the impression that we're a couple?"

"I hope not, but maybe to Kenna it seems that way."

"Why should that bother her, whether we are or we're not?"

Jenny looked up from scrubbing a skillet, "Cause maybe she's interested in you."

Erik tipped his head back and laughed, "She is not interested in me."

Jenny looked closely at him. "You are rather handsome. Especially when you eat potato chips and pieces of them dribble down your shirt."

Shaking his head, Erik looked down at his shirt and wiped off the crumbs. "I am not. Just stop it. Anyway, she's interested in other kinds of guys. Not someone who would treat her well." Erik placed another chip in his mouth.

"Not as handsome as Tom, but you are pretty good looking. Sure you are. Any girl would be a fool to not be interested."

Erik stopped wiping dishes and set down his towel. He was quiet.

"What's wrong?"

"When I first arrived here on the island, I wanted to be your super hero."

"And now?"

"Now I know that could never happen. I'm not Tom. I could never love you like he did."

Jenny grabbed a towel to wipe off her hands. Tears were in her eyes. "As much as I do love you, Erik, it's only a matter of time before we both find new people in our lives."

Erik pulled her close, reaching his strong arms around her, and hugged her. Like a brother.

Kenna had heard only parts of their conversation, but she'd watched it all from the kitchen doorway. Jenny deserved someone special like Erik. This family didn't need her and her bad influence. She hadn't even noticed she'd ignored Taylor today. She needed to leave.

"But Kenna, dear," May wrung her hands on her apron, "I thought you liked living with Jenny. And she's been so kind to you."

"I know and I do," Kenna sighed, "but I just can't anymore."
May looked around her kitchen as if in search of just the right words
to say to the young girl pleading for a place to stay.
"Something's happened. I don't want to intrude anymore on them."
"C'mon sweetie, let's talk this over with some tea."

———————

May shook her head, "Oh Kenna, I don't know..."
Kenna hated to plead, but as the day grew old she knew she didn't
want to be out on a park bench again. She'd had enough of that. "I'll
work around here. Maybe that could cut down on my room fee."
May clucked her tongue and held her hand up to cover her mouth.
Kenna needed to talk her into this. Just for a few nights until she knew
what to do next. "Please, May."
"Honey child, I wish you would tell me the truth. Why are you so
determined to stay on this island for the summer? Don't you have
family? Don't you have a job?"
Kenna shook her head. "No."
May added, "*Mmm, mmm, mmm*. You are a corker."
Kenna added a big smile.
"Oh no, girl. Oh No. You don't go adding the charm to that
request." May put one finger in the air and wagged it at her.
Kenna laughed. "Please?"
"Honey, I would like nothing more than to give you a room for the
entire summer. I would put you in it, and lock it up. I'd straighten you
around until you started telling me the truth, you hear? But, I have to
have a certain amount of income from each room to last here on this
island all year. I only have a few summer days to do that. You don't
understand island life. That's just how it's got to be."
Kenna wanted to beg more, but she knew May was right. She hated
taking advantage of this woman. She'd been mean enough at the
beginning of her stay to last a lifetime.
She turned to leave. "Okay, May. I understand."
May grabbed her arm on the way out of her warm, sweet smelling
kitchen. "How 'bout one night?"
"Okay? One night."
Kenna nodded. "Thanks, May. I'll go looking for someplace else
tomorrow. I promise."
They walked together into the lobby of May's small establishment
and May handed her some keys. "Lighthouse beam room. Up the stairs,
second room on the right."

"Can I pay you in the morning?"

May nodded.

"Hey, just one more thing?"

"Kenna, you're gonna kill me."

"I'm sorry," Kenna reached out and patted the old woman's hand. "Thanks, May. I really, really appreciate this."

As soon as Kenna reached the top step of the stairs May went back into her kitchen.

She picked up her cell phone and dialed a number, "Erik. This is May. What have you done to that girl? She's here again.

Chapter 19

The next day, Kenna put on her running shoes, a pair of shorts, and a skimpy t-shirt. She trotted down the stairs of May's business and headed out the door. Clouds hid the sun and the usually visible bright, blue sky. The fudgies must have stayed mainland today, only a few tourists bicycled through town.

Kenna began to jog down Main Street, passing row after row of souvenir shops and fudge-making stores. The smell in the air hinted of chocolate mixed with peanut butter. She never missed the smell coming out of the fudge shops. Jogging around people and dodging bicycles was a harder task than walking around them.

She followed the path leading around the island perimeter, passing a sign that said, *M-185*. Kenna grinned. A bike path labeled as a Michigan highway. She'd not noticed that before.

M-185 wrapped around the entire island. Kenna had once borrowed Jenny's bicycle to take a ride on it. Today she figured jogging the eight mile path could get her quota of exercise in for two days.

Soon the crowds thinned to just one or two bicyclists with walkers every thirty feet or so.

As she jogged, she found herself thinking of Blake and Taylor. She'd actually enjoyed spending time with them the last few weeks. If Jenny needed to get out of the house for a few minutes, she'd sit and color with Taylor. She loved talking to Blake as he sat in his high chair eating his afternoon snack, even though his vocabulary consisted only of "boat."

Another jogger pounding the pavement behind her caught her attention. Turning, Kenna found Brock approaching her at a breakneck speed. She tried to speed up, but soon he was right beside her.

"Hey, didn't you see the speed limit back there?" He smiled and winked at Kenna.

"Speed limit?" Kenna huffed, "I don't think I'm jogging over it. Believe me."

Brock laughed. "Where have you been, Kenna?"

Kenna continued to increase her speed just a bit with each step. "Sorry." It was a lame answer, but that was all she could think of to say.

"I understand. You got scared." The man looked her up from bottom to top. "Where you off to today?"

"Well," Kenna found herself out of breath while trying to talk. She wasn't sure if it was from not jogging in a while or who now joined her step for step. "I wanted to follow this path around the whole island, but now that I've begun, I'm not sure I can finish."

Brock grinned and motioned to the beach and some rocks. "Why don't we take a little break? We can start again in a few minutes."

Kenna didn't know if she really needed a break at this point. Afraid of where this could lead again, she almost refused the offer. What could happen out here in front of the whole world? Maybe she owed him at least a few minutes.

The two joggers walked over rocks to a large boulder sitting just a foot or two away from the water. The waves crashed on shore. The rock proved big enough to give the couple a cozy seat. Large rocks along the shoreline made excellent places to put your feet in the water and enjoy the view.

Brock sat down first. "What have you been doing all day?"

Kenna pulled out her ponytail band and shook out her hair. "I've been pretty busy."

"Busy?" Brock used his hand to wipe the sweat off his brow and leaned back to show his tight glistening abs. His temples glowed around the edges of his dark hair.

Kenna slicked her hair back and pulled it up again into a neater ponytail, tugging it apart at the back to bring the band closer to her head. "Oh you know."

Brock took a finger and traced it down her arm. "No silly, that's why I asked."

Kenna knew good and well that he didn't care anything about her life or what she was doing. She felt a twinge of fear, but her attraction to Brock electrified again. His high cheekbones, broad smile, and blue eyes probably gave every girl this man touched, a thrill. "I need to keep running."

Brock turned on the rock to face Kenna and inched a little closer. They now touched, ever so slightly, at the hips. "After our run, do you want to stop by my apartment again? We could finish where we left off."

Kenna smiled and then looked down. Did she want this kind of attention from Brock again? Yet it was the middle of the day. Lots of people surrounded them. His apartment was miles back in town.

She felt Brock touch her chin and pull it up to look into her eyes. What could possibly happen out here? On the beach. There was one thing that always got Kenna's heart racing. And that was kisses from this handsome man.

She looked over at the bike path just a few feet away. No one passed by at the moment. Perhaps if she gave him a little attention, he'd leave her alone for a while.

Brock then pulled her chin back to face him again. Their lips were now just inches apart. Without saying another word, Brock kissed her, slipping a little tongue into her mouth.

Startled, Kenna jumped back and put her hand over her mouth. "Brock, please. I don't want to do that out here."

Brock snickered, "No one can see from the bike path."

He reached for her leg and rested his hand on her thigh.

Kenna wasn't sure what to do at this point. Brock slinked his arm around the back of her. He pulled her outside thigh around the rock until they faced each other. She could smell his aftershave and the sweat trying to cover it.

"Kenna," he reached both arms around her and pulled her closer. "Kiss me again."

Kenna wasn't sure this was something she wanted to do, but his grasp on her was strong. She wanted to wiggle free but thought she would make him angry at ditching him twice.

He kissed her again. This time long and hard. Like the night before. Yet today, Kenna was thinking clearly and prepared to stop him.

Brock reached down and grabbed her waist. Kenna looked over at the bike path one last time. She didn't know how to pray. She wasn't sure if she even had a connection to God at that moment, but she tried anyway. She asked for a way to escape. Her imagination now worked, but she didn't like to think of what could happen.

She soon felt Brock's hand rising from her waist to around the back of her tank top. He pulled her in close and as he did his other hand inched up from her waist. He would soon be touching her just like last night.

She threw her head back and laughed. That was all she could think of to do at that moment.

Brock pulled back and grinned, "What?" His arm fell off her back, her tank top no longer hiding his roaming hand.

This was her escape. She knew she needed to move quickly. "I think I'm refreshed now." Kenna slipped off the rock and started jogging up to the path. She heard his steps on the rocks behind her.

"Kenna, wait up!"

As she approached the path, a group of bicyclists turned the corner and headed right toward them. Kenna breathed a sigh of relief.

She'd escaped this encounter, but there were six more miles to go, and not a single bathroom window in sight.

"Should I take a day and go to the island, too?" Samuel asked his older brother, after the two finished cleaning the milking machines that morning. The odor of ammonia mixed with hay made him blink.

"I don't know what you could find that I didn't, Sam. The island's not large. Anybody'd get lost in all those people."

"Did you ask people that live there? Year round?"

"A few. They were hard to find among all the tourists."

Samuel took off his gloves and slammed them into the ground. "I hate seeing Mother like this. She's lost weight. She's tired all the time."

"I don't think she's sleeping all that much."

"Duh!"

Michael sat down on a stool propped up against one of the barn walls. "I know. I know. I hate seeing her like this, too."

"Maybe we could go to the police again. It's been almost two months. Maybe they could do something now..."

"No. They won't. She's too old. To them, she's just another runaway."

Samuel shook his head. "I hate that."

"Legally, she's an adult, but she's not an adult. She's just..." Samuel had always been the emotional one in the family.

"A baby?"

Samuel nodded and sat down with his back on the barn wall. "Yeah." He fought back tears.

Michael added, "We just need to hope that despite her stupidity, our ineptness, and the whole insane situation, that God will keep her safe."

Samuel nodded and wiped off his mouth and then each eye. "I hate being here. I feel so inadequate."

Michael patted his little brother on the back. "Me, too, brother." He stood to leave. "Me, too. But like Claire says, God can protect her much better than us. We need to always remember and believe that."

"Easier said than done."

"I know, I know."

"I hope," added Samuel, "that one day I can find a sweet girl like Claire."

"Me, too. I'm a lucky man." Michael smiled.

Kenna grew tired. She wasn't used to jogging this many miles. When she started she thought she could walk for a while but with Brock close by, she wasn't so sure she wanted to walk. He might try something again.

Coming upon the sixth mile marker, Kenna found herself struggling to keep running. She'd need to hold out for two more miles.

The path around the island proved to be a smooth, narrow, and paved. Many twists and turns took the jogging couple past stone monuments and other tourists, but as the moments passed, she knew she'd have to stop again. If she stopped, she needed a crowded place.

Waves on the shore at their left and deep, dense woods at their right, the path stretched out long and sparsely populated in front of them. They now jogged around the back east side of the wide island.

"Kenna. Why don't we take a break here?" Brock pulled her off the road and onto a small wooded dirt path. Before she knew it he had pulled her farther into the woods. Panic set in. She couldn't escape him now, his grasp tight on her wrist.

"Brock, where are we going?"

"I know this little path that goes up and over the island. Let's take that route instead of the path around the back."

Kenna somehow went along. Her feet followed his. His grasp not letting go of her wrist. Somehow she knew that this situation could turn out not in her favor.

The path grew narrower. They soon were much farther away from the bike trail than Kenna wanted to admit. She couldn't do this. Kissing was one thing, but this man had other things on his mind.

A narrow path led off the dirt path they had been trudging up. "I want to show you a view, Kenna. It's a pretty spot on the island." He turned and winked at her.

The wink made her cringe.

What would she do now? How could she get out of this one? For once on the island she wished for Erik. Despite his love for Jenny, she longed for him to find her, save her, keep her from the harm that might be about to happen.

125

She also knew Erik worked today. Without a thought of her, he pushed his horses, delivered his guests, and surely didn't have her in mind.

If only he did. If only she had stayed closer to downtown. She knew at this moment that her city girl act hadn't been the best of ideas. She'd disappeared fine. Maybe she'd gone too far.

She pulled on her wrist. "Brock. I need to tell you something." Brock turned to her and stopped walking. "What?"

At that moment he didn't look scary. He even looked a little innocent.

"Can you please tell me where we are going?"

"I told you," Brock pulled her close and soon their bodies touched.

"No, you didn't."

He kissed her cheek. Then he kissed her nose. Then he gave her another full mouth kiss.

Kenna pushed on his chest after the kiss was over. "Brock. You need to know one thing."

Brock put his finger over her mouth. "No Kenna, don't tell me here. Just wait a few minutes." He again grasped her wrist and pulled her down the path some more. His grip had grown more intense and much stronger. It started to scare her.

Brock pulled her off the regular path and into the brush. His attention was no longer playful or sexy. This was a mistake.

As soon as she figured out what was happening, Kenna came to life. It was one thing to willingly do things, but this was another thing. This couldn't be happening to her. She summoned every ounce of strength she had.

As Brock did his best to get what he didn't receive two nights before, Kenna realized one thing: she wanted to be home. The ache from losing her father grew into a hard lump in her chest. She knew the past month would have made him so disappointed in her, but she never dreamed that her desiring freedom could end up so costly.

Erik pulled the horses to a stop at the top of the hill. The last bunch of passengers delivered, he would soon put them up, brush them and call it another day.

"Hup, Butch. Hup, boy." As the horses began their descent down the hill, something along the side of the path caught his attention.

"Whoa Butch. Hold up, boy." He pulled back on the reins and focused on the spot by the side of the road.

The path led from the cemetery at the top of the island. Someone was sitting at the end of the path. He squinted in the sun to see. As he did, his eyes focused on the blonde mop of hair sitting with her legs pulled up with her arms around them. As the blonde hair came into focus, he knew exactly who it was.

He jumped down and ran to the small figure by the path. He stooped down to see her ponytail all askew and her face buried in the top of her knees. He bent down slowly, "Kenna?"

When Kenna looked up, he saw swollen eyes and a bloodied, cut lip. Her clothes were torn in pieces, especially her t-shirt that had been ripped down the front. She did her best to pull it shut, but he could see her pink undergarment underneath.

"What happened to you?"

Kenna shook her head as the tears fell down her hot, red cheeks. "I'm okay, Erik. I'm okay."

"Who did this to you?" Erik felt like he could rip someone apart at this moment. Kenna looked just like a little girl in front of him, but he didn't want to envision what had happened to her.

She looked up into his eyes and shook. "Can you take me home, Erik? Please."

Erik scooped her up off the ground and raced her to the carriage. His heart pounded inside of him. He gently laid her on the bench of the carriage and grabbed a blanket from under the seat. "I'm gonna put this over you, okay?"

Kenna blinked and then nodded.

He covered her small body on the seat and then jumped to the seat and grabbed the lines. "Hey, boys. Let's go."

Chapter 20

"Erik, I'm so glad you found her." Jenny sat down in a chair in her living room. "I think she's resting now. She's pretty beat up."

Erik nodded. "Do you think...?"

"She won't say. I don't even want to think what's happened to her, Erik. It's too hard."

"I took the horses too fast down the hill. I was afraid the carriage would tip, but I did it anyway. I just wanted to get her to the medical center. But she refused to go. She just kept saying, "Take me to Jenny.""

"I don't even want to think what's happened to her, Erik. It's too hard."

He got up to leave. As he walked out, he slammed his fist into the wall. The framed photos shook and the glass rattled on the shelves. Jenny gasped. She watched him sit down on the top step of the porch and put his face into his hands.

Jenny knew she had to let Erik cool off a bit. She looked at him through her screen door. No one wanted bad things to happen to Kenna, but Erik was taking this pretty hard. She slowly opened the door and sat down on the step beside him. Jenny watched as Erik's hands clenched two, and then, three times.

She laid her head on his shoulder. "This is what I was afraid of. Let's just see what she can tell us. We need to find out from her what actually happened."

Erik rubbed his forehead. "I won't be able to let this one go. Kenna's a flirt. She's proven to us that hanging out at the bars and dressing provocatively is something she wants to do, but that doesn't mean anyone has the right to assault her."

Jenny nodded.

"Erik. Let me talk to Kenna." Jenny rubbed his back. "We need to find out details. Maybe she knows the person who did it and maybe not."

"Why won't she see a doctor?"

"We can't force her to, but I do plan on taking her to the police department. Someone needs to be charged with assault. We have no clue how old Kenna really is, but even that doesn't matter. She needs to report this crime. Other women may be in danger."

Erik nodded. "I hope we never find out who this was, cause he'll have to answer to me."

Jenny sighed.

"She isn't who she portrays to be in those short mini-skirts or hangin' at the bar. There is something real and simple about her. She can't be from New York City. Any big city. She knows about horses, bridles and she didn't scream bloody murder when she stepped in horse manure. I love talking to her when she stops putting up the stupid," he motioned quotes in the air, "act." He shook his head. "There are other moments when I can't help myself. I want to stroke her cheek, hold her. When I saw her by the side of the road I can't explain to you how angry I was. What does that mean?"

Jenny leaned back, placing her elbows on the porch. She didn't want Erik seeing her, "It means you are a decent man."

Erik stood, hands clenched and glaring at Jenny. He turned away and folded his arms. "I promised myself I wouldn't like girls like her again. They're trouble. Just trouble." He turned again to Jenny. "You're laughing."

Jenny stifled a giggle, "No I'm not."

Erik winced, "Yes you are."

"Okay," Jenny tried hard to not smile, "Maybe a little."

"Why?"

"Cause right at that moment, Erik Matthews, you sounded just like your big brother."

Erik's shoulders slumped. He sat down again by Jenny who was now also fighting back brimming tears.

"I'm sorry." Erik shook his head.

"Why?" Jenny sighed.

"Cause I don't want you to be reminded of him. Especially hearing me rant like this."

Jenny shook her head, "It sounded sweet to my ears."

"It would be so much easier with Kenna if I could just keep my wits around her. But she does something to me. Despite how she keeps up this act, I find myself falling for her." He now buried his head in his hands. "Ugh!"

Jenny put her hand on her younger brother's shoulder. "I know, Erik. I know."

———

Somehow she knew something was wrong. Erik and Jenny looked up as she approached the porch in the dark. The tip-tap of her shoes, the clunk of her cane and her heavy breathing revealed who it was before they could actually see her. May clucked her tongue.

"Erik. Jenny. I'm so glad you are both here."

May came closer and took one look at Erik. "What's wrong?"

Jenny answered first. "It's Kenna."

"Well that's what I'm here for. Where is that child? She's supposed to be in her room at my place, but," May looked at Erik. "What happened?"

"We don't know. She's got a pretty beaten up face and her shirt was torn nearly off, but that's all. She won't talk."

"We need to get her to the clinic?"

"She won't go."

May rung out her hands, twisting them together. She turned and sat down next to Erik on the porch. "What do you think happened?"

"When did you last see her?" Erik began questioning just like it was his formal investigation.

"Last night. She begged me to let her stay. I gave in." May sighed. "Again."

"I don't know why she left us," Erik said.

"Where is she now?" May asked.

"In her room." Jenny added. "May, why don't you go in and try to talk to her?"

"Me?" May backed away a bit, "She doesn't want to talk to me. I'm old. She's young. She's never been nice to me or even wanting to hear what I have to say to her. Except her whole demeanor seemed different last night. As though..."

Jenny asked, "As though what, May?"

"As though something had happened to her heart. Do you really think she'd talk to me?" May pulled off her hat.

Jenny smiled, "It's worth a try. Go ahead."

Erik nodded.

She got to her feet, turned on the step, and walked up and into the house.

––––––––––

May arrived at Kenna's door out of breath. She stopped long enough to catch her breath and whisper a quick prayer with another acknowledgement of, "I know, I know...I'm doing my best," directed toward heaven. If the girl was sleeping, May didn't want to wake her. She put her ear to the door.

May leaned into the door and it creaked as she opened it farther. "Kenna, it's May."

The small figure on the bed, covered by a blue homemade quilt, faced away from her. She tip-toed around the bed to the other side, and as she saw Kenna's face she put her hand to her chest. The swollen face looking up at her barely resembled the blonde with perfect make-up and a perky nose that asked her for a room just that morning.

"Oh, child," May gently sat on the edge of the bed. "What happened to you?"

Kenna rolled over a bit and fluffed up her pillow to sit up better. "What do you think?"

"*Mmmm. Mmmm.*" May shook her head. She looked to heaven and said, "Give me grace."

Putting down her cane, she reached for a damp towel on the bed stand and rung it out in the cool water basin beside the bed. She reached out and gently laid it over Kenna's black eye.

Kenna winced.

She patted her shoulder. "Sweetheart, you need to go to the police."

Kenna shook her head. "No, May. It wasn't anyone's fault but mine."

"What are you saying, Kenna? You didn't do this to yourself."

"No. But I caused it. I wanted to know what it was like to have a man look at you. To walk into a room and be noticed. I guess I just didn't realize that in trying to get that kind of attention, it could lead to something like this."

"It shouldn't end like this. This kind of attention isn't given from a good, honest man. This kind of attention only comes from men who want something they can't have and they seek to get it with their fists. Kenna, I've been on this island for years. I have watched girls seek out attention in all kinds of ways. But no young woman should get attention in this way."

Tears began to fill Kenna's eyes. May reached out and rubbed her shoulder. "Kenna? When are you going to open up? We've grown to like you around here and we hate seeing anything bad happen to you."

Kenna shook her head again.

"Kenna? I need you to listen to me very carefully. This, as a friend. Someone that cares about you. If you let this person get away with this, he may do it again to someone else. Do you understand?"

Kenna nodded, but didn't speak.

"There are many girls, just like you, here during the summer. Any of them could have had this happen to them. We need to keep you all safe. You must report this to the authorities."

Kenna pulled the damp cloth off her face and looked into May's eyes. "He didn't do anything but beat me up, when I refused to go further with his advancements."

May took the cloth and rung it out once more. "He didn't..."

"No," Kenna talked loud and determined. "He didn't rape me. He was in no shape to do that after I kicked him."

May smiled and laid the damp cloth over the girl's eye again. "Good for you, child. Good for you."

"Growing up with brothers sometimes comes in handy."

The two women sat in silence for a while, May just rubbed Kenna's shoulder. She wanted to ask about Kenna's brothers, but something made her hesitate.

"May? Can I ask you one thing?"

"Sure dear. What do you need?"

"Can you tell Erik and Jenny? Tell them that I'll be fine and they don't need to get the police involved in this. I voluntarily went into the woods with the man."

"Okay."

"I not only went into the woods with him, but I kissed him, too."

"But Kenna, that doesn't give him any right to hit you or try to assault you."

"I know. But maybe I needed the lesson. Maybe I needed to finally realize what I was doing."

"Kenna, you should still let the police know."

"I can't, May. Not yet."

"I don't understand."

"Others might find me."

"Sweetheart, why do you want to hide?"

Kenna just shook her head and whispered, "No. Not yet."

May wanted to get to the bottom of why Kenna was on the island. Why she felt her need to hide but instead she just got up to leave. "I'll be home if you need anything, but you stay here tonight. You're safe here. Erik will see to that."

———————

May hobbled down Jenny's steps and out onto the porch. Erik stood as she came out the door.

"Well?"

May sighed. "She's a mess."

Erik turned away from the woman and looked down the street, leaning on the porch rail.

May came closer to Jenny. "But I know one thing."

Jenny came in closer to May, "What?"

"My assumptions are right about this girl. She has a past and it includes brothers."

Chapter 21

As she rose in the morning, the bed squeaked, and every bone in Kenna's body throbbed. She stood, and shooting pain went through her right leg.

Grasping for the doorknob, she proceeded to turn the handle and felt pressure back from the other side.

"Kenna, can I help you?" Kenna found Jenny peeking around the door. "Can you walk okay?"

"I'm a bit shaky."

"Here," Jenny held out her hand. "Let me help you."

Kenna held tightly to her hand, as Jenny held her arm, too. Walking down the hallway, the two women reached the bathroom. "I'll stay right here. If you need me, just holler, okay?"

Kenna nodded. She couldn't believe the kindness of Jenny and Erik. She'd slept pretty well the entire night with only a few times waking as she rolled on her sore arm. But as she went to wash her hands, she finally got the first look at herself in the mirror. She did look awful. Brock had hit her several times on both sides of her head. She cringed at the thought, but she was so thankful her foot had been free enough to protect herself during the attack. And for once, she was thankful she'd been raised with a bunch of roughneck brothers. She raised her hand to her eye and touched it. It would probably take a few weeks for it all to heal. She wondered if Jenny would mind if she stayed hidden at her home for a while.

She turned the handle, and as she did Jenny opened the door. "Here, give me your hand again."

Kenna looked into Jenny's face. Jenny smiled and pulled her arm close as she took her hand. "I'll help you back to your room. Taylor and I made you breakfast. She wants to deliver it on a tray to your room."

Now concentrating on her walking, Kenna sighed. "You are being so good to me."

"It's no more than I would do for anyone else on the island."

"I know." Kenna squeezed her hand. "You are so nice."

They proceeded back to Kenna's room and she could thankfully settle into her bed again. "I hope I'm not putting you out."

Jenny raised Kenna's feet up on the bed and covered her again with the quilt. She fluffed her pillow and helped her get comfortable. "How's that?"

"Perfect. Thank you."

"Kenna? Can I sit down for a moment?"

"Your house!" Kenna then heard the tone in her voice and she knew she would need to begin using the manners she had been taught to use. "I'm sorry. Of course you can."

Jenny sat down and leaned forward toward Kenna on the bed. "Kenna, we need to talk."

"You want me to leave, don't you?"

"No. Please, let me talk to you."

Kenna nodded.

"I don't know what really happened yesterday, but May filled us in that you weren't sexually molested. Is that true?"

Kenna nodded again.

"Good. But I just want you to know that Erik and I totally agree that you should report this."

"I can't, Jenny." Kenna sighed.

"Can you tell me why?" A perplexed face replaced Jenny's normal happy one.

Kenna shook her head. "No, please. Don't make me go to the police. Perhaps other women could be in danger of this man, but it was partly my fault. I led him on. I teased him and he just wanted to go farther than I now realize I wanted to go. When I said no, that's when he hit me."

"But it isn't right. It's not your fault. You're allowed to say no."

"I know, I know. But Jenny, you just don't understand. I can't go to the police. I just can't."

"Can you tell me why?"

Kenna knew this would happen. Jenny deserved to know. She needed the truth, and Kenna was fairly certain that she would be okay with it all. But she still hesitated.

"Jenny, if I promise to tell you soon-not now, but soon, after I've healed a bit-would that be okay?"

Jenny nodded. "Sure. But Kenna, would any of this put my children in danger?"

"No. He wouldn't hurt you or the children. Like I said, it was partly my fault."

Jenny shook her head. "I don't think so, Kenna. A man has no right to hit a woman. Ever. Do you understand that?"

Kenna answered, "Yes."

Jenny stood to leave. "Jenny? Can I ask you for a favor?"

"Surely. What can I do for you?"

"Can I stay here until I'm better? After that, I'll leave, I promise."

"Of course, Kenna. You can stay as long as you need to. You don't have to leave."

"Do you think Erik will be all right with it?"

Jenny stood in the doorway. "I think it's my house, but to put your mind at ease, I think he'll be just fine with it. Ask him."

Erik met Jenny in the kitchen as she came from Kenna's room. "How is she?"

"She looks worse than yesterday. Her eyes are turning dark blue, but her lip isn't quite so swollen. She seems to be limping a bit, too. She needed help to the bathroom."

"Do you think I should take her to the clinic?"

"I don't think she'll go for that."

"Mommy, Mommy, look! Uncle Erik went out and picked these daisies for Kenna's breakfast tray."

Erik shrugged. "I wish I could do more."

Jenny went to Taylor and bent down to her level. "They look beautiful next to the bright yellow, scrambled eggs you made."

Taylor grinned as she tried to get the tray off the kitchen table. The orange juice sloshed and the jar of flowers nearly toppled to the floor. Jenny reached out for them, just in time.

"Whoa, baby. Why don't you let Mommy help you?"

"Yeah. It's kinda heavy."

Jenny giggled. "You can come with me to take it to Kenna though."

Taylor danced and jumped in the middle of the floor. "I'm so glad she's back, aren't you Uncle Erik?" Taylor grabbed for his hand and twirled under his arm.

"Well you better settle down though. Kenna doesn't need you too jumpy. You need to be very quiet for her."

"We are gonna help her get better. Mommy said."

"You bet. Just be a quiet helper though, okay?"

Taylor tip-toed, put a pudgy finger to her lips and whispered to Erik. "Okay."

Erik reached out to touch Jenny's arm before she headed upstairs. "Do you think she'll let me see her?"

Jenny nodded. "Maybe. But why don't you give her a little time."

"Tell her I'm sorry for what she had to go through."

Jenny shook her head. "No Erik, I think that should come from you."

Chapter 22

Kenna looked out the window by her bed. A slight breeze blew her curtains out of her view and she could see the ferry boats entering the harbor every fifteen minutes. She now wondered if she still wanted to stay hidden? Was it even such a big deal anymore? Now she knew if they found her, their disappointment in her would be worse than how she felt now. Tears brimmed her eyes as she thought of what her father would think of her actions since being on the island. For the first time since his death, she was glad he wasn't here to witness her alcohol binges, clothing choices or her relationship with Brock.

Since her attack Kenna thought more about her family. Her mother. As strict as she was, she'd never hurt her. The only real hurt Kenna ever felt from her mother was when she wanted to talk to her and was scared to even approach her. Kenna would run to her father for advice or just to talk, never her mother. Kenna couldn't talk to her mother about adult issues as well as she could talk to her father. So was that really her mother's fault or hers?"

If she ever tried, her mother's response was always, "Alisha, you're much too young to worry yourself about things like that." At certain times, Kenna did miss her. She just now began to realize how much. Her mother was a take-charge kind of woman. A woman who knew the answers to almost every situation that came up on a farm. She rarely questioned herself. For the first time in her life, Kenna realized she was much like her, in many ways.

She'd dressed today, but her head still ached if she sat up too long. She hated looking at herself in the mirror each morning and avoided it during the other parts of the day. A reality lesson invaded her thoughts every time she snuck a peek at her bruises. Another thought kept creeping into her thoughts. Her brothers would be so angry to see her so beaten up. Brock wouldn't stand a chance against them.

After her sudden departure and not contacting them about whether she was safe or not, she wondered if they still cared enough to protect her. Would they still desire to keep her safe? Maybe their hovering wasn't as bad as she once perceived it, just a few weeks ago.

A small tap interrupted her thoughts. "Door's open."

The door squeaked ajar and she heard Erik ask her if he could come in.

"Okay."

The door creaked opened further.

"Hey," Erik entered her room, then approached her bedside. "How are you feeling?"

"Better. Much better. My head just hurts if I sit up too long."

Erik nodded and looked down at his feet. He cleared his throat again. "I'm sorry, Kenna."

Kenna wasn't sure what he meant, "About what?"

"You know," He shifted again. "the attack."

Kenna shook her head, "That wasn't your fault, Erik. A lot of it was mine." She looked out the window again for fear her tears would erupt as the vision of Brock's eyes in her face and the roughness of his hand against her cheek would return.

"Why would you say that? What happened?" Erik walked over to her window and pulled back the curtains to look out. "Kenna, can you tell me who did this to you?"

Kenna shook her head so hard it began to hurt again. "No, Erik."

"Why not?" Erik came back to her bedside and pleaded.

"Because you would want to get revenge."

"And what's wrong with that?"

"Because part of it was my fault. My clothes. My flirting. I caused some of his actions. He just wanted what I was suggesting through those actions. I led him on to believe that he could have...anything. Everything. Even when I knew good and well that I wasn't about to give it up."

"Kenna, we can control ourselves. Men can stop. This is not all fault. He could have really hurt you. He might have killed you. He might try and hurt someone else in the same way."

Kenna shuddered. "I don't think he would have done anything to me, if I hadn't of led him on all these weeks."

"Maybe not. Maybe so. Either way, it doesn't give him the right to hurt you like this."

"Men want one thing from a woman. And if they don't get it..."

"Real men aren't like that." Erik came back to her bedside. "Real men respect women."

Kenna nodded. "I get it now. You're right."

"I am?" Erik looked surprised. "I mean, I am. Kenna, you're a beautiful young girl."

Kenna sighed. For some reason it bugged her that at this moment, even Erik thought of her still as a young girl.

"Okay, well..." Erik went toward the door. "Get some rest. Don't worry, I'm gonna sleep here tonight, on the couch."

"That's not really necessary," Kenna said, but relief filled her heart. Thoughts of her father flooded back into her conscious. Her father would do something like that for her mother. Michael would do the same for Claire. At that moment Kenna realized, those are the kinds of men she needed in her life. Not losers like Brock.

The evening sunset made Kenna's room blaze with an orange glow. The coolness of the evening made her get up from her bed to shut her bedroom window. Yet she didn't close it fully, because she loved the cool evenings on the island, hearing the long drone of a ship's horn echoing through the night.

She stood at the window for a while looking out onto the lights of the island. It was a beautiful place at night. Quiet and serene. Not at all like the congested, overcrowded tourist spot of the daytime.

An occasional bat flew past her view in the trees at the back of the house. Bats were everywhere on the island. It felt eerie just walking down Main Street at night. They swooped down, precariously close. She watched them through the window, flying from perch to perch, as she drifted off to sleep each night.

She went back to her bed, pulling the covers back to snuggle down under the quilt. Adjusting the fluffy pillows, she nestled her head, feeling safe lying there. What was so wrong with being herself? She could wear fashionable clothes and do her hair different, and still be a small town girl. Maybe, after all this time, that's the only reason she left home in the first place. To find herself. Perhaps that was what her father had been trying to tell her all along.

Kenna recalled an afternoon, just two short years ago, and a talk she'd had with her father as they leaned against the house, under the windowsill.

"She doesn't understand me."

Her father sighed, "Alisha, she does love you."

"Maybe. But she doesn't understand how I just want to find myself. How I want to be free to maybe change my hair or wear fun clothes like the girls at school."

"She worries about things around the farm, dear. She wants things to run well. Efficiently." Her father put a blade of grass in his mouth and chewed on it.

Alisha leaned forward, "But she never even tries to understand me. The minute I bring up buying a curling iron or even going shopping, she stares at me like I'm a moron. That if I had the opportunity, I'd run out and get a tattoo or pierce something."

"Alisha, your mother's parents were very strict with her. She had never even gone to a movie until the day I took her to one when we were dating."

"But she lets the boys do things."

"That's different."

"How?" Alisha shuddered with frustration. "Why can't she just let me pick out a cute outfit at the mall? A real outfit, not something made from one of her sewing patterns."

"Sweetheart," her father pulled her close. "I'll talk to her."

"It won't do any good. You know how she is. I'm gonna never have a guy even look at me dressing like this." Alisha looked down at her stained blue jeans, patched with her mother's sewing stitches. "The girls continually tease me. I hate looking like this."

Her father pulled her closer, "Alisha, you are a beautiful girl. You don't need curly hair or latest fashions for anyone to know that."

Alisha shook her head. "Yes, Daddy, I do. Ask the girls at school. Every girl needs to be pretty."

"You can't find true beauty in fancy clothes or curly hair. True beauty isn't just being pretty. Look at your mother."

"Exactly!" Alisha wrapped her arms around her knees.

"Oh Alisha. Someday you will figure out the real difference between being beautiful and being pretty. Many girls are born pretty. They dress pretty, even act pretty, but being beautiful comes from here." Her father pointed to her heart. "Acting pretty is easy, being beautiful comes from long hours of working on your spirit. Your personality. Your thoughts of others. Beautiful is how God wants us to be."

"Oh Daddy, you just don't understand." Alisha added.

"No, I've never been a girl," her father hugged her closer. "And you probably won't understand this until you are much older. Look at women like your mother and Claire. They are beautiful women."

"Claire?"

"Claire has a true, strong heart and she loves your brother very much. That's what makes her beautiful. Many girls can be pretty, Alisha, but only a few can be truly beautiful. Like Claire and your mother."

"I don't want to be just beautiful, I want to be gorgeous. Radiant." Alisha smiled. "Amazing. I know I can be, if mother would just let me."

"Mother knows best, Alisha. For right now, Momma knows best."

Before Kenna drifted off to sleep she finally began to grasp what her father had been trying to tell her that day. Tears filled her eyes as she thought about how trying to be pretty had gotten her. She even began to wonder what kind of girls Erik would possibly like. Probably girls like Jenny. Beautiful girls.

Then she remembered one last thing her father had told her, "You know, Alisha, you remind me so much of your mother when you're like this."

Chapter 23

Kenna grew stronger each day, but began feeling bored with staring at the four walls of her room. Day after day her head began to heal and it didn't throb anymore when she stood, but more than anything Kenna desired to get downstairs. Even to eat in another room.

One late morning, she decided to venture downstairs to see what was happening in the kitchen. While she stood at the top of the stairs, she heard Taylor and Jenny's chatter from the kitchen, followed by the sound of a mixer. She could see Blake stacking blocks one at a time in his playpen in the living room.

She eased one foot at a time down the stairs. The pain in her leg wasn't as intense as the first day after the attack, now it just felt sore as she made her way down the stairs.

Blake looked up and pointed. He burbled out a greeting and then smiled. If falling in love with a toddler was possible, Kenna knew Blake to be her only true love at the moment. Today he had on a bright red shirt with a boat appliquéd on the front. His bright blue shorts and blonde, tousled hair made him look like a sailor, just off a boat, at the marina. He squealed in delight.

"Hey, Blake. How's my buddy?"

She heard Taylor from the kitchen, "Mommy, who was that?"

"It sounded like..." Jenny emerged from the kitchen just as Kenna reached Blake's playpen, "Kenna!"

"Kenna's downstairs?" Taylor rushed in from behind her Mommy standing in the doorway. "Kenna!" she shouted.

Jenny grabbed Taylor's arm before she could rush forward and knock Kenna to the ground. "Whoa girl. Take it easy."

Kenna smiled and held out her arms to the little girl. "C'mon kiddo."

"Careful, Taylor. Careful." Taylor tiptoed to her, making her burst into laughter.

"You silly girl."

Blake babbled louder from his place in the playpen.

Kenna looked up and over the little girl who now squeezed her legs in a hug. She held onto the playpen for support with her left hand but wrapped her other arm around the small, excited, little girl.

"You feeling a little better, today?" Jenny wiped her hands on a towel.

Kenna nodded. "Even better now."

As the days went by, and Kenna continued to heal, she loved sitting on Jenny's front porch swing to read. The island, the crowded tourists, and even her fears faded away when she grabbed hold of a story plot and immersed her senses into a novel. Jenny had many lying around. Kenna loved to sit and allow a novel to take her away.

That's where Jenny found her one afternoon as the tears streamed down her face reading one of Jenny's books.

Jenny laughed, "You okay, Kenna?"

Kenna laughed back as she grabbed a tissue out of the box close to her on an end table. "Of course. It's just this stupid book. This is a really good one."

Jenny sat down opposite Kenna on the sofa. "Which one is that?"

"It's a Karen Kingsbury, the one about the September eleven attacks in New York City."

"That is a good one."

"My mother would love them." As the words left her mouth, Kenna knew she'd said too much. She instantly looked up at Jenny.

"She would?" Jenny looked back at Kenna.

They stared at each other for a while. Jenny broke the silence. "Kenna, where is your mother?"

Kenna laid the book in her lap. She inserted a bookmark into the page she was reading, and shut the novel. "That was a big slip up, wasn't it?"

Jenny nodded. "But we're friends now. Right?"

Kenna looked up. "Yes."

Jenny smiled, "Will you tell me who you really are, Kenna?"

Kenna knew Jenny to be her friend. She knew she could trust her. She'd been so kind to her for so many days, especially since the attack.

"Jenny. I'm not who you think I am."

"I know. I've known that from almost the first day I met you." Jenny smiled, "Although, Erik has known it much longer than I."

Kenna was surprised to hear Jenny tell her that. Maybe she hadn't been fooling as many people as she thought. A horse carriage stopping out front ended her questioning.

Both women looked up to find Erik stopping his carriage on the road just beyond the sidewalk. Taylor ran from the living room calling, "Uncle Erik." She continued jumping, even adding a twirl or two.

Erik smiled as he made his way up the sidewalk to the front porch. "Taylor, you are so silly."

Taylor giggled more.

"What are you girls doing out here on this lovely Michigan afternoon?

"Kenna and I were just talking. What are you doing out of work this early?" The breeze caused Jenny's hair to blow into her face. She tucked it behind her ear.

"Just checking on y'all. Heading back to the stables to unhook for the day."

"That's cool. Why don't you take Kenna back with you? I'm sure she would love an afternoon change from sitting on this porch and crying," Jenny laughed as she looked at Erik with hopeful eyes.

"Um, well..." Erik tried to stammer out an answer.

Before he could say anything more, Kenna added, "That would be fun."

Jenny stood and took Taylor by the hand. "We can talk later, okay?"

Kenna nodded. Erik sat down on the swing beside Kenna. "You really want to go to a stinky stable with me?"

Kenna shrugged her shoulders, "I guess."

"Do you feel up to it?"

Kenna felt especially better today and laughed. "I think so."

"Good. Do you want to change?"

Kenna wore blue jeans and a pink, flowered top she had borrowed from Jenny. It wasn't quite as revealing as her other clothes. "I just need my shoes."

"Where are they?" Erik stood. "I'll get them."

"Upstairs. In my closet."

"I'll be right back."

The door slammed behind Erik as he headed into the house. A sudden nervousness coursed through her body. She felt warm all over, despite the cool breeze of the morning.

Erik came back onto the front porch and stopped. "Kenna? What's the matter?"

She must have shown her nervousness. "We aren't going close to downtown, are we Erik?"

Erik shook his head. "No. And I'll be with you the entire afternoon. I won't leave you."

Kenna nervously tied her left shoe, but began to struggle trying to bend over to tie her right shoe. Erik kneeled in front of her and took the strings out of her hands. "Here, let me help you."

Kenna knew he saw her shaking hands. After tying her shoe, he stood, folded his arms and told her, "I promise to stay beside you. Don't be afraid."

Kenna nodded as they rose to leave. Erik called back into the house, "We'll be back soon, Jenny."

Erik's carriage horses, Butch and Buddy, stood beside the fence waiting for visitors to climb aboard. Erik took her hand. His grip was firm and sure helping her up beside his perch on the front bench behind the horses. He reached in for the lines and handed them to her. "Hold on until I can get up there beside you."

Kenna caught herself wanting to appear nervous at this task, but she'd handled plenty of horses. At that moment, she knew trying to pretend now would be silly. Erik landed close beside her in the seat and took the lines from her hands. "Good job, little horse woman. I think they are beginning to like you."

"Does that mean they won't drop something for me to step into?"

Erik laughed, "Can't guarantee anything, missy, but as long as you're up here with me, you're out of range." He clicked at the horses. "C'mon boys."

Kenna watched as Erik maneuvered the horses through throngs of people. Erik would respond with a smile or a tip of his hat. The horses flicked their manes in the wind as though they felt they owned the road. Erik urged them into a trot as he neared the hill just below the Grand Hotel. He slowed them at the corner and then headed the team upward toward the looming hotel.

Kenna loved this street. The moment she had arrived on the island and had gone up it as a passenger, it seemed to hold the essence of the island. She breathed in deep the cool island air. Never a day passed on the island that there wasn't a cool breeze mingled with the heat of a Michigan day. Despite the smell of horses and the crowds, the air remained fresh and pure.

Soon they came to the Grand Hotel porch lined with flapping American flags. Kenna heard Erik say, "Would you like a tour of the hotel?"

Kenna had wanted to venture farther into the hotel or just sit on the porch overlooking Lake Huron. She'd been so busy pretending and trying to get Brock's attention, she'd forgotten how much. She smiled at Erik, "I'd love that."

The horses came to a halt just at the foot of the Grand Hotel steps. Another carriage driver came and took the lines from Erik. He jumped off the carriage and held out his hand for Kenna. "Can I help you, miss?"

Kenna took Erik's black gloved hand to get down off the carriage. "Thank you."

"You're welcome, my lady. This is the Grand Hotel. It's waiting for you to get a first-hand view."

"I thought we were going to the stables."

Erik smiled. "Not quite."

Tourists pay ten dollars for a guided tour of the Grand Hotel, but Erik's employment offered special benefits. "What would you like to see first?"

Kenna smiled at Erik as he took her hand and placed it over his arm. Erik smiled back. They ascended the stairs leading up to the porch.

"Let's begin on the most prominent part. The porch is six hundred and sixty feet long and, as you can see," Erik waved in the direction of a few hotel patrons, "it is the favorite for many of the hotel's guests." White pillars held up the front edge of the porch where red geraniums cascaded out and over the edges.

"I love the white rocking chairs. The red geraniums are just beautiful," Kenna admired the view. Lining the porch, American flags flapped in the island breeze.

"You have to turn around now." Erik turned so Kenna could look out at the view from the front porch of the Grand. The clear, blue waters of Great Lakes surrounding the island stretched as far as she could see.

Directly in front of them, a set of steps led down to the street. Across the street, a set of wooden stairs disappeared into the bushes. "Those lead down to the front lawn and pool," Erik told her. Sprinkling fountains and animal-shaped sculptured shrubs graced the front lawn. Off to the right of the front lawn was the famous Grand Hotel pool.

"Have you ever heard of Esther Williams? She was an actress from the early thirties. She was in a few movies with stars like Bob Hope and John Wayne."

Kenna shook her head. "I seem to remember my father talking about her, but I'm not sure."

"Well, she swam in that pool in a movie, *This Time for Keeps*. The pool is named after her. Your *Somewhere in Time*, movie wasn't the only one made at the Grand. Wanna go inside?" Erik pointed to the doors of the hotel.

The front lobby's charm verged on grandeur.

"This is the front lobby." Erik motioned around the room. On the deep, green carpet with only an occasional hot pink circle every few feet, sat pastel green and hot pink captain chairs. Gold chandeliers hung from the ceiling in various places, giving the front lobby sophistication and elegance. A concierge greeted Erik at his front desk. "Hello, Erik. Who have you brought with you today?" He stepped forward and held out his hand.

"Kenna. Hi."

"Oh madam, the pleasure is all mine."

"I'm just going to show Kenna around a bit."

"Don't get lost, my friends. It is a large hotel with only great things to see."

Erik led Kenna off to the right and through the lobby up to a set of library-type doors. One was propped open to look into the main dining area of the hotel. Bright green-and-white-striped chairs were placed around round tables which sat on both sides of the room, sitting atop gleaming, hardwood floors. Pastel green curtains offset peach walls.

"Maybe one night we can all come up here for a meal. Would you like that Kenna?" Erik grinned. "C'mon, there's much more." As they turned to leave the dining area, Kenna looked over at Erik who seemed a bit off, almost nervous. "Let's take the elevator up first." Erik pushed the upward button.

"What's up? Just rooms, right?"

"Oh honey, the best spot in the Grand is on fourth floor."

The elevators doors opened, and Erik put his hand on her back and nudged her inside. "Push four."

Kenna did it and soon the elevator lurched upward. "I had no clue an elevator would be in this old building."

"That's it for the Grand. Some things are preserved for history and authenticity, but safety features and updates are law requirements."

The elevator car stopped on the fourth floor. Just off the elevator Erik led her to the left. They passed a few guest rooms, and a narrow staircase, and another level appeared in front of them. "Let's go up some more."

"What's up here, Erik?"

Erik winked, then nudged for her to go up the stairs. "You okay?"

Kenna grinned and nodded. "This place is amazing."

They reached a landing and then went up some more stairs and out onto what looked like a door to a patio. Kenna gasped at the view in front of them.

"You are now at my favorite spot in the hotel. Atop the Cupola Bar." Erik took Kenna to the middle of the little balcony room and they looked down onto a bar just a level below. A huge crystal-clear chandelier filled the space between the bar and the area just below. It had tiny pink flowers accented on each light post.

Erik led her to a purple couch which outlined the outside of the room. Little white round tables, with same-colored chairs, lined the outside of the room. Just enough for one person to sit at and the other person to sit on the purple couch. He sat her down on the sofa so she could turn and look outside the windows that encircled the room. The view took her breath away.

Erik leaned over her and pointed out the sights. "See the island over there? That's Bois Blanc." He pointed off to the right, "Over there is St. Ignace, connected to Mackinaw City by the bridge."

"It sure looks majestic from this view."

"Doesn't it? The bridge is five miles long."

Kenna nodded, trying to take it all in. She looked down onto the sight of the island right in front of them. You could easily see almost the entire Grand Hotel pool area. "Look, there's your carriage in the pool, Erik."

Erik laughed. "Yes, the image at the bottom of the pool is the same as all the Grand Hotel Carriages."

"That's awesome."

"Look over there." Erik pointed to another part of the lawn. It held a carriage, created and carved out of bushes. "I don't think Butch would like to pull that one. He'd get briars up his backside."

Kenna laughed. Erik then rested a hand on her shoulder. "Well, what do you think?"

"I've never seen anything so amazing. I've wondered so many times what would be up here in this part of the hotel."

"Hmmm. I might be just a carriage driver, but I'm also a great fudgie guide."

Erik sat down beside her as they took in the enormous view. They could see ferries coming into the island, one by one. Off to each side of them was the roof of the Grand. It made the whole building seem even larger than it did from the front.

Kenna looked over at Erik taking in his own amount of scenery. She hadn't noticed him in such an intimate way. She could easily lay her head on his shoulder. She smelled his aftershave and looked at his clean-shaven face. His prominent chin and high cheekbones were defined and strong. He was a very handsome man.

He turned to look at her. "What?"

Kenna looked out again at the view. "Thank you, Erik."

Erik leaned back on the couch and smiled. "For what?"

Kenna saw how his green eyes sparkled from the afternoon sun now shining through the windows in front of them.

"For this." She motioned with her hand. "This is exactly how I pictured this place to be. It's amazing."

Erik laughed. "Yes it is. One of the best."

"Thank you for showing it to me."

"Sure. No problem."

She couldn't believe how beautiful the Grand Hotel was. She'd missed so much by being in the island bars till dawn. For the first time since leaving home, she finally felt like just being herself and she also realized, it was so much easier.

"Well, what do you think?" Erik had shown her more of the lobby, taken her down to the pool, and walked her around the yard.

"It's better than I thought. Nothing is as modern as I assumed it would be. They almost kept the grandeur of what it would have been like many years ago. I like that about it the most."

"You know what I like about it the most."

Kenna shook her head and looked at Erik.

"I like it that I was the one to be able to show it all to you. You are a true fudgie."

"When do you stop being a fudgie?" Kenna grinned.

Erik thought as he walked back toward the Hotel. "For you, probably never." The porch lights began to flicker on as the afternoon now gave way to the evening. "You need to see the island lights as well as the Mackinaw Bridge lights from the Cupola Bar. Let's go back up and we'll get to see them."

Kenna nodded like a child off to see the neighborhood Christmas lights.

Chapter 24

They reached the Cupola just as a crowd of wedding guests left with a few stray customers finishing off their drinks. Erik led her to a corner couch right next to the windows that overlooked the orange sun setting in the western sky just over the Mackinaw Bridge.

He sat down and she sat down next to him on the couch. A waiter approached them and Erik ordered two non-alcoholic drinks. The waiter took the order then asked if they needed anything else. Erik also ordered two waters. He winked at Kenna. "I'm thirsty."

"Yeah, I could use some water, too," Kenna smiled. "Thank you for giving me such a *Grand* tour today." She winked when she said the word Grand, pronouncing it with the grandeur it deserved.

"You're welcome." Erik looked up and out toward the sunset. "You can see some great sunsets from this spot." He smiled, "Guests love sitting up here, many have told me, watching the sun disappear on another day and the sparkling lights appear on the bridge."

Boats slowed as they made their way onto the island, but now more were leaving than approaching. Kenna thought of all the tourists lugging home their belongings, fudge boxes, and souvenirs.

Erik sat quietly beside her on the couch, seemingly mesmerized by the view in front of him. She tapped him on the shoulder. When he turned to look at her, her heart ached to tell him the truth. For the first time since she arrived on the island, she felt drawn to finally tell someone about herself and why she so much wanted to stay hidden. But her secret now seemed insignificant and frivolous.

"What?" Erik grinned as he leaned into his arm resting on the back of the couch.

"Are you going to tell me?"

Erik turned his head from side to side, "Tell you...?"

"When do I stop being a fudgie?"

He laughed. "You?"

Kenna nodded.

"Never. You'll always be a fudgie with pink luggage."

"Thanks."

The waiter arrived with their drinks. Erik paid him and then lifted his glass.

"To the view."

Kenna held up her own drink and smiled, "Yes, to today." They both sipped their drinks and put them back on the table behind them.

The view changed from a crimson, bright sky, to the shady dark blue of night. The lights on the bridge began to twinkle on the horizon. Two strands of lights reached up to the towers from each end and both sets descended to the middle of the bridge and then up to the southern bridge tower and down again. Street lights appeared on the road below the towers. Tiny lights could be spotted just under the bridge from an occasional night time boater.

"I never get tired of watching the water," Erik broke the silence. "Even at night it holds a type of mystery to its darkness." He added, "I often wonder about the ships and where they are headed. What kind of life would it be to live on a ship. All summer."

"Not sure I'd like working on a ship."

"Oh, I don't know. Maybe when the weather gets rough or the October winds begin to howl, but on a warm summer night like this, I betcha it's magical."

Kenna nodded, "Maybe that will be the profession I take up next."

"Oh really," Erik laughed. "I can't imagine you ever being a ship mate." Soon Erik excused himself and told Kenna he would be back in a minute.

Kenna picked up her drink and just as she turned to set it back on the table behind her, she looked up to find Brock staring down at her. She gasped, "Brock."

"Well hello, little thing. Feeling better?"

"What are you doing here?"

Brock motioned around him with his hand, "Public place. Public bar." Then shrugged his shoulders and smiled down at her.

Kenna froze in her seat. She wasn't quite sure what to do, but moving wasn't an option. She murmured to herself for Erik to hurry back. Before she could force herself to move, Brock sat down beside her and she could smell the alcohol on his breath.

He got really close to her face and then whispered in her ear, "You didn't tell anyone about us, did you?"

Kenna glared at him and as she tried to move away, Brock reached around, grabbed her shoulder and pinched it. "Where you going? This time, I'm not so sure I want to let you go."

"You didn't let me go before. I kicked you, and then ran away."

Brock laughed. "Ah yes, that was a pretty fine move on your part."

She sat in silence and just glared at him.

"But..." Brock inched even closer to her. "There's something else I want to do before you try anything like that again."

He got close to her ear, as Kenna tried to pull away from him. "I want what you have been offering this whole summer. And tonight, my dear, I will get what I want."

Kenna looked up at the door leading into the Cupola and didn't find Erik charging in. She knew if he saw who she sat beside, he would figure out exactly who had assaulted her.

"So..." Brock breathed in her face. "Why don't we just leave this little scenic rest stop and head to a room? My room."

"Why would you have a room at the hotel?" Kenna tried to stall him. She would not leave the Cupola with him freely.

"I have a room here tonight. It's on the third floor. And if you ask me, the view is even better there." He smiled down at her. "Let's go see."

"But I like the view here. Right here. So much better."

"Well..." Before Brock could get out anymore, the waiter approached the table. He gave Kenna an odd look and asked Brock if he wanted something to drink. As Brock looked over at the table behind Kenna he must have seen the four drinks. "Aren't you alone?"

Kenna smiled. "There are much more eligible men than just you on the island. In fact, there are even good, honest men around."

Brock looked up at the waiter. He hovered over them either waiting for a drink order or a tip. "I'm over there. I'll be gone in a moment," Brock said.

The waiter left and Brock whispered again. "I'll find you Kenna. I'll find you alone again." He smiled and another whiff of his evening drinks wafted through the air, "Soon. Real soon."

Kenna looked after Brock as he left, and Erik returned to the table. She breathed in deep and took a long sip of her drink. She did her best to calm her nerves and appeared calm, but Erik must have sensed something was wrong.

"Sorry, but..." Erik sat down and put his arm around her. "Kenna, are you all right? You are as white as a ghost."

Kenna giggled. "I'm fine. Can we leave now though?"

Erik tensed up. "Kenna, what's the matter?"

Kenna looked up to see Brock wink at her from the doorway, just as he left. She began to shake. She fought back tears.

"Kenna. Look at me." Erik looked into face. "What happened? Talk to me."

"Please take me home. Please."

Erik stood, took off his jacket and wrapped it around her shoulders. "Okay, Kenna. Let's go."

Kenna snuggled close to him. She felt as if she could throw up, but she would not leave Erik's side until she was safe at home.

Once outside, Kenna breathed in the cool night air. It settled her a bit, but as Erik let go of her shoulders, she instantly reached up for his hand. He winced a little, but let her grip it tightly. They left the hotel and walked home. Kenna never let go of Erik's hand. She couldn't. She wouldn't.

She looked over her shoulder once. There was no sign of Brock, but Kenna somehow felt his presence. His aftershave still hung in the air.

Chapter 25

"I think he was there."

"How do you know?" Jenny sat down at the kitchen table after she set out their mugs of coffee.

"She just freaked out. I tried looking around for someone, anyone that I hadn't seen before, but every man there seemed to have another woman with him. All of them totally into their drinks and own dates. She gripped my hand so hard while we walked home and kept looking over her shoulder. I hate to think of her afraid. If only I could have seen him."

"It must be a regular on the island and not a tourist that assaulted her."

Erik nodded. "All I did was go to the bathroom and came back and found her a mess. It was horrible. If I ever get wind of who he is..."

"You'll call one of the island police officers, Erik. She needs to report this. Do you think he knows where she lives now?"

"Don't worry. I'll spend the next few nights on the couch here again. There is no way I want any of you to be here alone. I did keep a pretty close eye out last night as we walked home. I didn't see anyone following us, I'm sure I would have seen someone. And let's just stick close to home a little more this week. Okay?"

Jenny nodded. "Okay."

"You need anything, we'll go together. Not sure you or I can physically make Kenna stay home, but distract her from going out anywhere. If you can."

Jenny nodded.

Claire watched her mother-in-law peel fresh apples one after the other. She was especially pensive today. The apples peeled quickly and soon she began rolling out fresh pastry crust.

"I hope the boys like the pies tonight."

Claire smiled, "I've never known one of those boys to turn down a piece of your homemade apple pies."

Rita wiped the pastry flour off the front of her apron and then flipped the pastry over the freshly sliced apples in the pie plate. She crimped the edges of the pie and then took a sharp knife and slit the top for air holes.

"I hope these cook nicely today, despite the heat." She wiped the sweat off her brow. "I can't believe it has been almost three months since Kenna disappeared." The motion of the pastry roller hitting the dough hard, "She just loves apple pie."

Claire nodded. "I know."

Turning to Claire, her mother-in-law stopped working with the dough scraps. "Aren't mothers and daughters supposed to be close? We could never see eye to eye on anything. Ever." Claire could tell by her shaky voice, her mother-in-law was trying not to cry. "Claire? Doesn't she care about us? Even at all?" Turning back to the counter, with her back to Claire, she added, "Everyone talks about her. They ask me at the grocery store. Even the post office. This town is too small. Everyone knows everybody else's business."

Rita's shoulders sagged, and she began to weep. "I don't know what to do. I miss Grant more than anything, but Alisha leaving is so different. Not knowing how she is, if she's okay. I know he will never come back, I can only wish that someday, Alisha will want to come back. I need her, too."

Claire went to her mother-in-law and pulled her into her arms. "She'll come home soon, I'm sure of it."

"I'm not so sure. She's such a determined little soul. Ever since she was tiny, she would only go to her Daddy. Never to me. I was too hard on her, I guess. I just had a hard time raising a daughter. Boys are easy; girls...need protection. She's a pretty girl, Claire. If I had allowed her to wear the clothes other girls do around town, someone would have taken advantage of her. But now, I realize I didn't prepare her for the real world. I kept her close, too close. I just hope she learns quickly. I'm so scared for her."

Claire reached for the tissue box on the counter. "I'm sure something will click. She'll realize how much we all love her here. Something will happen to help her remember. That's been my prayer."

"I'm not so sure she needs to remember as much as she needs to realize it."

Claire nodded, "Perhaps you're right."

Kenna knew she needed to get to the store. She was afraid to venture too far from the house alone, and she'd noticed that Erik now took them wherever they wanted to go, but she really wanted to get this errand done and soon. For fear of seeing Brock, she wore Jenny's clothes and wrapped her hair in a scarf.

She tip-toed down the stairs soon after she heard Erik leave for the day. She slipped into her shoes and pulled down her sunglasses on her way out the front door.

As soon as she found the drug store downtown she went over to the hair section. She looked through box after box of shades until she found the right color. With the line at the counter short, grabbed her favorite candy bar below the counter, tossed it alongside the dye, then gave the cashier her money. It had been a few weeks since she had bought a candy bar. At this moment, she didn't care what a little chocolate did to her hips.

She left the store, grabbed the bar out of the bag, peeled back the wrapping, and slowly took bite after bite. It was the most delicious purchase she had made in weeks. Her main concern was a sudden glimpse of Brock, but thankfully tourists were in control of the sidewalk this morning.

She passed the local bakery as the most perfect smell drifted out from the door. She looked in through the front window to watch the baker fold a solid piece of pastry dough over a pie plate full of sliced apples. As he finished up that pie, he turned to the oven behind him and pulled out two steaming pies. The smell suddenly brought back memories of her mother's kitchen in the days following late summer and early fall. She let her head bump into the window in front of her. She closed her eyes and savored the familiar scent.

After just a few moments of breathing in the aroma drifting out of the Mackinac Island bakery, Kenna knew what she needed to do before heading up to May's for another favor. She turned from the bakery window, lowered her sunglasses and headed up to the library at the west side of town.

Erik steered the horses down through town for his last run of the day. Butch was eager to make it back up to the hotel and his stable. He kept pushing Erik to move forward even before all the final passengers made it onto his carriage. He lurched forward as one woman had just put her foot up onto the carriage step. She stepped back to the sidewalk, and Erik ran up to Butch, "Hey, fella. Settle down. Whoa!"

As he returned to the back of the carriage, he helped the woman climb aboard. "Sorry. I got a horse that wants to be done for the day." The woman only smiled and sat down in the carriage.

Erik rose to his seat behind the horses and gave Butch the okay to move ahead. The carriage lurched again. "Butch, c'mon buddy, take it easy."

Erik's cell phone chirped. Before he started his touring speech he picked it up. Jenny sounded frantic as her voice echoed from the phone.

"What?" Erik replied. "What do you mean she isn't home?"

"I didn't get a chance to catch her or change her mind. She left while I was feeding the kids their breakfast. That's not unusual for her, but it makes me nervous."

Erik sighed as he told Jenny to be patient and stay home. He assured her that he would be there soon.

As he headed the carriage north through town, he saw what appeared to be Kenna walking down the sidewalk toward him. She had her hair covered with a scarf and her sunglasses on. Jenny's clothes also changed her appearance. He slowed the horses and hollered her name. She instantly looked up and waved to him.

He motioned for her to come closer. "Kenna, I don't like you wandering around alone. I'm almost done with this shift. I'll be home shortly. Then I'll take you wherever you need to go."

"I was just at the library, but I do need to make one more stop before I go home."

"Why? Can't you go home and wait?"

Kenna shook her head. "No. Erik. I'll be fine."

Erik felt his jaw lock. "Where are you going?"

Kenna glanced up and gave him a determined look, folding her arms. He noticed a plastic bag dangled from one of her arms. She looked down at the sidewalk, then up again.

He softened, "Tell me where?"

Kenna giggled. "Mays. I'll be at Mays. Give me just a couple of hours. Then I'll be home. I'll be safe there."

Erik shook his head. "You are gonna drive me to drink."

Kenna laughed again and pointed to his water bottle in the carriage. "There it is, right there." She sauntered around him and headed back down the street.

Erik snapped the reins as Butch lurched forward. He had a horse wanting to go one way and a girl he wanted to protect, going another way. He said a quick little prayer for her as she got lost in a mix of island tourists.

Chapter 26

May leaned over Kenna, scrubbing her head with a dry towel. "It's been awhile since I did anything like this. I remember my sister begging me to do her hair when she was twelve. She'd seen Liza Minnelli on television the night before and just had to be the same shade," pulling the towel off her head with a swish. "Voila! A brunette."

Kenna leaned closer into the mirror on the vanity and smiled, "It's not quite the same shade, but it's pretty close."

"Same shade as whom?"

Kenna shook her head. "Myself."

"You're not a natural blonde."

Kenna grinned. "Not anymore." She pulled her blow dryer from her purse. "Where's your plug, May?"

"Right here, Kenna." May looked her over. "Not a bad job, if you ask me."

"Yeah. Thanks."

"I was a bit worried there for..." May stared into the mirror behind Kenna as she tossed her hair backwards away from her face. She wasn't wearing any make-up. "That's amazing. This new hair color has really changed your looks."

Kenna could see May squinting into the mirror at her. She pulled up her glasses that hung around her neck. "That's odd."

"What?" Kenna switched off the blow dryer. "What did you say, May?"

May adjusted her glasses and then continued to stare at Kenna in the mirror. "Oh, I guess it's nothing. It's just..."

"What, May?"

"I swore I've seen you like this before."

Kenna shook her head. "No, May, I guarantee you have never seen me as a brunette."

May turned to leave Kenna. "No. You're probably right. How would I have ever seen you as a brunette?" She waved at Kenna with her right hand as she left the room, "Must be just one of those *déjà' vu* moments."

Kenna continued to pull out her hair with a brush as she switched the blow dryer to the high position. She wondered what Erik would say about her change. The only reason she went back was to have a little more time on the island without Brock scaring her anymore. Her style was the same, but a different hair color might throw him off for a while. She'd be safer and so would Jenny and the kids. Maybe Erik would trust her more. It didn't matter anyway. Kenna looked at herself in the mirror. Being Alisha again wasn't nearly as bad as she thought.

Kenna tied a tight scarf around her head, carefully tucking in the wisps of brown hair around it so it was completely covered. She headed back to Jenny's house as the island was clearing of visitors, and residents headed out to do their evening errands.

She loved the island at these hours. Straggler tourists tended to roam closer to downtown, and the back streets of the island grew sparse as just a few people headed to their island cottages. The sun was aglow on the western side as it tried to peek through the island trees. Kenna could hear music coming from downtown. The bars were heating up early on this Friday evening.

She got to Jenny's. As she opened the front door, she heard Taylor scream from the kitchen, "She's home, Mommy! I just know it." The little girl scampered into the living room. "It is her, Mommy. Kenna's here."

Taylor ran for Kenna and hugged her knees. "You're okay. I'm so glad God took care of you."

"Seriously Taylor, what's up? Why are you so happy to see me?"

"Because we've been worried sick. All day." Kenna looked up to find Jenny in the kitchen doorway with Blake on her hip.

Kenna felt her face flush. "I'm sorry, Jenny. I didn't mean to scare you?"

"Where have you been?"

Kenna pulled her scarf off her head. Jenny put Blake down on the floor and came over to her.

"Kenna, what did you do?"

"I dyed it."

"Well, I can see that. But why?"

Kenna bowed her head as her hair fell around her shoulders, the style still the same, but the color quite different. "Do you like it?"

"Well, yes," Jenny circled her. "I think I do." She stopped in front of Kenna. "But, do you?"

"It's my old hair color. Until my real color returns."

"Why did you change it?"

She shrugged her shoulders. "Protection, I guess. I would hate for anyone to come for me and hurt you instead."

Jenny took Kenna's hands in her own. "Kenna, look at me."

Kenna looked up, "We're safe. You're safe. But you need to be sure to stay close to home."

"He was at the hotel the other night." Kenna couldn't help but confess to Jenny.

"He was?"

Kenna nodded. "It scared me. I know Erik is here to help us and keep us safe, but what about you guys. If I change my hair color, maybe it will stop him from trying to find out where I live. Probably not forever, but for awhile. You've been so kind and I would hate anything to happen to you."

"Kenna, perhaps you should report your attack to the police."

Kenna shook her head. "I'm sorry, Jenny. I can't. Not just yet. Please trust me."

"Can you tell me what brought you here, Kenna?"

"To the island?"

Jenny nodded as she pulled her by the hand into the kitchen. "Let's get some dinner. You must be starving."

Erik started the walk home. There were day when he missed his pick-up and today was one of those days. Although, he'd probably be driving it too fast if he did have it.

Kenna was driving him crazier than she ever had since her magical step onto island. Now he found himself longing to get home to see her at night. Their unexpected tour of the Grand had been a real turning point for his feelings. He always was intrigued with Kenna, but her childish behavior and teenage-acting ways was just such a turnoff for him. He wished he knew more about her life. Her real life.

What had brought her to the island? Why didn't she just leave? Summer would soon be coming to a close and he needed to make decisions about his own life. Would he stay here with Jenny and the kids throughout the winter? Did they really need him anymore? But even those thoughts were pushed aside when he began to think of Kenna again.

Erik pulled his wallet out of his pocket. He stopped and looked down as he ruffled through a few dollar bills and some receipts. He pulled out the ferry ticket stubs. Perhaps she'd consider taking them and using them this time. She'd probably be safer, off the island.

163

Erik ran up the steps of Jenny's house, pushed open the door, searching for Kenna. "Jenny, is she here?"

"In here, Erik." Jenny called from the kitchen.

Erik felt his shoulders sag. He'd been pushing hard to get home and he didn't realize that he hadn't even stopped to change out of his work clothes. He reached down to pull off his black high-topped boots.

Taylor ran out to greet him. "Uncle Erik. You gotta see Kenna. She looks different." Taylor helped pull off his second boot and took him by the hand. "Come see."

Erik held on to Taylor's hand and walked with her into the kitchen. The scene surprised him. Two women sat at the kitchen table with a box of tissues and an opened package of cookies between them.

"Hey, Erik. Welcome home," Jenny smiled.

Taylor pointed. "See. Look at Kenna's hair."

Erik glanced at the brunette sitting at the table, surprised to see it was Kenna.

"What do we have here?"

"See Kenna," squealed Taylor. "Isn't her brown hair pretty?"

Erik folded his arms and stood in the doorway. "Different. Very different."

Jenny rose, went to the microwave and popped it open. "Dinner?"

Erik grinned. "Sure," his stomach growled.

He pulled out the chair closest to Kenna and looked her in the eyes. He watched her blush and put her head down. "What's this?"

Taylor put her hands on her hips. "Uncle Erik. I told you. She's changed her hair. Her yellow hair is gone."

Erik laughed. "Yes, it is."

Taylor wiggled onto his lap, put her hands on each side of his face and said, "You need to tell her she's pretty."

"I do?"

Taylor nodded. "Yes."

"Right now?"

"Yes," She pointed to Kenna. "Now."

"Kenna, you're pretty."

Taylor sighed. "You can do better than that."

"I can?"

"Uncle Erik. Stop teasin'. Be nice to Kenna."

"Taylor. Can you get down one second?" She scooted off his lap and ran to Jenny who was just unwrapping his meal after heating it up for him.

"Kenna?"

Kenna raised her head and smiled at him. "You're beautiful."

Taylor giggled and buried her face in her hands.

Jenny laughed as well. "Why don't we let Uncle Erik eat? I think it's about time for bed."

Jenny set down Erik's plate, picked up Taylor, and kissed her cheek. "You're so silly," she carried her out of the room.

Erik could hear Taylor jabber all the way through the living room and up the stairs.

"Well," Erik picked up his fork and poked it in his mashed potatoes. He scooped up a spoonful and blew on it for a few seconds. "What made you change your hair color?"

Kenna sighed. "Do you like it?"

Erik nodded. He put another mouthful of potatoes to his mouth. "Do you?"

"It's what I've known my whole life."

Erik picked up a few strands of her hair and fingered them. He scooted his chair closer to her. "It looks natural. It's not fake. I like that about it."

"It's still fake, but once my real hair color comes back, you'll see there really isn't that much of a difference."

He took a long drink of water. "Why?"

"Cause I don't want to be fake anymore. I don't want to hide behind someone I'm not."

"Not just you?"

"No." Kenna pulled her hair behind her ears. "I'm sorry I left the house without letting anyone know, Erik. I didn't mean to scare you or Jenny. I just had to do this today."

Erik soon finished his supper and put his dishes in the sink. Approaching Kenna at the table, he held out his hand for her to take. "Let's go sit on the porch."

He wasn't quite sure how he would let Kenna know he hadn't had a comfortable day. His neck ached from the tension of worrying about Jenny and the kids.

As they sat on the front porch, Erik wanted Kenna fully aware of his day's frustrations. "Kenna, we need to talk."

165

She sighed.

Erik rubbed his hands together and then directly at her. "Today was awful."

Kenna shook her head. "Why?"

Erik sighed. "Don't you understand how dangerous things are for you now?"

"Well, yeah. That's one of the reasons why I dyed my hair."

She wasn't getting it. "Kenna. You're not alone here."

Kenna relaxed a bit, "I know. Thank you for that."

Erik stood. He paced in front of her. Back and forth.

"Erik, what's wrong?"

They both heard Taylor laughing from an open window on the second floor.

"That's what's wrong."

"Taylor?" Realization finally appeared on Kenna's face. "Jenny?"

Erik nodded. "I do care about you. I do care what happens to you. I hope you know that by now."

Kenna nodded.

"But those babies and their mother are my family."

Kenna looked into his eyes. The lines deepened on her face and she looked away.

He sat down. "Now. We've had this talk before, haven't we?"

Kenna leaned back against a step. "Yes."

"Kenna. My brother meant the world to me. He was my only brother. His death did something to me that I can't even imagine experiencing. My heart ached for weeks. Even today," tears sprang into his eyes. He cleared his throat before speaking again, "I feel like my left arm is missing."

Kenna nodded. "I know that feeling." She sat forward again and leaned her elbows on her knees.

"Do you have a family at home?"

Kenna sighed and then nodded her head slowly.

"How do you suppose they are feeling right now?"

Kenna gave him a puzzled look.

"Do you think they are feeling abandoned? Afraid?" Erik raised his hands in the air.

Lowering her head, "I don't know."

Erik stood again and crossed his arms. "Yes, you do."

"How would I know that?"

Erik raised his voice, "You just told me how you felt when your father died. I've watched you mourn him here. What difference is it if someone dies or if someone just up and leaves?"

The air was growing colder and Kenna rubbed her arms against the chill.

Erik wasn't sure he should dig into Kenna's life any more or not. Realization seemed to finally be getting into the little girl's head. "Kenna, how do I know you won't do the same thing to them?" He pointed to a second floor window.

"I would never hurt them on purpose."

"Oh no? Why not? You hurt the ones that raised you, gave you a good home and loved you to adulthood. Why would a family you just met be any different?"

Kenna stood. "Are you saying this about them or are you referring to something I might do to you?"

Erik crossed his arms and looked down. Then up again, "I refuse to allow anyone, not even you, to hurt them."

"You do love Jenny, don't you?"

Erik sighed and nodded. Before he could add, as a sister, Kenna stood, marched up the stairs and back into the house.

Chapter 27

May headed into town first thing that morning. She checked every driver of each Grand Hotel carriage. She had to find Erik. As a black carriage drove past, she glanced up at the driver who wasn't Erik.

Growing frustrated, she shuffled up one side street and then the other. Soon she found herself out of breath and needing a drink. She settled on a bench outside the bakery to think. What was her next move? Catching her breath now was an essential need. Passing out on the sidewalk wouldn't be the best option.

Hunger suddenly overtook her need to find Erik. She turned to find Bob in his store. Skipping breakfast probably hadn't been a good idea. Gaining full air capacity before moving, she got up from the bench and entered the shop which smelled of freshly baked cookies. Standing just inside the doorway, she assessed her purchase decision. She wanted a cream puff, stuffed full of the fluffy white whipped confection, but with the lack of air from her search of Erik, a healthy choice might be a better option.

The baker greeted her with his usual, "May, May. How are you this glorious morning?"

"Good morning, Bob. I guess I'll forgo the crème puff today and settle on that delicious bagel right there." She pointed to a whole wheat one at the back of the tray.

"That's two thirty-five."

"For a bagel?"

"Yes, May. Unless you want cream cheese with it."

"Is that cheaper?"

"No, that'll be twenty-five cents more."

"Oh for Pete's sake, Bob. Don't you have enough saved for those college educations yet?"

Bob turned from the counter, handing her the bagel. "No, May, not yet. You'll have to have a bagel every morning for every single guest at your bed and breakfast to get the youngest through college. She's at Yale."

"Well, get those kids to go to cheaper schools then. You and I would get along much better if your prices were cheaper."

May turned to leave and then turned back. "Hey Bob, do you remember that fellow, back a few weeks, who came into your shop showing you a photo of a missing girl?"

Bob grabbed his chin and rubbed it. "Hmmm. Don't think I recall..." then waved at May, "Hey, wait. Yeah I think I do."

"What color hair did she have?"

"Are you kidding, May? That was months ago."

"I know, I know, but think."

"Hmmm. I guess maybe a brunette."

"That's right, Bob." May waddled out of the store. "That's right."

"Have a good day, May." The baker called out from behind her.

"Oh I will, Bob. I will. You, too."

Erik could see the old woman waving to him down the street. He waved back. Clearly she wanted him to stop before heading up and out of town to the hotel. May stepped off the sidewalk and headed out into the street.

"Whoa, Butch. Take it easy. Here comes May." Erik eased the horses to the right side of the road, came to a stop and set his brake.

"What's up, May?" He called to May, who was waving like a mad woman in the middle of the street.

"It's her." May nearly lost a shoe as she lumbered closer to Erik and his carriage. She did manage to bump into a man trying to find his way across Main Street. "Oh, I'm sorry. I need to see this man in this carriage." She pointed up at Erik.

The man ignored her and kept walking. May shook her head and waved a piece of paper at Erik. "It's Kenna. Well, maybe not Kenna. This girl's name is Alisha."

Erik leaned out of the carriage to take the paper out of May's hand. "Kenna?"

"Yes. A man came onto the island a few weeks ago looking for a young girl. I didn't quite recognize her when he showed me the photo, but now I do. I dyed her hair yesterday."

"What man?"

"Tall, lengthy sort of an individual. Didn't fit the touristy type, but good looking. Seemed awful tired."

"May, now slow down. What are you talking about?"

"Yesterday...Kenna wanted me to dye...her hair. I did it." May gasped for air.

"Slow down and talk to me."

169

"I'm sorry, Erik. I should really lose some weight."

"When did you see him? What did he say?"

"Okay. So," May gasped. "This man came to my hotel and wanted to know if I had seen a girl. Well of course I had never seen this girl. She was a brunette, not blonde. And I thought she looked Amish."

"Someone came looking for Kenna?"

May nodded. "Yes. A few weeks back. I just didn't recognize her from the photo and I also didn't have my glasses." May put her finger to her lips, suddenly remembering. "Yes, that was it. I couldn't find my glasses."

"Did you get his name?

"No. Cause I had never seen the girl."

"But you are sure it was Kenna?"

"I'm almost positive."

"Did he say anything to you about her?"

"No. I don't think so. He just asked if I had seen her." May leaned down and pulled her shoe on tighter. "What are you going to do?"

"I need to get to the police station. Can you come with me?"

"I do have to cook today, but I can spare a few minutes. Why the police station?"

Erik got on his radio and asked for a quick backup driver. "This could be the man who hurt her. Can you identify him to the officer?"

May nodded.

Kenna knew one thing she had to do. At first she was furious with Erik, but soon his remarks struck home. He was right. Her family was probably worried. Somehow she had imagined them being relieved she was gone. The last few weeks before she left, her mother and her had been in all kinds of arguments. She now knew better. Erik knew what family was and how important it was to help them, not make their lives harder.

Perhaps she'd been selfish to leave home. She couldn't be the only person in her family grieving her father. Her heart ached when she thought of her home without him. It just hadn't been the same. Everywhere she went on the farm, reminded her of him. His ball cap hanging by the back door, his empty office chair, and how quiet the barns were without his whistling. Another reason she just had to get away.

Leaving Jenny's house felt wrong again, but she had to get to the library. Using a computer from there would help her stay hidden. She just couldn't face going home yet.

The library wasn't particularly crowded on this rainy morning. Crowds diminished on the island on bad weather days. She went directly to a computer at the side of the room. Plugging in her information, she was soon at her e-mail page. She flipped through e-mails from colleges and universities she'd applied to before leaving home. At the very top was one from Erica.

It read, *"Hey girl. I hope this finds you well. I miss you so much. Things are crazy here. Your mom and brothers have been here harassing me almost every day for a week."* Kenna glanced at the date. It was shortly after she'd left home. *"But don't worry. I haven't told them a thing. I wish I knew if you were okay. When you said you wouldn't e-mail or call or anything, before you left, I thought you were kidding."* Kenna sighed. *"Obviously not. Please be safe. I know I said this was a good idea, but the look on Michael's face scared me. He looked horrible. Well, like I said, be safe Alisha. Love, Erica."* She had added their usual *"BFF"* at the bottom.

Tears brimmed from Kenna's eyes. How could she have been so naïve? Erik was right.

She pulled out a small paper from her pocket where she had jotted down Claire's e-mail address and inserted it into the *To* field portion of the e-mail. It might be too late and they'll probably not want anything to do with her excuses, but she had to tell them she was safe. Being gone three months now, maybe they didn't care anymore. A small portion of her thought maybe she wanted them to care. She hoped she still mattered to her family. But were they angry, and how long would it last?

"Tell him, May." Erik began to pace in the law enforcement office.

"Dan, this man came to me a few weeks ago. He asked if I had seen a girl. He showed me a photo of her."

"Oh wait. I remember him," the officer Dan added.

Erik jumped. "You do?"

"Uh yeah. He wanted to know if I had seen the girl as well."

"What did you tell him?" Erik leaned on the officer's desk.

"What I tell everyone looking for someone. There are thousands of tourists on this island every summer. How could I pick out one person?"

"Then what did you do?"

"I sent him to May." The officer pointed to the heavy-breathing woman in front of him.

"He didn't look familiar to you? Perhaps an island resident?"

"No. Not at all." The officer leaned into his desk. "In fact, he looked nothing like a tourist. More like a farmer."

Erik squinted, "A farmer?"

"Yes," May added, "he did. Looked like he came right off a farm in Indiana."

"That doesn't make any sense." Erik rubbed his jaw. He'd been awful hard on Kenna for leaving her family, but maybe she had someone to run away from. Maybe the person after Kenna was someone from back home.

"Thanks for your help."

May moved in front of Erik to leave the office. She stopped on the sidewalk outside. "Do you think he could be the one that hurt Kenna?"

"I can't seem to put this all together. I thought the person who was hurting Kenna was on the island."

"He seemed very determined to find her," added the officer.

"I think I need to talk to Kenna again. Who is trying to find her?"

Kenna wasn't sure she should stay another day at Jenny's house. She felt safe there. She trusted Jenny, but worried about the family's safety. Maybe she should head to May's again. But then she'd be putting May into danger.

As she reached the porch to the bed and breakfast, she couldn't make up her mind. She sat down on a step. It had been weeks since she'd had a drink, but at this moment she wanted one. Not really wanting to get drunk, but just the calm that followed that first drink, somehow seemed appealing. Hesitating for just a moment, Kenna fought the urge to head downtown. She stood up and turned the doorknob.

Inside she found May working at the front desk. May looked up and stood, "Kenna?"

Kenna felt a chill, despite the eighty-degree day outside. "Hi May. Are you busy?"

May shook her head and smiled. "Well. I need to get some cooking done, but no dear. Not too busy for you."

"I just wanted to thank you again for helping me with my hair yesterday."

May leaned into the counter. "You're welcome. I like how you styled it."

"Thanks." Kenna hesitated for what seemed like minutes instead of seconds. "Can we talk?"

May smiled. "Of course, sweetie. Let's go have a cup of tea."

"I've done something awful," Kenna blurted out before her courage disappeared.

May poured her a cup of tea. Kenna didn't really like tea, but somehow May's sweet tea always made her feel better. "Thanks."

Sitting down beside her, the old woman seemed to ooze kindness. Kenna had been right to come here. "Well, tell me about it all."

Kenna explained how she felt smothered at home. She told May about her mother, her brothers and even about Claire. "Before Daddy died, he would always be the one to fix my life. We were super close. He understood how protective my mother was and would always convince her to lighten up on me. When Daddy died, things changed. It got bad between us. I sometimes wondered if she would put me in my room and lock the door."

"Your Daddy's death must have been horrible for your mother. I've lost two husbands now. It's lonely and can be frightening."

Kenna nodded. "I guess I didn't think of that. I just wanted out. Once I graduated from high school, life was so dull and boring." Kenna looked at the old woman taking in all of their conversation. "May, cows never take a break."

May laughed, "I've heard that."

"My brothers expected me to pick up more work 'cause I wasn't in school anymore."

May nodded and sipped her tea.

"I just couldn't take it. So I began devising this plan to run away. For a while I wasn't sure where I'd go. But after my graduation open house, I got quite a bit of money from gifts. My mother told me I had money in a bank account. Lots of it. Her and my Dad had wanted me to have the chance to go to school in the fall. May, it was a lot of money. They must have been saving for years. I couldn't believe it. It was more than I had ever had in my whole life.

"I kept imagining more and more. Then one night I was sitting watching my father's favorite movie and it came to me. Mackinac Island. My father wanted to visit this place so badly. We would sit down and watch the movie together and he would tell me, 'Someday, Alisha, we'll go there, just you and me.' I believed him. I couldn't wait. When I sat on the couch that day watching it alone, my heart wouldn't stop hurting. Then it hit me. I could go there. I could run away to our island."

May shifted in her seat, "Why did you think the island would be the place to go?"

"I just knew. It drew me almost like I was drawn into your place just now. I know that sounds weird, but as soon as the boat came up to the dock, I knew I had made the right decision. But I had to change. I knew my brothers would find me if I didn't. If I could disappear, yet still be fully able to live a new life, I knew I would have it made."

"So you changed your looks?" May sipped again.

"Yes. Not only my looks, but my entire personality. Believe it or not, I am not a party girl. Granted I always imagined myself being one, but my parents would have never allowed it."

"Are your parent's religious?"

"We used to go to church. When I was little. But the farm got busy. Life got in the way. My sister-in-law goes now. Usually alone. My Dad always wanted us to go, but mother always said we were just too busy."

May nodded.

"We're just old-fashioned folks. Farmers. We basically believe that living a good life and believing in God is enough. Right?"

Smiling, May shook her head. "Lots of people believe that, but that doesn't mean it's the truth."

Kenna wasn't sure what May meant by that. "So here I am. When I got attacked, it scared me. I never thought serious danger lurked past our dirt road or our farm. I thought it was something parents told you so you wouldn't leave home or run away. I just wanted to hide, not have to hide in fear as I'm now doing."

"Many young girls feel that way, Kenna. But danger does lurk, even for old women like me."

"I wish it didn't have to be that way. And now, my problems have been passed on to Jenny and the kids." Kenna winced. "They've been so kind to me. They don't deserve to have to stay home for fear something could happen to them. That's wrong."

May nodded again.

"I can't leave yet. I don't even know that anyone at home wants me. I've probably made them hate me."

"You can't run away from problems, sweetie. They follow. No matter where you go." May patted her hand.

"I know that now."

May stood to pour some more tea into her cup. "You want some more?"

Kenna shook her head.

May sat down again. "Kenna, can I tell you a story?"

Kenna wasn't sure she wanted to hear a story. Answers to her problems would be much more helpful at this point, but she trusted May. "Okay."

"There was once a boy who wanted to do the same thing you did. Run away. He hated living on a farm. But he wasn't wealthy, just young and full of ideas. Kinda like you." May smiled.

Kenna began to listen. The old woman had humored her by listening, so it was the least she could do.

"He asked his father for his inheritance. Early. Before he really deserved it. So the father, knowing full well he wouldn't be able to stop him, gave him his inheritance. The father had another son, so he gave him only half of it.

"The young man was thrilled. He took the money and went into a close town. Soon he had gained dozens of friends. They had wild parties. He enjoyed it all. Just like you enjoyed your first few weeks on the island."

Kenna lowered her head. If only she had it to do over again.

"Life seemed good. Almost perfect, until something horrible happened. He lost it all. He was broke. Soon he was not only looking for a place to live, but was so poor, he didn't have anything to eat."

Kenna didn't have that issue. She was much lower in funds than when she had come, but not close to being broke yet. "What'd he do?"

"Well he didn't have a nice family like Erik and Jenny to take him in. In fact, all his friends just disappeared. He was alone. And hungry.

"One day while walking around aimlessly, he found a farmer, much like his own father. Before long, he found himself eating slop right out of the troughs he now filled. Standing in the muck and mud of the pig pens, he thought about his new life. He thought to himself that his father's servants had it better than he did right now. They weren't hungry and they had a bed to sleep in every night. The only alternative was to go home. Beg his father to hire him. To be a servant. At least then he wouldn't be dining with a pen full of pigs."

Kenna shuddered. But May was right. Her younger brothers had nice trucks and homes due to working for her father for so many years. "So what'd he do?"

"He did just that. He went home. Walking home he realized the stupidity of leaving home. Yet every step made him more afraid of what his father would eventually tell him. He knew a scolding was due. Inevitable. But he also knew he could handle that as long as he wasn't so hungry anymore."

Kenna hadn't experienced hunger, yet May's story seemed all too familiar.

"As he came over the top of the hill toward his house, he realized his father was out working in the field. He could see his father working a job he probably would have been doing, if he were still home. This made it worse.

"As he drew near to his father, several servants looked up to see him coming. They spoke to one another and then one of them said something to his father. The son stopped dead in his tracks. This was it. This was the moment he had dreaded the whole time he considered going home in the first place."

"So what did his father do?" Kenna asked.

Tears began to form in May's eyes. Kenna wasn't sure she wanted to hear. "His father began to run."

"Away?"

May shook her head. "No. His father began to run to him. Slowly at first and then faster and faster. And you know the best part of this story is this. He was running," May opened her arms and held them wide open, "with his arms wide open."

Kenna began to choke up over the story, "He wanted him home, didn't he?"

May nodded. "Yes he did. In fact, he called to the servants to celebrate! Create a feast! Have a party! Go kill the fatted calf, for my son was lost and now he is found."

"Kill the fatted calf? That sounds like a...," Kenna smiled.

"A Bible story? That's right, dear." May patted Kenna's hand.

"Are you gonna tell me the moral of the story now?" Kenna giggled.

"Yes. I am. The moral of the story is this: no matter what you do or where you go, there is a special place in a parent's heart for his children. It's right here." May pointed to her heart. "Nothing you could ever do will take away that love. Nothing, child."

Kenna smiled through fresh tears.

"Just like God. God loves us so much he gave his only Son to die for us. To die for the bad things we do. Like...run away from home. For me, it's this ol'e gossipy tongue that gets me into more trouble than I can even imagine."

"God?"

"Yes dear. God. He loves us and wants an intimate relationship with us. Not just a portion of your life and our life's ambitions, He wants all of it. Our dreams, our ambitions and our hearts. He wants our love. Every single day. He wants to hear from us and He wants us to read about Him in the Bible. Read stories like this one and apply the lessons in it to our lives."

Kenna nodded.

"Honey, your problems and your sins are not new. There have been young ones all down through time that wanted to see if the grass was greener on the other side of the fence. Believe me child, I know this is true because just a few short years ago, May laughed now, "Kenna, it was me sitting here listening to this story from another old woman.

"It seems like yesterday, but every single day I look in the mirror and see this old woman staring back at me, I know that it has been much longer. When I was your age, I ran away, too. Sometimes we get smart, find ourselves and go back. Other times, some people don't go back. And believe you me, dear, they regret it their whole lives. They often spend the next few years and beyond wondering what they could ever do to make up for their stupidity."

May took Kenna's hand. "That's why dear, I take such great pride in finding out about all you young ones on the island during the summer. You are not the first one to come across that very doorstep," May pointed to her front door, "and I realize why they are here. God sends them. Sometimes one at a time, but usually two or three. And I do my best to love them until they get their act together." May now sat back and sighed. "Kenna, I have to tell you one more thing."

"What?"

"Someone has been here to find you."

"Who's been here?"

"Not sure. But I think it may have been one of your brothers."

"When?"

"It's been a while now, but he was here all right. Looking for you. I didn't recognize your photo, 'cause you weren't the same in it."

Kenna stood up. "I can't believe it."

May stood, too. "Well honey it's true. Took me a time to figure it out. I'm so slow these days. But when I dyed your hair yesterday, it finally hit me."

Shock penetrated Kenna's senses. "Are you sure?"

"They want you back, dear. Trust me. I think they're waiting with open arms."

Kenna looked back at her friend and hoped in her heart she was right.

Chapter 28

"Michael, come here."

Michael looked up from the newspaper to see the look on his wife's face as she sat at their home computer.

"Another messed up accounting figure?"

"No." His wife stood up and pointed to her chair. "You gotta read this."

"What?" Michael rose from his lounge chair and went to his wife's chair.

"It's an e-mail."

"From who?" Michael sat down, looked at the name on the e-mail and read it over again. "It's from Alisha?"

Claire nodded and smiled.

Michael read the e-mail out loud. "*Dear Claire. I hope this e-mail doesn't freak you out. I just want you to know that I'm okay. I'm in a place that I feel safe and comfortable. I think you deserve to know. I won't care if you share this with Mother or the boys, but I just need you to know.*"

Michael wiped the sweat now forming on his brow. "That little..."

Claire touched his shoulder. "Finish reading."

Michael went back to reading. "*I apologize and I'm sorry. I didn't mean to hurt anyone. I just needed to breathe. To find my own way. Believe me when I say that I'm safe. I will keep in touch. Love to you, Alisha. P.S. Give the baby a kiss for me. I'm sure he is so big now.*"

"Michael, what did you say?" Their mother stood in the doorway to the living room. She dropped the dish towel from her hand and she crumpled to the floor, hitting her head on the door frame as she fell.

Claire gasped and Michael jumped to help his mother now passed out in the doorway.

"Erik." Jenny walked out onto the porch the next night as Erik was sipping his after dinner coffee.

He turned, nearly spilling his coffee down his shirt.

"I'm sorry. I didn't mean to startle you."

Erik laughed. "I shouldn't be so jittery."

Jenny sat down beside on the step. "It's okay. We need to talk."

Erik didn't look her in the face, but continued to sip his coffee.

"I'm sorry, but I overheard your conversation with Kenna last night."

Erik shrugged his shoulders. "It wouldn't have changed what I said to her."

"I know. You aren't one to mince words. You lay it all out. Black and white."

Erik knew what she said was true. It had always been a bad part of his personality. His brother had told him many times.

"Erik, we gotta face facts here."

"What facts?"

"Tom is never coming back. I'm getting used to that fact, but you can't seem to move on."

"I'm not saying that Kenna didn't need to hear your lecture last night, but did you realize the impression you left her with?"

"That I'm mad at her?" Erik took another sip. "I can't deny my feelings. I hate that she is putting you in danger."

"Erik, do you really believe whoever tried to assault Kenna will come back and hurt me or the children?"

Erik nodded. "Maybe. With Tom gone, now it's my job to protect you."

Jenny stood up. "Your job? I don't remember hiring you for that job."

Erik stood to face his sister-in-law. "You didn't? Well what in the world have I been doing here for the past three months?"

"Erik," Jenny calmly looked into his eyes. "I think we have been mourning him together. But as far as the protection goes, after Tom left for Iraq, you weren't here. No one was here. I was alone. Really alone. Two weeks after he left, I realized that my protector is not my husband. He is a God who always knows where I am. What I'm doing. God will protect my children long after I will be able to, cause He loves them even more than I or you do. Nothing can happen to me that doesn't go through His hand first."

Erik bowed his head.

Jenny touched his hand. "Erik, I do appreciate all you have done for our family. I will be eternally grateful for your love and all the comfort your presence has been for me. My life would have been horrible if you hadn't been here with me. But your talk with Kenna last night revealed one thing to me."

Erik looked up into her eyes.

"She thinks you are not only my friend, but she thinks you are in love with me."

"I didn't say that."

"Your lack of an answer did." Jenny turned and began to walk up the steps of her house. "She loves you, Erik. She is young but she does know her mind. And I think," she went to the screen door and slowly opened it, "I think you like her, too."

Kenna needed to sit on the bench by the water that day. She thought about all May had told her about. May was right. She was a prodigal. The whole conversation reminded her of a storybook her father used to read her when she was a little girl. It was about a lamb who wanted to try and get to the other side of the fence to try the fresh grass there. He was too little to climb the fence and too tall to walk under it. He tried to squeeze his way between the posts time after time, but to no avail.

She thought of the pictures of the book and how they depicted the lamb trying to crawl under and over the fence and the warnings his mother gave him every time she caught him trying to get to the fresh grass, especially because it was outside the protection of the barn yard fence.

Not being able to remember the ending, Kenna knew the story to reflect much of the story May had told her. She contemplated whether she should pack her bags now and head for home. Perhaps her family would be there with open arms.

Ferries continued shuttling passengers back and forth from the island. Despite the late part of the season, all kinds of tourists still roamed the island's walkways and paths. School would be starting soon. Life on the island would turn quieter. This year she wouldn't be heading back to school. That seemed odd for her to imagine.

All her lessons of being on her own weren't in vain. She'd learned to live on less. Spend her money wisely. Jenny and Erik had taught her the importance of family and how never to take it for granted. And May's love and her words were always not far from Kenna's thoughts. Maybe once she got home, she'd encourage her family to go back to church again. If they wouldn't go with her, she'd go with Claire and baby Nathan.

Those were good lessons. She also learned to always be herself, trying to be someone else got tiring. Hanging from bar windowsills wasn't all that fun.

But only one thing bothered her more than wondering if her family wanted her back. Would she be able to live at home again, in the absence of her father. The months after his death had left so many memories of him being close. She then realized, there was only way to find out.

———————————

"Hey girl, what're you doing out here?"

Kenna turned to find Erik right behind her. "You love scaring people, don't you?"

Erik smiled and sat down, "Not really."

The sun began to set in the western sky casting orange glows over the water, and sending goose bumps down Kenna's arms. She would miss the views of Michigan's Great Lakes. As her father would say, "Northern Michigan is this side of heaven."

Erik leaned into her. "What're you thinking about?"

"How much my father would have loved to see this place."

"It's a beautiful place. Especially when the crowds go away and the water is like glass."

"I wish he could have seen it. We would sit for hours after watching our movie and dream of the day we could ride horses or take a carriage ride around the lake's edge."

"You got all that from just watching *Somewhere in Time*?"

"Kinda." Kenna smiled. "I would send off for the brochures advertising the island. When they'd arrive in the mail, we would scour over them deciding what we would do if we ever got to visit here."

"Why didn't he ever take the time to bring you here?" Erik adjusted his ball cap on his head.

Kenna hesitated and then said, "Working on a farm doesn't allow you much time off. He was just beginning to be able to leave the boys to do all the work, but he hadn't been brave enough to leave them. Especially for just a vacation."

"You do live on a farm. I knew it."

Kenna was surprised, "How did you know that?"

"You didn't scream."

"When?" Kenna laughed.

"Your first step on the island. You remember that. You didn't scream. A girl from New York would've hollered like a baby." Erik leaned back and put his hands behind his head.

"I also have five brothers."

Erik tilted his head back and laughed, "Five? Wow."

"Michael, Samuel, John, Phillip and Luke, a sister-in-law named Claire and a brand, new baby nephew. His name is Nathan."

Erik seemed surprised and overwhelmed by the news, "Wow. That's awesome."

All was quiet except for the chirp of a few grasshoppers and a distant clip-clop of horse hooves.

"I'm really gonna miss this."

"Going somewhere?"

"Erik, I think I'm gonna go home. May and I had a long talk today. She told me the story about a man that once left home."

"The prodigal son?"

"How'd you know?"

Erik smiled. "May would be the only one who could tell that story well."

Kenna smiled.

"I gotta tell you something and ask for your forgiveness," Erik leaned forward.

Kenna looked over at him. "Forgiveness? What for? I'm the one that should be asking..."

"I asked first."

"Is this a game?"

"No. No game."

"Kenna, will you forgive me for giving you the wrong impression of Jenny and my relationship?"

"Impression?"

Erik nodded. "I'm not in love with Jenny. I love her, but I'm not romantically in love with her."

Kenna fidgeted on the bench. "I really don't think that is something you need to apologize for. In fact, it's really none of my business."

"Well, I just wanted you to know."

Erik stood to leave.

Kenna knew he would be one of the only ones to help her with her grief. She asked abruptly, "Erik, how did you stop grieving your brother long enough to continue living?"

Erik sat back down. He looked over at her and then down at his shoes. "It wasn't easy."

Kenna looked at her friend. She asked, "I hate home now. Every place I turn, I see him. His chair remains empty at our kitchen table. My mother has yet to clear out his clothes from her closet. I sometimes," Kenna nearly choked from emotion, "go into their walk-in closet and just close my eyes and sniff the air." Kenna shook her head. "So stupid, isn't it? I just smell him there."

Erik looked up into her eyes, "I have something in my pocket." Erik reached into his pocket and pulled out a piece of paper and unfolded it. "It's a note. The last note from my brother." Erik handed the worn paper to Kenna.

Kenna began reading: *Dear bro. I love you man. I just needed you to know that. We are in heavy battle here today. I'm afraid to close my eyes tonight. Can't shoot an enemy with your eyes closed, but I'm so tired, I think I might faint. I just want you to know that. Give Jenny and my babies my love. Kiss them and love them for me. Love you lots, Tom.*

Erik pointed to the note still in Kenna's hands. "They found this on him. That night was his last." Tears welled up in Erik's eyes and Kenna watched him wipe them and apologize.

Kenna handed him back the note, "I wish I had a note."

"But that's the point, you do. Maybe you can see parts of your Dad in every one of your brothers. Each one must have a trait of his."

Kenna laughed. "Yeah, they all do. Michael pats the cows on their butts after milking them, just like Daddy used to. Samuel plows the fields in the exact same way as Daddy, and I often find him talking to the tractors as he fixes them, just like Daddy did. You're right."

"I'm sure if you asked one of your brothers, they'd tell you they see him in you, too."

Kenna nodded.

"Their memories live on. I see Tom in Taylor and Blake every single day. The way Blake tilts his head when you talk to him and the way Taylor stomps her foot when she does something wrong. That's their Daddy."

Smiling, Kenna patted Erik's hand. "You're right."

"Be thankful you have the farm to return to. Without it, you may have to forget your father way too soon. God gives us little reminders every so often to remind us He has them in His care." Erik squeezed her hand back, "We really haven't lost them after all. They live on, in the lives they have touched."

"Alisha!" Claire sat straight up in bed. Sweat dripped from her forehead. She couldn't believe she was just dreaming. The vision she had just seen sent ripples of terror through her entire body. Her nightgown clung to her body.

"Claire sweetie, what's wrong?" Michael leaned over to his wife and tried to wake up. "I think you're dreaming."

"Oh Michael, it was horrible! I'm so afraid."

Michael tugged her down and back under the warmth of their bed covers and cuddled her close. "It's okay. You just had a bad dream."

Claire shook from head to foot, but the warmth of her husband's arms calmed her down a bit.

"Michael. I'm afraid."

"I know sweetie, it was just a dream."

"No. I think it's worse than that."

"What are you saying?"

"I think you need to try to find Alisha again."

"We'll talk about this in the morning, dear. Try to go back to sleep."

"No Michael," Claire turned her face toward her husband.

"What?" Michael blinked several times and then looked into his wife's face.

"You have to go again. To the island. I think she might be in real danger."

"How do you know?"

"I don't. I just have this feeling." Claire pulled herself again as close to Michael as she could get. "Please Michael. Promise me."

"Okay, Claire. But what about mother? She's just now getting her strength back from her fall."

"I'll take care of her. She's managing much better now. Please promise me."

"Yes. I promise."

Soon Claire could feel her husband's body relax against her. She knew sleep would not come quickly as the urge to get Michael back to Mackinac Island only grew stronger.

Chapter 29

Kenna knew she'd have to talk to Jenny about her life. Her old life. Jenny was reading a magazine, and Kenna decided to be bold one evening. This woman knew about grief. She knew the heartache of losing someone especially close. Maybe she could relate better than even May.

She decided to plunge right into the subject. "I somehow thought that if I left home, my sorrow would disappear."

"Sorrow?" Jenny asked.

"I lost my father last year," tears began to well up in Kenna's eyes. She hesitated a moment and then wiped them away with her fingertips. "He meant everything to me. He kept me sane."

Jenny nodded, "I know that pain."

"We live on a farm. A dairy farm. I've never remembered anything else. Early milking hours, even on Christmas morning. Never a day went by where I didn't see my father leave the house early in the morning and sometimes not return until after I went to bed at night. Our time together..." Kenna choked up a bit, "it was short, but I loved him very much."

Kenna sighed again and shifted in her chair. "He died suddenly one afternoon. He was walking out to the barn after having an afternoon coffee break with my mother. He died in the driveway."

Jenny stood up, came next to Kenna and took her hand. "It was," Kenna again choked up, "the hardest day of my life. No one can replace him. We used to sit out on the front porch at night and listen to the crickets. He wasn't much of a talker, but he loved having me with him. He would laugh at all my jokes, would listen even though I knew early morning hours caused his yawning, he knew that I loved a bouquet of white daisies from the field and would always bring me some whenever he brought Momma some. We had a special place to sit together and I used to hide there, cause I knew he would find me. He always made me feel like his princess."

Jenny stroked her hand as tears streamed down Kenna's face. "I didn't know what I would do without him. I didn't know if I could live without him."

"How did the rest of the family take his death?" Jenny asked.

"That was the problem. Everyone seemed to just," Kenna motioned with her hand, "go on. Without him. I felt as though my world stopped the afternoon he died. I went through all the motions of the viewing, his funeral, everything, but everyone else just seemed more worried about that stupid farm. The boys had to figure out Daddy's schedule and start doing his jobs. Michael was more concerned about his pregnant wife than about mourning Daddy's death. They all made me really angry."

"What about your mother?"

"She mourned in her own way. She grew quiet. We were never close, so she would eat dinner and then go up to her room. By herself. That's when I began to form this plan. I wanted out. I wanted to leave. Every time I would go out into the driveway, I would see the exact spot I found him. It haunted me. I would stand in the driveway every day and just stare at that spot. I couldn't get his body out of my head. So lifeless. So still."

Kenna put her face into her hands and sobbed, "I wanted him back. I couldn't understand why he had to die. It was that stupid farm. Hours and hours of his life gone for what..." Kenna sobbed some more and screamed, "Cows, Jenny. My father's life was cows. I wanted more for my life."

Jenny rose and got the tissue box from the kitchen and brought it back to Kenna. She blew her nose and wiped the tears from her eyes. "I know he loved farming, but it killed him, Jenny. He did everything for us. Why?"

As tears continued down her face Jenny reached again for her hand. "Kenna, I know this is hard. But sometimes a man does exactly what he needs to do. I begged Tom not to reenlist before his last deployment." Tears now began to fall down Jenny's face. "He said it was his duty. I knew that, but somehow I had a feeling about this time. He'd gone twice before, but this time seemed final to me."

"See, that's what I mean. Why do they do that?"

"Because they're good men. They're honorable. Loyal. And, they want to take care of us."

"How was that taking care of you?"

Jenny shook her head, "He fought for our country, giving the ultimate price. So we would be safe."

"It's not fair!"

"You're right, Kenna, it isn't fair. But war and heart attacks are a part of life. God meant for your daddy to die that day whether he was a hard worker or not. He also meant for Tom to die, fighting for his country."

"Why would God take away people like Daddy and Tom?"

"I don't know. I may never know if I will ever make sense of death, but I do know this. It doesn't change their love for us."

Kenna went on, "So that's why I left home. I couldn't take it any longer. I hated the cows, I hated my mother's quietness, I despised the boy's attitudes toward the farm. Then my nephew Nathan was born and everyone looked at him as Daddy's replacement. How could a little baby replace my daddy? Our secret spot was so empty without him."

Jenny shook her head. "You're right. No one will. But Kenna, remember this. No one will replace your daddy, but that little baby probably helped your family to remember that life goes on. That's exactly what I see and love about Taylor and Blake. There's a part of them that is Tom. He lives on in them. Maybe Nathan is helping them all cope. Your brothers are probably overwhelmed with all that they are now in charge of. Your oldest brother and his wife have a new child to care for. They weren't replacing your father, they were just trying to look to the future. No one will replace him."

"Watching you, Erik and the children, I see that more now. I wanted to disappear. Change myself. Forget the past, but unfortunately, the past came right along with me. I still mourn my father here, even more so. No one here even knows him."

Jenny nodded.

"I don't want them hurt anymore. I know I've probably made them worry. I didn't want to do that, I just wanted to be away from the hurt."

"They'll understand, Kenna."

Kenna looked up at Jenny. "Do you think so?"

Jenny smiled back, "I'm positive."

"I'm proud of you, Kenna." Jenny left Kenna, picked up a toy left on the floor from Taylor and threw it into Blake's playpen.

"Proud of me? Why? All I've done is cause my family heartache and fear. I'm ashamed of what I've done."

Jenny sat in a chair across from her young friend. "The best part of making mistakes is to fix them. We all make them, we just need to be sure they get fixed the right way. God offers second chances all the time, His mercy is great."

Kenna smiled at her friend. "It's a good thing, 'cause I need lots of it. Life is too crazy."

"Believe me, I understand that completely. If it wasn't for Erik, I'd be in a much more hysterical state than I am now. I don't know what I would have done without him. But even more than Erik, I cling to God and His love."

"Erik is your family."

Jenny smiled, wiped the remaining tears from her cheeks. "That's it exactly, and I would guess they want you back just as much."

"So, when do you leave?"

Kenna shrugged. "Soon."

Jenny sighed. "Okay. Keep me posted on the plans." Before she left the room she turned to her young friend. "We'll both be okay, but we need to not run away from life when it hurts. Hurt only follows you and somehow, in time, if you face your heartache, it makes you wiser and always your faith stronger."

Kenna took a walk shortly after talking to Jenny. She had to think about what Jenny had said. Before she could get her thoughts wrapped around forgiveness, she saw Erik driving the horses up the hill to the Grand Hotel. Busily he was reciting his speech for the visitors aboard his carriage. He didn't see her standing on the sidewalk at the edge of the road.

She watched as he put his head back and laughed at a visitor's comment on the carriage. His hands were steadily hanging onto the horses. Her immature actions as of late, made her feel like a child beside him. Despite the fact that he was a few years older, she imagined a life with him. A permanent one. She scolded herself for the thought. Yet, at this moment, she couldn't help but envision herself as more to him.

He'd helped her through so much of this silly adventure of hers. And despite her doubts of whether he would ever like her for more than a friend, she couldn't help but smile to herself remembering the moment he helped her...under the windowsill. Just as her father had done for her whole life.

She'd ruined her chance to be more to him than just a little sister or a frustrating teen. Because that is exactly what she was.

The next evening Jenny was fixing dinner when her phone rang. "Hello?"

Kenna picked up Blake who was fussing at Jenny's feet.

"May, what's the matter? Yes, I'll be right there." Jenny turned off the stove burner, even though dinner was not finished. Jenny hung up the phone. "Kenna, May needs me. She's having breathing problems again and sounds pretty panicked on the phone. Can I leave the kids with you for a few minutes to go check on her?"

Kenna nodded. "Sure, is she okay?"

"This happens from time to time. We just need to get her breathing treatment going. I shouldn't be long. Will you be okay?"

"Sure. I'll finish up dinner."

"Thanks." Jenny slipped on her sandals and told Taylor to mind Kenna while she was gone.

Kenna waved. "We'll be fine." The front door slammed behind Jenny as she rushed out of the house.

Michael packed the last of his shorts and t-shirts. He hated to think of leaving his family again to find his sister, but Claire seemed so agitated and fearful over the past twenty-four hours. The last time he'd seen her like this was just hours before she gave birth to Nathan.

Claire stood at their dresser and began tossing socks in his direction. "Pack a few extra of these. Your feet get so sweaty in those work boots, you'll appreciate an extra pair."

Michael nodded, "Are you sure you want me to do this again?"

Claire came across the room, drew close to her husband and held his face in her hands. "So sure, it almost frightens me to think of you not going."

"I don't get it," Michael added as he tucked the socks into the open spaces around the outside edge of his suitcase.

"Neither do I. I just know that you have to find her. Your mother can't take much more. Her fall last week scared me. I can see her getting worse if you don't hurry up and bring Alisha home."

Michael nodded. He'd seen the same decline in his mother's health and demeanor. If he could find Alisha, maybe bringing her home would help her recover faster. The doctor said it took weeks for a concussion to heal. The worry over Alisha wasn't helping her recovery.

"What if I don't find her again?"

"We gotta trust God will help you."

"How do you know He will?"

Claire kissed his forehead, his nose and then his mouth. "I wish I could tell you that you will positively, without a doubt, find her, but I don't know. But this tug in my heart to send you is stronger than my doubts."

Michael knew not to doubt his wife. She'd proven many, many times that her premonitions were real and sincere. His love for her almost made him think he could do nothing but what she asked. Ever.

"Okay," he sighed. "I'll go one more time. But this is it. Not again. You better get on those pretty little knees of yours and pray I find her this time."

Claire nodded. "My knees are already beginning to hurt." She smiled and kissed him again.

All Michael could think of was how much he loved this tiny woman in his arms. If God could help him this time, maybe he'd go to church with her once he returned. He needed greater help in raising this family than even Claire could give him.

Chapter 30

Brock came into the bar with gaunt, bloodshot eyes. He'd asked for two bottles of whiskey and Carl told him to go find them elsewhere. Everyone knew he was a trouble-maker, but this evening, Marty's supper was completely disturbed by the man screaming at the bartender across the bar. Everyone in the whole restaurant heard him scream profanities and then shove money into the bartender's apron pocket.

"I'm not gonna sell you any more whiskey, my friend," Carl calmly answered.

"Oh yes you are," Brock pulled on the man's arm which stiffened in defiance.

"No Brock."

He heard more profanities across the bar as the two men continued arguing.

Soon Marty stood, as did other men, just in case Carl couldn't regain control of Brock. Many knew Brock's temper and knew they didn't want patrons or any guests on the island hurt or offended by the often-drunk gallery owner.

Brock soon stumbled out of the bar, without his drink, swearing loudly.

Carl stood at the bar and shook his head, then made a phone call.

Marty sat down again and asked another guy about the incident.

"His gallery is going under. I saw the banker put up a foreclosure notice in his window today."

Marty felt bad for the man, but knew he would soon be under lock and key due to the conversation now between Carl and the island police. He heard Carl add, "He's headed up North Street, but I'm sure you'll find him back at his shop before long. That is, unless he passes out in the meantime."

Many comments like: "That guy is a jerk. He needs to leave the island. He's nothing but trouble" were being murmured around the bar.

"Feeling any better yet, May?" Jenny placed the breathing mask more securely to May's head.

She nodded. "Thanks, dear."

Jenny agreed. "I think you'll be okay now. Just breath as normal as you can."

"What do you think about Kenna now, May? Do you think she means it?"

May shrugged her shoulders. "Who knows, Jenny. I hope so. She needs to be home at this age." May breathed in deeply, "Starting out her life with a family who love her."

May nodded. "Indeed."

Jenny smoothed back May's hair from her forehead. "Your color is getting better now. I should get back to Kenna soon. I left her with dinner half done and the kids."

May patted her shoulder. "I'm fine now. Go ahead and head home."

Jenny sat down at May's kitchen table. "I want to stay just a few more minutes until your breathing is back to normal."

May smiled at Jenny.

Blake babbled at the television playing in the living room where Kenna and Taylor sat on the floor putting together a puzzle. Kenna giggled at the little girl's eagerness to finish it as fast as she could.

"You like puzzles, don't you Taylor?"

Taylor grinned up at her with a smudge of peanut butter on her chin. "Yes. I love puzzles."

"You are good at putting them together."

Blake interrupted the conversation with some of his own toddler made-up words and smiled when Kenna looked up and grinned at him.

This wasn't her ideal job. She'd grown up a little while on the island realizing that some jobs needed to be done whether you want to do them or not.

A knock at the front screen door startled them all. Kenna looked up at the door and couldn't quite see who was knocking. She put another puzzle piece in for Taylor and stood to go to the door. As she did the door swung open and in walked Brock. He smiled as soon as he saw her.

Michael departed the ferry with a much smaller crowd than the morning boat he had taken on his first trip to the island. He intended to get some food and begin his search for Alisha in the morning. He hoped May would have a room for him at her bed and breakfast. A surge of departing passengers lined up on the dock ready to head back to the mainland. Several had sunburns and bags of souvenirs. Toddlers cried and elderly people seemed anxious to get on the boat to head for home.

He got to the sidewalk in front of the boathouse and looked both ways again. His last visit to the island made it easier for him to know what to do. Maybe he'd stop off at the police station first before heading to Mays for the night. He hoped the police chief remembered him from before, and had possibly seen Alisha since his last visit.

He hoped Claire's premonitions were right but he didn't even know for sure if Kenna was even on the island.

"Brock. What are you doing here?" Kenna stepped between the man in Jenny's house and the children.

"Surprised?" Brock smiled. He gave her the glance that once sent a shiver up her spine, but this time it was colder, bringing fear into her heart.

"Um, yeah."

"Where've you been? I haven't seen you around lately."

"I've been busy." Kenna pushed her hair behind her ear.

"And the hair." Brock reached out to touch it and Kenna flinched backward. "I think I like it better blonde."

Kenna shrugged her shoulders. She could feel Taylor's body leaning against her legs.

"Kenna, who is he?" Taylor tightened her grip around Kenna's legs.

Brock kneeled down and held out his hand to Taylor. "Hi, little one."

Kenna kneeled down to pick up Taylor and positioned her on her hip. "What do you want, Brock?"

Brock stood again and put his hands in his pockets. "Oh, nothing really." He turned and looked at Blake still babbling from his playpen.

"You need to leave." Kenna squeezed the tiny little girl in her arms. She had to think fast. Harming these children was the last thing she wanted. As scared as she was having this man in the living room, she knew she had to keep her wits and think fast about how to keep them safe.

Brock laughed. "Leave? Uh…" Brock put his head back and laughed loud. "No."

"Brock, these are not my children. I'm just watching them."

Brock proceeded to get closer to Blake. Kenna moved with Taylor still in her arms, putting herself between the playpen and this mad man. "Leave them alone."

"Okay," Brock again put his hands in his pockets. He looked horrible and the whiff of alcohol followed him into Jenny's home. "I don't want to hurt anyone. Especially..." he smiled, "children."

Kenna turned to put Taylor in the playpen with Blake. She cried a little, clinging to Kenna's neck, sensing danger. Soon she loosened her grip, left Kenna and clung to Blake who fussed at her closeness.

"Let's go for a walk." Kenna reached down and grabbed her sandals. "Let me just put on my sandals."

Brock smiled. "Okay, but hurry up." Brock moved to the door and looked back out onto the front porch. He'd stopped smiling. "I said, hurry up."

"Do you promise if I go with you, you'll leave the children alone?" Kenna slipped on her second sandal.

Brock nodded. "Of course."

Kenna knew there was only one thing for her to do. As scared as she was, she would not let Brock hurt Jenny's children. She led Brock through the kitchen after telling Taylor to stay in the playpen and wait for Erik. She prayed silently that the children would be safe until someone arrived back home. She then whispered the same prayer for herself.

"Do you remember me?" Michael asked the police officer sitting at the desk. The guy grinned and shook his head. Michael wasn't even sure if it was the same officer he'd seen in June. "Well, my sister is missing. We've been looking for her all summer." He again held out the photo of Alisha to the man.

The man smiled, "I don't remember you, but I do know who this girl is."

Michael sighed and smiled, "You do."

"Sure. Is her name Kenna?"

Michael's shoulders dropped, "No. Her name is Alisha."

"Well she sure looks more like Kenna to me. I'm not really allowed to give you much information about her, but that's Kenna all right."

The police officer's cell phone rang. "Yup. Okay, be right there."

The officer stood and quickly took out a pen. He jotted down something on a piece of paper. "I gotta go, but check out this address." He handed Michael the note. "If May hadn't been in here asking about you the other day, I wouldn't be handing out this address so quickly."

"Thanks," he said as he took the paper from the officer.

195

The officer called over his shoulder, "I know how much you are probably worried about your sister. I'm sure Erik would appreciate having her found. Especially by her brother."

"Where are we going?" Kenna could feel and smell Brock's breath over her right shoulder.

"You just keep going." Brock pulled her arm up behind her back sending pain searing through her shoulder. He meant business. She knew the children would be safe as long as she could keep Brock away from Jenny's house. She also felt something sharp prick her back. "Don't make me do something we'll both regret."

Kenna shook her head. "I thought you didn't want to hurt anyone."

"Innocent people," Brock sneered, "And you, my dear, are not innocent."

"Don't scream or draw attention to us or this will go into you faster than anyone can get to us to help you."

Fear like she never knew before began to overtake Kenna's soul. "Brock, what do you want from me?"

"Oh honey," Brock hissed into her ear. "You know exactly what I want."

The day had grown chillier as the sun began to set on the island. Erik drew the horses up to in front of Jenny's house just in time to hear the children crying from the front room. He jumped off his perch and tied the horses to the nearby post. "Stay boys," he called as he took the steps faster than normal.

Erik found both children in the front room. Taylor screamed from her spot inside Blake's playpen. "Uncle Erik. I need you." Her face was red, as if she'd been crying for a while. Blake screamed the same piercing cry as his sister.

"Guys, guys." Erik picked up Taylor who immediately put her head down on Erik's shoulder and sobbed, smearing her wet nose on his jacket. "What's wrong?" He reached out another arm for Blake and scooped him up as well. "Where's Mommy?"

Taylor hiccupped and said, "I don't know, Uncle Erik. I need you."

"I'm here, sweetie. I'm here." Both kids began to sniffle and whimper. "Mommy didn't leave you here alone, did she?"

Taylor raised her head and shuddered, "No. Mommy left. Kenna went that way." Taylor pointed to the kitchen.

"Kenna?"

196

"Yes." Taylor again put her head down on Erik's shoulder stifling more tears. "She left us."

Erik sat down on the couch with both children on his lap. Blake now sucked his thumb and leaned into his chest and Taylor still clung to his neck. "Taylor, sweetie. Where did Kenna go?"

"I don't know." Taylor picked her head up. Erik watched more tears flow down the red cheeks of his niece.

"Why would she leave you?" Erik's confusion over Kenna's actions didn't seem quite right. She knew the young woman to do stupid things, but leaving his niece and nephew alone just didn't sound plausible to him. Not after her latest changes.

"Did she tell you where she was going?"

Taylor sniffed again and wiped her nose with her hand. "No. She just told us to stay there." Taylor pointed to the playpen.

Erik pulled a napkin from his pocket and began to wipe Taylor's cheeks and her nose. His heart ached for his niece. She seemed more afraid than he'd ever seen her.

"Uncle Erik?"

"Yes, sweetie."

"Who was that man?"

Erik's heart turned to stone. "What man?"

"The one who came and took Kenna with him." Taylor hiccupped and squeezed Erik tighter around his neck.

Chapter 31

Kenna could feel her arm grow numb as Brock continued to pull it up from behind her. A point still pushed sharply into her back.

"When I get you to my shop, you'll do exactly what you've been hinting you'd do all summer."

"Brock, I'm not who you think I am."

"I know good and well who you are."

"No. You don't. I'm only nineteen. I'm not twenty-one, nor am I from New York City."

"Oh, even better." Brock again hissed in her ear.

"Please, don't hurt me."

"Oh, I won't hurt you. I just need you. I've needed you all summer. Took me a while to find you again, but you aren't going to get away from me this time. We'll have fun, you'll see."

Kenna was led through crowds and crowds of tourists leaving the island. All seemed too busy to see her need of help. She heard a little girl scream across the street for her Daddy. An ache of despair filled Kenna's heart. If only she could do the same.

Jenny's cell phone chirped just as she was about to leave May's house. She saw it was Erik and immediately answered. "Hey."

"Jenny? Where's Kenna?"

Erik's urgent voice scared her. "Erik, what's wrong?"

"Where's Kenna?"

"She's home watching the kids. I had to run up here to..." Erik interrupted her.

"No. She isn't here."

"Taylor! Where's Blake? She's supposed to be watching them."

"She's not here. I'm at your house. No one is here but the children."

"Are they?" Jenny's hand went to her mouth. She grabbed her purse as May hollered after her as she left the building.

"They're fine, Jenny. Scared, but fine. Hurry up. I need to go find Kenna."

"I'm on my way."

"Brock, you're hurting me."

"Honey, I don't want to hurt you." He pulled her closer. "I just want you."

Kenna felt her body trembling. She grew cold from the night air. She wanted to be warm, but more than that, she wanted to be safe. Remembering the small and simple prayers she would overhear Taylor recite, she began whispering her own.

"What are you whispering?"

She stayed silent and just kept murmuring to herself. Soon Kenna saw Brock's gallery come into view. She knew where he would take her. If she could kick and cause a little more attention, maybe someone would stop Brock. Twisting her arm a little she tested what she could do. Fairly quickly she felt a bee sting pinch into her back. Something warm trickled down her back. His grip grew tighter.

"I wouldn't do anything crazy, little one. I have a knife at your back. It won't take me long to sink it into your ribs and all I have to do is pretend you're a drunken girlfriend just fainting from a night of fun."

Kenna now knew her fate was sealed. She prepared herself for the fear of what was to come. Her greatest regret about the whole thing was how she would never be able to make it all up to her family, never see her mother or brothers again. She also longed for Erik, but knew he would still be working. This time her hero would not be just under the windowsill.

Chapter 32

Kenna felt Brock pull her toward his art gallery. A closed sign was on the door, as well as a posting of some kind. She knew this could be her only time to escape. Looking around she tried to find someone close by. A little attention from another was all she needed.

Another summer sunset reflected across the waters of the straits. It was so dim now that anyone she gained eye contact with wouldn't be able to pick up the fear in her eyes or the urgent message she pleaded through her facial expressions.

Brock fumbled with the door handle as the front door to his shop swung open. He hadn't even locked the door. He pushed Kenna through the doorway and into his shop. This was her opportunity, but he thrust her so hard forward, she fell to the floor of the shop. She knew she could never get up in time.

Brock shut the door to his shop and that was it. Kenna felt her fate slam shut, just like the door. She would probably be raped, maybe killed. Every muscle in her body tightened and her head grew achy.

Never did she believe this would be her destiny. She thought back to her last few days with Erik. Growing to love him, wanting him to be the one to love her made this moment even more hurtful. Tears began to slip down her cheeks as she watched Brock lock the door behind him.

Brock approached her as she sat on the floor. "Don't worry, little one. Don't you remember what I've told you? I want to show you love. Real love. That's all."

"This isn't love."

"How do you know? You are a virgin, aren't you?"

Kenna looked down.

"Ah, you are. C'mere little one."

Kenna felt Brock pick her up and she knew this was it. As he carried her up the stairs she knew of one thing, she wasn't going to do this willingly and without a fight. She began to thrash and hit him. He only laughed, holding her tighter.

———

Kenna felt as though her body was somewhere else. She dreamed of being back on the farm watching her father milk the cows or playing with baby Nathan on a blanket. She seemed to somehow escape as Brock ripped buttons off her shirt and pulled down her jeans. She tried to kick him again, but he laughed and grabbed her knee. "Not this time." The evil in his eyes made her feel like she had now escaped from island heaven to earthly hell.

Chapter 33

Jenny picked up Taylor as she entered the front door of her house. "Erik, what happened?"

Jenny hugged Taylor. "Sweetheart, where's Kenna?"

"She left with a man, Mommy. She left us all alone."

"What did she say to you?"

"Nothing. I was so scared."

Jenny hugged her daughter tighter and looked over at her son now playing again in his playpen. She watched as Erik pulled off his riding boots and jacket, and put on his running shoes.

"Erik, what are you doing?"

"Going after her."

"You need to call the police."

"You do that, I don't have time."

Jenny pulled her cell phone out of her pocket, just as Erik left through the kitchen.

Darkness had settled on the island. It was silent. Erik felt cold and tense as he made his way down one of the streets. He had no clue where to go. Suddenly, he heard a whippoorwill in the bushes. It startled him. Taylor told him they had left out the back of the house, through the kitchen, so he headed down a side street behind the house. Frustration filled his soul as the only sound he heard, was the hoot of an owl.

He knew it may be too late to find Kenna safe, she'd been gone from the house for about a half hour. He looked through bushes and into alleys secluded and far away from the normal bustling main street of town.

The bars were full of people. He looked into each one as he headed down the street. There was no sign of her. Fear like he hadn't known in a while gripped his heart. Would he find her? Would he find her in time?

Upon turning a corner downtown he heard someone holler his name from behind. He jumped as he felt every muscle in his body tighten. He turned just in time to see Marty jogging toward him. "Erik, where you going?"

Erik shook his head at his friend, "Kenna's been kidnapped from Jenny's house."

"What?" Marty looked behind him as if he were looking for her too. "When?"

"Just about thirty minutes ago."

"Oh man. This has been quite the night. Cops just came into the restaurant I was in to check out a man who was..." Marty stopped in mid-sentence.

"I gotta get going." Erik left Marty looking puzzled.

"I can help."

Erik turned, "Thanks. You go that way," pointing in the opposite direction.

"Got it."

Looking through each gift shop downtown, at a glance, Erik worked his way down Main Street. Crowds were thinning from another busy tourist day. Several times Erik crashed into one and got dirty looks.

Never did he imagine his need for super powers would actually become reality. He longed to soar over the island to just get a tiny glimpse of Kenna, stand silent and listen for her, look past shop doors, through nearby horse stables, and see her. He realized how stupid that was. Super heroes were fictitious. Made up. Pretend. He wasn't brave like Tom.

Turning from the dock, he glanced up and down Main Street and shook his head. This was impossible. How would he ever find Kenna in these crowds? Frustration filled his heart. He'd prided himself for months on keeping others safe from harm. Especially Jenny, his niece and nephew.

A helpless feeling began to overwhelm him. He glanced down toward the marina and then back the other way. Shaking his head and putting his hands on his hips he felt small in the midst of the evening island crowds. No one was trying to crawl out a window. No small figure sat on the side of the road waiting for him to come along to rescue her. He could no longer protect this young woman from harm and a sudden surge of anger began to penetrate his heart.

He sat down on the edge of the sidewalk. In the midst of the bustling street activity, Erik Matthews bowed his head and began to pray to the only One who would know the whereabouts of the young girl.

"Lord, I have no clue where she is. I can't protect her from all harm, but you can. Take care of her. Bring her back to our family safe." Stopping for a moment he felt something different in his heart begin to emerge. This young woman wasn't his to protect. She wasn't even a member of his family, but at that moment he began to realize how much he wanted to protect her. It could only mean one thing.

A loud crash ripped through Brock's house. He stopped his lewd act against Kenna and stood. She thrashed again and fell off the bed, hovering in a corner of his bedroom. She pulled a blanket over herself and watched Brock head for the stairs. Kenna shivered in the corner, trying to figure out her next move. She looked to the window, but knew that Brock's upper level was high and just above the front sidewalk to his shop. Dropping down would be impossible.

As Brock descended she heard stomping up the stairs to him. Kenna heard him grunt and moan as if someone was hitting him. Maybe Erik did know where she was. Who else would be there to rescue her? She issued another prayer that whoever it was, he'd win.

Moments passed as the bodies slammed against walls and slaps of fists centered on possible jaws from the floor below. Kenna reached for her jeans and pulled them on, she wrapped a blanket around her torn shirt. She went for the window. If she could get it open, it was her only means of escape.

Silence came from the floor below. She wasn't sure who had won the scuffle. If it was Brock, she'd soon be in trouble again. Adrenaline raced through her body as she tugged at the window to push it up. She ripped three fingernails off, but she kept trying to pry the window open. Footsteps began to ascend the stairs. Again fear penetrated her senses and forced her to look for a chair or something heavy to break the window as the winner of the lower level fight came to the top of the stairs.

She turned just in time to see her brother Michael peer around the corner. "Alisha?"

Kenna saw blood dripping from one of his eyes, but a face she never believed would be there to rescue her came closer to her. "Are you okay?"

She ran to him and wrapped her arms around her big brother's neck and began to sob. "I'm okay." Michael grabbed the blanket tighter, squeezed her as he kissed her cheek.

Out of breath and desperately needing a drink to fill his cottony mouth, Erik stopped again to see a crowd forming outside the art gallery at the end of the street. He saw many police officers leading a man out of the gallery in handcuffs.

Erik headed to the gallery, but soon was distracted by a couple heading up the hill toward Jenny's street. He stepped into some bushes bordering the street. Erik could see Kenna's head. He was sure it was her.

He followed close behind him. She stumbled a bit, but the man grabbed her arm to steady her.

Erik was nearly behind the couple when he heard Kenna say something to the man. "I'm okay."

Some mysterious emotion surged through Erik as he came directly up behind the man. Grabbing his arm, he wheeled the man around to face him by twisting his arm behind him. The man winced in pain, "Hey!" Kenna turned.

"Erik."

"I have him, Kenna." The man now faced Erik and started to squirm.

"Erik, stop." Before Kenna could finish her words, Erik drew back his fist.

The man raised his arm to block Erik's fist.

"Stop Erik. This is my brother."

Erik stopped and looked at the man's beaten up face. Blood was already coming from a corner of his mouth and one of his eyes was red, puffy and on the verge of being completely closed.

"Michael. This is Erik."

The men's faces were inches apart. Erik stepped back and lowered his fist. "Michael?" Kenna nodded. "Your brother?"

"Yes. Don't hit him."

Erik stepped back. "I'm sorry. I thought..."

Michael raised his hands in surrender. "Please don't beat me up anymore. I think I've had enough for a while." He smiled, "I am her brother."

Erik looked at Kenna who seemed shaken up but fine. "Are you okay?"

"Now I am." Without hesitation, Kenna moved closer to Erik.

Erik felt his body relax. He put out his hand, "Hi, my name's Erik. Sorry for almost..."

Michael smiled and wiped the spit now coming from the outside of his smile, "It's okay. I appreciate your concern for Alisha."

Erik looked at Kenna, "Alisha?"

Kenna shrugged and nodded. "Alisha."

Chapter 34

Jenny looked relieved to see Kenna coming up the steps to her house. She pulled her close.

"I'm okay," Kenna whispered into her ear.

Taylor instantly wrapped her arms around Kenna's legs and hugged her. "I'm so happy you are back. Momma was crying and praying."

Kenna picked up the child and kissed her on the cheek, "Taylor, I'm so sorry I left you alone."

"It's okay. Momma said you saved us."

Kenna looked at Jenny and whispered an apology. "The police let me head here before asking me any questions so I could be sure the kids were okay." Jenny only smiled and hugged her tighter.

Erik appeared shaken and frustrated as he raked his hand through his hair, now standing it on end. "Jenny, this is Alisha."

Jenny looked puzzled as Erik motioned toward Michael. "This is her brother, Michael. I just about decked him."

Michael moved closer to Jenny, she noticed blood trickling down his face from his swollen eye. "Erik!"

"I didn't hit him, I said I just about did."

Jenny motioned for Michael to come into her house. "Come in sir, looks like you can use some ice." Michael followed her into the house. Taylor followed Jenny into the house.

———————

Erik looked at Kenna. "Alisha?"

Kenna nodded. "Yes."

"That's a beautiful name."

Kenna smiled. "Thanks."

"Are you really okay?"

"Thankfully, yes. As frightening as the whole thing was, I couldn't stop worrying about Taylor and Blake. Are they...?"

"They're fine."

"I'm sorry I left them alone. I was afraid what Brock would do to them. I had no choice. I'm sorry Erik."

Erik shook his head. "Alisha?"

"Yes," tears were now brimming in the young girl's eyes.

"I'm so glad you are okay. The kids will be fine. You kept them safe the best way you knew how."

"If I did one thing right this summer, I hope that was it."

Erik nodded his approval.

Alisha took the ice packs from Jenny and gently laid them on Michael's swollen eye and another on his scraped and bruised knuckles.

"I'm so sorry, Michael. How in the world did you find me?"

Michael had his eyes shut and slowly opened his good eye. "I followed you."

"Followed me?"

"Yeah. A police officer knew you after I showed him your photo. As I approached the house, I saw that man pulling you down the sidewalk from the back of the house. As soon as he led you around the corner at the block, the sun reflected off the blade he had to your back. I knew you must not be going willingly."

Kenna shook her head, "You guessed right."

"I followed you close enough so I knew where you went, but I was afraid if I got too close he would see me. As he entered the store, I just waited so I could follow you, but when I got to the door, I realized he had locked it. So I did what every good farmer knows how to do."

Alisha laughed. "What?"

"I broke the door down. I wasn't sure if the guy would come at me with a knife or not, so I grabbed a piece of the broken door frame before heading up the stairs. What I heard scared me. The jerk came bounding down the steps and that's when I was thankful I'd grabbed a piece of the frame. I whacked him as soon as he hit the last step. Unfortunately, it didn't knock him out cold, it just dazed him and he came after me. I took a right hook to my eye and then it took me a little longer to finally get him finished off."

"Thank you."

"Claire was right. As always." Michael moved the ice pack over the bump forming at the side of his temple. "She told me you needed me. She knew. I am so glad I stopped at the police station first. I would have missed seeing you leave the house."

"How long have you been on the island?" Alisha asked.

"About an hour."

Erik sat down opposite Michael. "I'm sorry, man. I thought you were the guy we thought was hurting Kenna."

Michael sat up, "Who?"

"Alisha," She looked at Erik.

"Uh, yeah. Alisha." He smiled and squeezed her hand.

Michael asked. "That's what Dad used to call you, isn't it?"

Alisha reminded him. "It's Daddy's pet name for me. After the woman from the movie, 'Somewhere in Time.'"

Michael nodded. "You guys loved watching that movie."

Kenna kneeled and put her head on her brother's knee. "I miss him, Michael." Her brother put his hand on her head. "I know, so do I. We all do."

Chapter 35

Alisha arrived at Jenny's house the following morning after filing the police reports, with Michael by her side. Michael was also questioned regarding his part in the episode. On the way home, Michael told her how hard her leaving home had been on their mother.

"She fell last week," Michael told her. "The doctor said she probably has a concussion."

"Did she have x-rays?" Alisha asked.

"You know mother. She refused them when the doctor told her there really wasn't anything they could do for them, but bed rest."

Alisha was quiet. She knew her disappearance had probably added to her mother's anxieties.

"Alisha, we need to get home. Will you come with me?"

Alisha looked up at her brother and nodded.

"Can we go in the morning?"

"Yeah, but let me tell everyone myself. Okay?"

Michael nodded. "Sure."

"Michael, I'm really sorry about how I left home. It wasn't fair to you, the boys or mother. I just felt so smothered. I'm nineteen now. I don't mind helping around the farm, but I want to think about doing something different, too. Can you understand that?"

"Yes, I can. I'm sorry we didn't give you a little extra breathing room. But Alisha, you gotta know, we didn't do it on purpose. I just got so caught up in Daddy's dying, having to take over the farm and caring for Claire and Nathan. I was overwhelmed. Unfortunately, you were the last person on my list to worry about."

Alisha nodded. "I know. I just made matters worse. I'm sorry."

Michael looked at her and then hugged her. "Don't worry. Next time, talk it out with one of us first. Maybe we can help you figure life out. Running away from your problems doesn't make them go away."

"I know that now." Alisha put her head down. "I just missed Daddy so much. I couldn't stop the hurt. I tried and tried, but that farm was his life. Wherever I went, held a memory of some kind. I miss him so much, it sometimes suffocates me."

Michael sighed. "I know. Me, too."

Alisha hadn't considered anyone missing her father more than she. It dawned on her that maybe she wasn't the only one missing him. "The pain never goes away."

"I know," Michael began getting choked up. "I see him every morning in the barn. Then I suddenly realize, he won't be milking today. I see him getting on a combine," Michael stopped for a moment and then added, "And then I remember that it's now my job to get someone to plow the fields, plant the crops. Everywhere I go on that blasted farm, I see him. I remember how well he took care of things and I get discouraged, 'cause there is no way I can take care of it as good as he did."

Alisha reached for his hand. "What are we gonna do?"

Michael squeezed her hand back, "We're gonna keep going. We're gonna keep the plants growing and the cows milked. We're gonna remember him by doing our best to keep things running. As smooth as we can."

Alisha nodded.

"'Cause that's how he would want it. But Alisha, we gotta have you to help us do that. None of us can sense a birthing cow like you. We need you home. For now."

Alisha began to say something, but Michael added, "But soon, when we get things going again well, we'll give you the space and time to make a decision whether you want to continue with us or not." Michael squeezed her hand again, "Okay?"

Alisha looked into the eyes of her brother who now resembled her father more than anyone else on earth and smiled, "Okay."

Alisha had packed all her clothes the night before. Once home, she'd have to sort through them to see which ones she wanted to keep or sell at a resale shop in town. She'd left most of her old clothes back at home and she found herself longing to wear sweat pants and t-shirts again. She wondered if her mother would allow her to keep some of the newly purchased sundresses.

She came down the stairs with her suitcase to find everyone sitting in the living room waiting to tell her goodbye. This would not be a fun day on the island.

Taylor bounced up to her and hugged her around a leg. "I don't want you to go, Kenna."

Alisha stooped down to her level and hugged the little girl, "Taylor, my name is Alisha. Can you say that?"

"Lisha." Taylor grinned.

"Good job." Alisha hugged her a little tighter.

"Can I still call you Kenna sometimes?"

Alisha laughed, "Sure."

The little girl then began to skip around the room chanting the two names, "Lisha, Kenna, Lisha, Kenna."

Jenny stopped the little girl and asked her to go find a snack in the cupboard. Off she bounced, into the kitchen, still chanting the two names as she skipped.

Alisha stooped and gave Blake a kiss on his forehead as he stood in his playpen. "Bye, Blakey."

He grinned and waved goodbye with his right hand. Everyone laughed.

Jenny came up to her and gave her a hug. "We're gonna miss you around here."

"I'm sure you are. No one to keep you up late at night, worrying whether I come home drunk or not." Alisha looked over at her brother who was glancing at his watch. She wondered if he heard the drunk comment.

"Life will be anything but dull now."

"Jenny, I'm sorry I was so difficult."

Jenny hugged her again. "No worries. I'm glad you could be with us for a while." She stepped back, "Erik had to work this morning, but he wanted me to tell you goodbye."

Alisha's heart sank. "He's at work?"

Jenny nodded. "I'm sorry. He was going to try and stop by before you left, but I'm not sure that he'll make it in time."

Alisha nodded. "I understand. Tell him goodbye for me, too."

Just as she said it, May knocked loudly on the front door. "Yoo-hoo. Anyone home?"

Jenny went to the door, "Hello, May. Come in."

"I just," the old woman leaned into her cane, "Wanted to tell Kenna goodbye."

"You mean, Alisha?" Jenny corrected her.

She nodded, "Yes, Alisha."

Alisha went to her and held out her hand, "Goodbye, May. Thanks for everything."

"Oh child. Come here." May opened her arms wide.

Alisha hugged May. "I'm gonna miss you," she whispered in her ear.

May pulled back and smiled. "Me, too, sweetie. Will you write me?"

Alisha nodded. "Sure."

"We'll be praying for your trip home and for your Momma." She pulled Alisha close again, "Don't worry, sweetie. She'll be there waiting, just like we talked about."

Alisha thanked her. "Thanks for being there for me."

"Just doin' my job, baby girl. Just doin' my job."

Alisha glanced around the room at her friends. They had grown to mean more to her than even she realized. But now, as she was about to leave, she wished she could stay a little longer to reciprocate some of their love back.

Erik did his best to get home before he suspected Alisha would leave for home. He'd spent most of a restless night convincing himself how important it was for her to go home. He did want to tell her goodbye, but working that morning wasn't an option.

He turned down Jenny's street in the carriage, urging the horses to move a little quicker. They weren't interested in hurrying anywhere.

He noticed Alisha and Michael waving goodbye to everyone now standing on Jenny's porch as he came over the hill toward Jenny's house. For some reason he pulled back on the lines. The horses whinnied complaints as they came to a halt.

Erik watched as Alisha pulled at the handles of her pink luggage and headed down the street away from the carriage. They were heading for the docks. Erik didn't try to wave them down or stop them. He just let them walk out of sight as he sat on his carriage bench and watched. It was best, he thought. He sighed.

Chapter 36

As they drove home to the farm, from the airport, Alisha rolled down her window and turned on the country music. She admitted to herself, this was part of farm life she really had missed.

The farm loomed small on the horizon. As they got closer, Alisha began to tense up and imagine what now awaited her. Would the family not want to see her? She'd talked to Claire on the phone before leaving the island. Claire seemed happy she was heading home, but what about the boys? Alisha looked over at Michael who sported much more than a black eye now. He looked like he'd been in quite the fight. The bruise made Alisha feel guilty, and they also brought her relief and thankfulness. He loved her.

As they neared the driveway she grabbed Michael's hand. "Are they gonna be mad?"

Michael shook his head. "Not sure, kid. But I do know they have all looked forward to this day all summer."

————————

Claire was at the door to hug Alisha. Before she could say anything, Alisha whispered, "I'm sorry Claire."

Claire pulled away from her and smiled, "I understand, but you did scare all of us."

Alisha nodded. Each of her brothers stood in the kitchen. She looked at each one and saw pain etched on all their faces. Two of her brothers were looking down at their boots.

She lowered her head and said, "Before anyone says anything, I want to apologize. I want to ask your forgiveness. It was horrible for me to leave like that." She looked up again, "Please forgive me."

Samuel was the first to step forward, "Accepted." He pulled his little sister to him and hugged her tight. "I'm sorry we didn't pay more attention to you. Will you forgive us?"

Alisha pulled away and nodded.

The other boys just looked at her.

"How's mother?"

They all looked around the room. "She's had better days, but she is anxious to see you," Claire said.

Michael came in behind Alisha and put down the luggage and then pulled his wife close for a kiss and hug. She pulled his face down and kissed his stitched brow. "You are such a hunk!"

The brothers grumbled and murmured.

"Oh stop, you guys. You're just jealous that I have a sexy wife and you don't."

"Could be," added Samuel. The room erupted in laughter.

Alisha asked Claire, "Is she in her room?"

"Actually Alisha, she's in your room."

"She hasn't slept in her room since you left."

An ache filled Alisha's heart. She never realized her mother would care so much about her being gone. Regret now replaced the ache, for all the things she'd done to hurt her family. "I'm gonna go see her."

Alisha took each step as though she was going to stand before a judge for a crime. Fear gripped her heart, yet she knew she'd caused pain that she needed to make right. Before she left the island, Jenny had told her to be brave, fix her mistakes in a good way. Do what's right. Mend the hurts she'd caused like an adult, and soon others would see her as one. She raised her head as she took the last step. She breathed in deep. Missing Erik now was a part of her agony, but facing her mother seemed to be the worst thing she'd have to do in her whole life. Would she yell at her? Make her feel even more guilty? She knew she deserved everything she might have to face. She slowly went to her bedroom door and before turning the knob she closed her eyes and whispered a short prayer again of forgiveness. Tapping on the door she waited for a response. Soon she heard her name, "Alisha?"

Alisha opened the door to find her mother sitting up in bed with her arms wide open. "Alisha!" Relief on her face. The words of May came flooding back as if she had just talked to her yesterday. The story she'd told her was true even in Alisha's life.

She sat down on the side of her mother's bed and hugged her as she did when she was a little girl. "I'm so sorry, Alisha. I was so wrong. I didn't pay attention to your hurt for fear you'd see my heartache. And," tears began to stream down mother's cheeks, "in doing that," she pleaded, "I lost you and we both mourned apart, instead of together."

Alisha hugged her mother tight, "It's okay, except I need to apologize for leaving like I did. That was also wrong and disrespectful. I'm sorry, Mother."

"Well," her mother pushed her away, "let me look at you." She put her hand to Alisha's cheek and stroked it. "You are beautiful."

"Do you like my haircut?" Alisha tested the waters.

Her mother pushed a strand of hair behind her ear, "Yes. I think your father would like it as well."

Alisha smiled, "Really?"

Her mother nodded.

"Alisha, let's start over. This time, I'll remember you are a grown woman. I will give you more space, just like your father wanted me to do for years. I know how important it is now."

"And I, will learn to be a better daughter."

The pair hugged and cried together. Her mother smiled, "So, tell me what happened to you on Mackinac Island. Did you meet any new friends?"

Alisha knew from that moment, her mother had changed. Perhaps now they could share more moments together, just as her father had done with her in the past. "I learned more about myself than I thought I could in a few short months. What I thought I wanted to be is nothing like what I really want to be. I realized how important all of you are in my life and it's just not me wishing for Daddy back. I can be myself. I do love cows, and horses, and I missed getting up early to see the sunrise and watching a new calf come into the world. I saw myself through someone else's eyes. He taught me that I can be myself and still have fun. The whole experience made me realize how much I need you, and the boys, and Claire, in my life."

Her mother smiled but tears started caressing her cheeks."That's a lot to learn in one summer."

"It will be a summer I will never forget." Alisha laid her head down on her mother's lap and sighed.

Chapter 37

Jenny found Erik sitting on her front porch. He'd been so quiet since Kenna left the island. He pretended to not care she was gone, but Jenny knew differently. She opened the squeaky front door and held it carefully so it wouldn't bang shut. Blake had just gone down for his nap. She sat down beside Erik who looked up with his normal, pleasant smile.

"Well," Jenny asked?

"Well, what?" Erik looked at her with a puzzled expression.

"I've decided to leave the island." Jenny finally decided to acknowledge out loud her latest decision.

Erik turned and pointed to her house. "What about the house?"

"I think I'll sell it. It will give me enough to live off of for a while and also help with a substantial down payment on a house in the lower peninsula."

Erik nodded.

"It's time to go out and find your own life now, Erik."

"I can't imagine what that could be." Looking up at her, Erik continued. "You know...when I first came here all I wanted to do was be your hero." Picking up a small stick and snapping it, he added, "I even imagined there could be more for me here than just that." Erik looked over at his sister-in-law, "But that's okay. I make a better Uncle than I do taking over my brother's life."

Jenny grabbed the hand of the young man who now looked lost and alone. "I'm sorry, Erik. I didn't mean to disappoint you. For all you've done for us," she patted his hand, "I will never be able to repay you. You gave me comfort and security when I thought I'd lost it all. But, you're right. You will never be Tom."

Erik smiled and gripped her hand, "I know that now. I'm not sure why I have to come to everyone's rescue. As hard as I've tried to be everyone's hero, only God can keep people safe from the horrible sin in this world. I overstepped my bounds in trying to be everything, to every woman."

Jenny kissed his hand now, "Oh Erik. You haven't been as horrible as you make yourself out to be. Look at Kenna, I mean Alisha. She

217

would have gotten herself in more trouble if you hadn't have been here to help her."

Erik shook his head. "I think I overstepped my bounds, even with her."

"How so?"

"She didn't need a hero in her life as much as she just needed to see, in me, a good example of a man. God's kind of man. So she could see the difference between Brock and I." He put the piece of stick down and picked up another one. "Instead, I denied the fact that she didn't scream when she stepped in horse manure or hesitate when I asked for a special rein. It was then I should have questioned her and got her back on track. In the beginning, a part of me wanted to see her fail, because of how she was acting."

"That isn't how we should be to others, especially when they are lost, like Alisha."

"I know that now. Now I only want to see good come from her life. From her experience on the island."

"That's what May says." Jenny smiled. "She's always told me, she only wants young adults to find God through their experiences with her."

"May does know how to influence them."

Jenny acknowledged with another tilt of her head. "Okay Erik. So you aren't interested."

"In Alisha?"

Jenny nodded. "Yes, Alisha."

"She doesn't want me in her life."

Taylor screamed from her backyard swing, "Uncle Erik? Uuuunnnncclllleee Errrrrriiiikkk! Come push me."

"See," Erik moved to the side yard, "I make a much better Uncle than even a boyfriend."

Jenny knew the pull in his heart would continue until he found out for sure.

The morning started early as Alisha helped Michael deliver a calf at four a.m. She was in the barn cleaning when Samuel approached her from behind. "Hey chickie- poo...," he stopped, "I can still call you that, right?"

Alisha laughed. "Yes Sam. If I can still call you stinky butt."

"Speaking of stinky," Sam went to the barn wall and lifted a pitch fork off a hook on the wall. "I better get busy cleaning that stall. What was it?"

"What was what?"

"The sex of the new calf, silly girl."

"Oh...it's a bull."

"Good. We need more bull around here."

They both laughed.

Sam picked up a pile of straw with the pitch-fork. "Do you hate being back?"

"No, not as much as I thought."

"You know, sis, we're just a bunch of moron guys who sometimes think that girls are just something to watch on a hot day at the fair."

"Sam. Please don't say anymore." Alisha started to grin.

"No. Really. We care about how short their shorts are. Or how pretty their hair glistens in the sun. If they like farmers or are the hoity-toity girls from town who could never do some of the things you and Claire do on a regular basis."

"Okay, okay. I know what guys like."

Samuel nodded as he picked up another clump of hay.

"And...I never want you to look at a girl like that again. Just how her hair glistens or how short her shorts are."

Samuel stopped his motion. "Why?"

"Cause there's more to a girl than that. Look for someone like Claire. Or like Jenny who I met on the island. Those are the girls who will not be afraid to pick up a pitch fork if needed and they'll be awesome wives, too."

Leaning against his pitchfork, Samuel smiled. "Such wisdom from such a little squirt."

Alisha went over to her brother and tried to kick the pitchfork.

"Yes, that is pretty good wisdom."

Alisha gasped, nearly stumbling in her muck boots. "Erik?"

Erik came in closer to Samuel and held out his hand. "Name's Erik."

Samuel pulled off his gloves and shook the hand of the stranger in the doorway. "Name's Samuel. How do you two...?" Samuel motioned from Alisha to Erik.

Both answered at once, "The island."

Samuel dropped his gloves and adjusted his hat. "Alisha, is this the good guy or the one Michael beat up?"

219

Erik raised his hands, "Kenna...I mean Alisha, tell him I'm the good one."

Alisha knew it was her opportunity to reclaim some dignity, "Hmmm, it's kinda dark in this barn. I'm not so sure."

Samuel began to move closer to Erik.

"Kenna!" Erik backed up.

Alisha tipped her head back and began to laugh. Loud. Catching the fear in Erik's eyes made her laugh even harder.

Samuel picked up his gloves and began putting them on and walked back to another stall needing to be cleaned.

_____

Erik breathed a sigh of relief. "Why'd you do that?"

Alisha walked closer to him, "I love seeing the fear in your eyes." She took off her rubber gloves and looked down at her blood stained overalls and pulled on her ponytail. Looking up at Erik, she shrugged her shoulders. "Sorry. Delivered a bull this morning."

Erik grinned, "A cow?"

"No, Erik. A bull." She looked Erik over from the tip of his own cowboy boots to the flannel shirt keeping out the cool weather of the fall Iowan air. "Nice boots."

Erik looked down and pulled up a pant leg. "Do you like them?"

Kenna nodded. "Yeah, they're cool. But what do you need cowboy boots for and what are you doing here?"

"Well, you see. They shut down the island to tourists in the fall."

"You mean fudgies?"

Erik grinned. "Yeah."

"So that means you had to leave 'cause you are a fudgie."

"Jenny moved to southern Michigan with Taylor and Blake. My future was empty of plans. Can't live in paradise forever."

Alisha crossed her arms. "You didn't answer my question, Erik. What are you doing here?"

Erik looked down at his boot. "I wanted to try out my new boots. On a farm. And I guess I wanted to get to know Alisha better."

Alisha folded her arms, "Oh really."

"The real Alisha, not the pretend Kenna."

"Well, this is a good day to see how I look on most days."

"Beautiful."

Alisha smiled, feeling thrilled to hear Erik say she was beautiful. "What did you say?"

"You're beautiful. From the ponytail to the straw in your hair."

"What does that mean?"

Erik moved in closer, "That means, Kenna, I want to get to know Alisha. I want to see what makes you get up this early and go to a stinky barn. I want to know what you are like in your family and how you react to real life."

"What if I don't want you to?" Alisha put her hands on her hips.

Erik sighed. "Well, I guess you can tell me to leave."

Alisha lowered her arms, "You can stay, only if you promise one thing."

Erik studied her like Michael did with Claire. "What?"

Raising her chin in defiance, "You'll never call me a fudgie. Ever again."

Erik shook his head, "I can't promise that, Kenna."

Alisha walked up to Erik and got right in his face, "Okay. But you need to promise to start calling me this." She held out her hand, "Hi Erik, my name's Alisha."

Erik grabbed her hand and pulled her close.

"Erik, you know when I first realized that I wanted to get to know you better."

Erik shook his head, but smiled. "No, when?"

"Under the windowsill, being my hero."

Made in the USA
Monee, IL
01 October 2020